LIES IN

REWIND

D1262030

a novel by
TALI ALEXANDER

Copyright ©2015 Tali Alexander
Formatting and interior design by JT Formatting
Cover design ©Andrea Bat

Tali Alexander Books Inc.
For information email Tali Alexander at:
TaliAlexanderBooks@aol.com

Printed in the United States of America
Library of Congress Cataloging-in-Publication Data

First Edition: June 2015
Alexander, Tali
    ISBN-13: 978-0996052931
    1. Lies in Rewind—Fiction   2. Fiction—Romance
    3. Fiction—Contemporary Romance   4. Fiction—Suspense

Adult Content Warning!
The content you are about to read includes adult language and graphic descriptions of nudity and sexual activity. This book is intended for adult readers 18 years of age and older. Reader discretion is advised.

A Note from the Author

Thank you for purchasing **Lies in Rewind©**. This is the second book in the Audio Fools series that follows the love lives of two best friends, Emily and Sara. This novel could be enjoyed as a standalone, however I would recommended to first read and meet these characters in **Love in Rewind©** (book one) prior to reading this book, for a more complete experience.

To help you, the reader, have a more complete experience of **Lies In Rewind©,** there are words/songs within the novel that will include a superscript number. This number will reference a web-link within the LINKS page located within the back of the book. Please feel free to browse to the referenced link of any of the song titles mentioned within this novel while reading to be directed to: **www.TaliAlexander.com** where you'll have the opportunity to read the lyrics and hear the songs mentioned inside **Lies In Rewind©**.

Life is made up of sobs, sniffles, and smiles, with sniffles predominating

– O. Henry, *The Gift of the Magi*[1]

St. Lucia

William

"**Y**ou're a great singer Emily, that was wicked. I've never had anybody sing naked for me before. From now on I will always think of you when I hear this song."

She's jumping around on my bed with her beautiful hair and knockers swinging up and down, and I don't think I've ever smiled for this long in my whole entire miserable life. This woman, this beautiful woman, is a bloody godsend.

She finally gets tired and flops down next to me on the bed. I've had a hard tool for hours and I would give anything to have some relief. How sweet a revenge it would be if I banged his wife? He ruined my sister and I will ruin his wife, an eye for an eye, arsehole. I'm still floored by how I could've possibly hated this beautiful, innocent woman. She's a bloody saint, it's him that's the devil; she only knew him, fucked him, loved him. She had no experience, no idea what kind of life she could have without him. I could give her everything and I could love her in ways that bastard doesn't even know how. He's not capable of loving one woman, just cheating, lying, and eventually, destroying anything beautiful that he gets his dirty paws on.

I know she's currently smashed, but the way she smiles at me—she wants me, she *need*s me to make her forget that arse. *Liam, you can do this, make the first move,* I try to motivate myself. If she says *no* I'll back away and go wank off in the loo. This is it; I've waited to touch her all day. I start by taking her small hand in mine and turning it so I can kiss the inside part. *Touching her is heaven.* I watch her eyes as they slowly close in pleasure. I didn't think it was possible, but my dick just got harder; next level will surely be rapture. I continue kissing the inside of her arm, and her skin feels like pure silk. She smells of beach and pineapple juice. Emily had at least ten Malibu Bay Breeze cocktails while telling me everything there was to tell about her love life on the beach today. I lower my head to her stomach and give it a nibble. She starts giggling as my hair falls and grazes her skin. I look up to see her smiling with her eyes shut, and the sound of her laughter is the best sound in the world. *Does she make him feel this good?* I'm delirious just being alone with her.

I look at her sprawled before me and I want to suck and squeeze her tits, but I'm worried it'll be too much, too soon for her…I don't want to scare her. I know she's bloody naked in my bed with only her knickers on and everything she does is turning me on. I'm nuzzling her stomach dangerously close to her pussy, but she's most definitely intoxicated. *I should just tuck her in and perhaps give her a friendly goodnight kiss,* I think as I get a whiff of her arousal. My mouth actually waters and I may ejaculate prematurely just imagining how wet she is. I've been dying to kiss her perfect lips from the moment she told me her husband was cheating on her. How could that bastard ever want or need anything but her? All I want is to stop her from crying and kiss her so hard she forgets Louis fucking Bruel ever existed and that she happens to be his wife.

I can't help myself now, my hands have a mind of their own, and they're touching her beautiful tits and squeezing those hard nipples that I'm salivating to suck...as she moans, "Oh, Louis, please don't stop."

New York

Sara

I'm at my usual table eating my usual Nutella-filled chocolate croissant and sipping English breakfast tea with milk and two sugars. I look down at my favorite navy Prada suit paired with my nude colored Jimmy Choos. I smooth over my hair that, thanks to my useless alarm clock, I didn't have time to deal with this morning; therefore, it's pulled back. But I made it, I'm here and I wait. I wait almost every single day. I've only missed seeing them while I moved to London for a few years, but other than that—rain, snow, or shine—I'm always here.

The staff at Joanna's restaurant are incredible; I have been coming here almost every day for seven years and they just leave me to my business. They don't ask me what I want, they already know, they just nod their hello and bring me my usual. I sit in my customary tiny table by the window as I wait to see him leave his house. I have the perfect view of his brownstone from this angle. He sometimes looks up toward the corner restaurant before getting into his car, almost as if he senses me watching him.

I look down at my watch; it's almost half past seven and he still hasn't left his house. I finish my flaky brioche and wonder for the millionth time how they fucking get all that velvety smooth chocolate inside without marring the pastry, *must be a syringe*, I conclude as I devour the last bite and look out the window just in time to see his black car pull up. A minute later, he finally emerges, clean-shaven and hair still slightly damp. I inhale as if I'm standing right next to him. The three of them get into the back of his chauffeured SUV and drive off.

Time's up! I think sadly to myself and whisper "*See you tomorrow, JJ,*" to no one in particular.

I finish my tea, collect my things, and leave. *I love the suit he had on today*, I think stupidly and smile to myself. Another day in the delusional make-believe world I live in, where I see off my beautiful love every morning as he heads to work. In my mind, I sometimes even fix his tie.

New York

45 Days Later

Sara

"Here Comes The Rain Again[2]" by The Eurythmics

It's official; this is the worst week of my life. How can an educated, self-sufficient woman be this dumb? My stupid ex-husband, Gavin, has just evicted me and announced that he sold our Gramercy Park penthouse. *Fuck!* After all the things I've done for him, after everything we've been through, he has the gall to sell my place. I let him keep our flat in London because he promised me I could keep his place in the city. This marriage seemed perfect when he proposed it and is now slowly turning into a nightmare. We were supposed to fool everybody, not mislead each other. As usual, a good deal came along and his promises went out the goddamn window. I know the penthouse was legally his, but since I asked him for nothing from our worthless, bogus marriage or divorce, the prick could've at least let me keep the place I've been living and calling home for the past year. I'm on the verge of tears as I try to pack up all my shit.

I still haven't spoken to Jeffery today. I should probably start figuring out a place to crash for tonight. It's nice to come back home in the morning from breakfast to find a stranger standing in your house, telling you to pack your crap and go. I'm not moving back with my parents—that's for sure! If I move in with my brother, Eddie's wife, Michelle, will somehow inform the whole Upper East Side that her loser sister-in-law has been evicted by her loser ex-husband, and is now officially homeless. *Fuck, fuck, fuck!* Why am I crying? *Sara, stop fucking crying. Everything will be all right.* But I know that's just bullshit. There is no freaking way anything will ever be all right for me. Look at my pathetic life; people with half my problems require tons of drugs to survive…I'm beyond drugs. I should go straight into Bellevue and reserve a private suite in the psych ward.

I'm in a dark nook at my favorite corner bar. This place is not just a bar, it's my little secret portal to escape reality and feel the past exuding and mingling with my sad reality, and I feel at home as soon as I sit at my beloved booth. Most of the college students who frequent this place don't appreciate the fact that William Sydney Porter—AKA O' Henry—once wrote *The Gift of the Magi* in this very booth over a hundred years ago. That story of comic irony about foolish lovers and their foolish gifts to one another mirror my own idiotic existence. Thank God I have this little place to come to, a safe refuge to feel sorry for myself and get drunk at least once a week. Bruce, the owner, treats me like his own flesh and blood; truthfully, he treats me better than my own flesh and blood treat me. He would never let me walk home alone to my building around the corner on Irving Place—*well, it's no longer my building,* I think dismally to myself as my dire situation becomes abundantly clear.

Here I am, crying into my Irish cream-spiked coffee, plotting the murders of Gavin—my ex-husband, and Jeffery—the person who's ruined me and my life forever, while ultimately, trying to understand my own worthless existence. *I should text Emily.* I pick up my phone, which I've set to vibrate just in case Jeffery decides to call, which is my way of ensuring I don't get any of his calls until I have a plan. But I've checked my phone three thousand times since I told him we're over for the umpteenth time last night, and I can't believe he hasn't called or texted me back yet. My phone starts vibrating in my hands—it's Emily. Emily always has the sixth sense to reach out to me just when I need her most. I really don't have anybody but her. I've lied to her about so many things that sometimes it's almost impossible for us to stay friends. When I moved to London and married Gavin, I tried to cut all ties with her and we've only really started talking again a month ago. Thank God for her; if I didn't have her to talk to, surely I'd need drugs and much more booze to continue living.

"Emily!" I say with my fake everything-is-perfect-in-my-world voice.

"Sara, I've been calling your house for hours. I need you pronto! I'll meet you at your place in a half hour." She sounds like she's already on the move. *Shit, I don't have a place anymore. Fuck, what do I tell her?* I'm hands-down the shittiest divorce attorney on the planet. I can negotiate properties for my clients that they have no knowledge of, and yet I can't even negotiate to keep the place I've called home for the past year.

"Emily, wait! Let's meet somewhere else. Maybe at your house." I feel like shit! I look like shit! But hey, what choice do I have? I don't have a home anymore.

"We can't meet here! I don't want Louis or anybody else hearing our conversation." She whispers into the phone, ensuring nobody overhears her.

"Are we throwing Louis a surprise party? You know he's recovering from a heart attack. I don't think he'll appreciate a surprise party." I try to be funny in the hopes of maybe eluding Emily and avoiding her seeing me until I get my shit together.

"Don't be stupid, no parties. I have a problem. I need your help," she answers back, still in a hushed tone.

We should all have Emily Bruel's problems. Thirty years old, looks like she's twenty-one, more money than she could ever spend in one lifetime, two stunning children, the love of a gorgeous husband who had a freaking heart attack because he thought she left him, a supportive family, and drum roll please...the best set of boobs I've ever seen. As much as I should hate her, I can't, I don't. I've always wanted Emily's life but not in a catty bitchy way, more like in a looking up to your sister kind of way. I always imagined my life would somehow unravel and fall into place the way her life has. She is the kindest best friend any girl could ask for. I wish her the world, and I know she wishes me the same. I love her, plain and simple. I would do anything for that girl. People like Emily get a happily ever after. Liars like me deserve pain-in-full, and I have plenty of that.

"I was actually about to text you," I tell Emily as I marvel to myself at her uncanny ability to always know to check up on me at my lowest point.

"A song I hope?" she says and I can hear the smile in her voice.

"Yep," I answer, smiling back.

When Emily and I grew apart, it was hard not being able to just say the name of a song to someone and know beyond the shadow of a doubt that they got me. Emily and I created our own language. The song lyrics would do the talking for us. We are so completely in sync with each other that we don't have to elaborate on our feelings or experiences further than just mentioning the title of a song and who sang it and *boom*—the other person knows exactly what's happening.

"Okay, now you can tell me instead of texting me. Is everything okay, are you still in bed? You sound a little off," she questions as she senses my state of devastation over the phone. If she only knew how off I really was. I don't think there's a song out there that could depict how fucked up my life currently is.

"Here Comes The Rain Again[2]" by Annie Lenox was the best I could give her.

"Are you drunk? Why did you just say that? Oh my God, Sara, did you just say that 'Here Comes the Rain Again' is by Annie Lenox? You know that the song is by The Eurythmics!" I could almost hear the alarm bells sounding off in her head. That's how well I know my friend.

"Well, Annie Lenox sang it, so technically it's by Annie Lenox." Who was I kidding; my subconscious just sold me out.

"Where are you?" she asks in her no-nonsense voice.

Physically and emotionally I'm in Hell, but I tell her, "Pete's Tavern…it's this little—" she doesn't let me finish.

"I know where it is, I'll be right there." And she hangs up.

Great! I should've told her I wouldn't be staying here for long. This place is not Emily's style. Okay, I guess we'll need to address my problems first before I get to hear about hers. Here we go, when she sees me, she'll go into her Dr. Oz, Dr. Phil, and Judge Judy mode on me. *Fuck!* She will zero in on all my issues and see right through me. My life just keeps getting worse.

Half an hour later, Emily Bruel walks into Pete's as if she's a regular. Even in leggings and a T-shirt, she's stunning. I can see her eyes widen and her mouth form a "what the fuck" expression when she starts walking my way and spots my luggage scattered on the floor all around the O' Henry Booth I'm occupying. I try to smile as brightly as I can so that maybe she won't notice the bags, the weight loss, the red eyes, and my colored hair.

"Sara, did you forget to tell me something? Are you in the witness protection program, or are you bailing on me, again?" she asks with wide, worried eyes, staring at me in shock and awe.

"No, Gavin had me evicted this morning after I wouldn't give him the keys to the apartment a few weeks back. He sold it, and well…legally it still has his name on it, and since we're no longer married, I don't have any rights to be there. And to answer your question, I never had that officially changed because he promised me I could stay in New York and live in his apartment as long as we get our divorce settled quickly." I know what she's thinking. I know I fucked up because I didn't want to deal with reality. I trust people and believe their empty promises, letting them take advantage of me. While my job is to protect everybody else, I always somehow fail to protect myself.

"Okay, so what's the plan? Where are you planning on staying? You know you can always stay with us if you'd like." She finally slides inside the booth to sit down. She reaches out her hand and we lace our fingers together. It feels soothing to have another human comfort me, and yet an overwhelming amount of guilt blooms in my gut when I look at our joined hands.

"No, you and Louis are still working out your own shit, you don't need me there. I was thinking I'd crash at the Pla—" *Oh shit,* I was about to say The Plaza. That's the place where Emily caught Louis with some ho. That was the place where the shit hit the fan and started a massive shit storm for the Bruels. "I mean, The Pierre. You know The Pierre is my favorite hotel in New York." Emily's eyes close for a second as I see pain etched in her pursed lips, and I knew my big, stupid mouth fucked me up once again.

"Was the song for Jeff? Are you guys still, you know …

6

together?" She manages to flip a switch and change the subject back to me.

"Yeah, I guess every song is about Jeffery. My heart wants any part of him that he is willing to give me. Apparently, the only part he wanted to share with me is his penis," I say with a wicked grin as we both finally crack a smile. Conversations about Jeff and myself never end well. I should therefore try to avoid them at all cost like I always do. The truth is, I sometimes don't even know what's true and what's a lie when it comes to Jeffery Rossi.

"Sara, he'll never leave her. They've been married for years and they have kids, and you know who her parents are. He isn't going anywhere." She sounds sincere and I know she means well, but if she only knew the truth. When it comes to my heart, there are only two people who are in the know. It has always been that way and that is how it needs to always stay.

"Emily, I know. I've had a front row seat to his life. I know what's important to him… Anyway, can we drop this shit? What did you want to talk to me about?" I need this Jeff conversation to stop. Talking about him won't change anything. I see the pity pass in Em's narrowed eyes, and I don't need her pity. I did this to myself.

"I know I keep telling you this, but something great is waiting for you. 'Don't Stop Believin'' by Journey. You will find happiness even if it's not with Jeffery Rossi." Happiness without JJ is not happiness, it's purgatory, and I know it all too well.

"Okay, my optimistic BFF. It's Friday, I have the day off today, so spill the beans." I need to hear someone else's problems. I'm sure I'm about to hear an *I-need-to-find-a-new-nanny* story that in Emily's world is the equivalent to mayday.

Emily looks around the empty bar as if making sure the drunks don't hear us, and whispers almost inaudibly, "I met a man while I was in St. Lucia running away from my overactive imagination." I'm not sure I heard her right.

"*What*?!" Okay, so maybe I keep misjudging my best friend. Clearly she's not as innocent as I think she is. This should be interesting; drama that, surprisingly, doesn't belong to me.

Sara

"Just Can't Get Enough⁴" by Depeche Mode

"**W**ait, I need to hear every fucking detail of this. If you think of leaving out even one nuance of what happened in St. Lucia, I'll show Louis the video of our sixth grade talent show, where you sang 'Wind Beneath My Wings' and did an interpretive dance." Em doesn't know, but I even had that video copied and downloaded on my laptop to make sure the priceless extortion jewel never gets lost.

"You wouldn't! You swore on a George Michael poster and a Wham cassette tape that you would never, ever show that video to anyone." The look on Emily's face is priceless. She really cares if someone sees that adorable video that I love.

"I'm a lawyer, I lied." I'm joking, but the truth is I've always lied. Anyway, this little bitch better tell me everything, and I mean *everything*, that happened in St. Lucia. I need someone else's life to think about. My own life is not worth fiddly.

"Okay, fine, I'll tell you everything, but this information does not leave this bar, got it?" She tries to scare me, which is a joke...Emily couldn't scare a fly. I nod my head and she proceeds. "This is what happened; I arrived in Le Spa in St. Lucia, which was recommended to me by some random porter at the airport. So I clearly didn't know where I was going." Emily stops, takes in a few deep breaths.

"Keep talking, you got to this spa place, hotel, whatever…then what happened?" I'm intrigued by where this story is going. My imagination conjures up images that need validation with Em's words. Emily closes her eyes and I can see her quietly freaking out by the rapid breaths she takes. Something happened in St Lucia, and it wasn't good.

"I didn't have a reservation and the manager was trying to help me. Sara, I thought it was over! I thought he left me! I saw Louis' old asshole friend and then he walked out with that beautiful woman. He hadn't touched me in months…and you see, the place was totally sold out. He felt bad for me and gave me his room."

What?! She must be on crack! I don't understand half of what she's mumbling about. "Who felt bad for you? What are you babbling about? Who gave you his room? Louis' friend, or are you talking about the manager?" She didn't make any sense.

"God, Sara, just shut up and listen. Will, the manager—I mean, the owner of the hotel in St. Lucia—gave up his room for me. I was a mess; I got so drunk on the flight over that I didn't know what planet I was on. When I got to the hotel in the morning, he just took pity on me. We started talking and I told him everything about what happened with Louis. My phone died, he gave me his cell to call home. Pam picked up and told me Louis didn't come home. I didn't know my husband didn't come home because he had a goddamn heart attack! I thought he left me. This guy offered to help me forget about Louis and we got drunk." She puts her head down on the table and I know she's on the verge of crying. This story sounds nothing like the Emily I've known all my life. This story sounds like one of my lies. Em takes a few deep breaths and continues. "I don't remember anything that happened after that point until I woke up half naked in bed with him." My mouth opens and I'm truly shocked that Miss

Prude USA ran away and ended up in someone else's bed while her husband back home ran around the city trying to find her, eventually suffering a heart attack.

I gather my emotions and ask, "With Will the manager, right?"

"Right!" She nods. "I woke up in bed with Will Knight."

Holy fucking shit is all I can think. *Holy fucking shit!* "He has a hot name…is he hot?" I ask instinctively.

"Sara, get your head out of your ass. Who cares if he's hot? I fucked up!" *Who cares if he's hot* translates into *he's not very hot*. Emily getting all worked up is abso-fucken-lutely priceless. My day is actually getting much better.

"Did you sleep with him?" God, of course she slept with him. She looks positively, one hundred percent guilty.

"I slept in the same bed with him, but I had my panties on and he said we didn't do it." Well, if he said it then it must be true. I want to laugh at how absurd this whole story sounds, but she really does look worried and scared.

"You believed him? Did he have his underwear on?" Hesitation followed by loss of eye contact translates into no underwear. "Okay, he was naked. Did he have a nice package?" This should completely throw her off-kilter.

"Sara, are you for real right now?"

"Yes, I'm for real. Don't pretend like you didn't check out the goods. I said every last detail and I meant it!" I will not relinquish that blackmail footage without mega details. I give her that *I'm not fucking around* look and she knows she'd better start singing.

"Fine, what do you want to know?"

Ha, I knew she'd cave. I want it all. "I want: length, width, color, proportion to scrotum, hair no hair, and circumcision status." I also want to know how it felt and tasted, but we'll get to that later…baby steps.

"Sara, remind me again why we're still friends?"

"Because whatever I just asked was exactly what you were thinking the first time you saw Will's willy. The only difference between you and me, besides your big tits, husband, and millions of dollars in the bank, is that I say out loud what you whisper inside. You need me to help you verbalize your thoughts." Our relationship in a nutshell.

"You forgot to mention that we're the last two remaining '80s song whisperers on the planet."

"Yeah, who but you would know that me naming the actual artist as opposed to the band they were in at the time they sang the fucking song, is equivalent to SOS-'my life is falling apart.'" Only Em would know that I know who sings every song that came out of the '80s. Obviously, if I said Sting instead of The Police sang "Every Breath You Take[5]," she would know that I'm in an alley somewhere stabbed and bleeding within an inch of my life.

"Only because I love you, I will go off course and describe his package for you." I'm as close to wagging my tale as humanly possible. "The man had a good-sized dick. It was thick, but I can't tell you the exact length; he wasn't really fully erect when I saw him naked. No hair, and nice, even coloring. He looked circumcised and he had the biggest balls I've ever seen. Not that I've seen many, but they were huge compared to Louis'." Wow, I didn't need the Louis comparison or the mental image I just got of her husband, but this guy sounds like a keeper.

"Did you play with it?" I'm sure she did.

"Sara, this has gone too far. I didn't start this conversation to talk about Will's willy. I have bigger problems that I need you to help me with." Maybe she's pregnant with Will's baby.

"Fine, you never let me enjoy myself anyway. I just started getting a little wet; can't you tell me a little more? Wait, Will! Does he have an accent? Like a British accent! *No!* Don't tell me, I don't want to know. If a man is well hung, owns a hotel in St. Lucia, and has a British accent, I may have to go there myself to find him. I didn't catch the name of that spa you mentioned, what was it again?"

"Sara, he's not in St. Lucia. He's here, now!" Emily says, dramatically pointing down with her fingers. I start glancing around and laughing. She only described his package, so I'd only be able to find Will if he was naked.

"Em, stop being cryptic. Where is here? He's clearly not here, as in *here*," I say, making exaggerated hand gestures at our surrounding space. "Did you bring him back with you as carry-on? How did he get here?"

Emily's pouty expression is hysterical. Is this woman really thirty years old with two kids? She looks twelve!

"He's the one who brought me back home from St. Lucia, Sara—" Her phone vibrates in her hand, interrupting her explanation. She looks at the screen, rolls her eyes, and presses ignore. "So, as I was saying, Will helped me get back home to Lou— Fuck! Is this man serious? He has been texting and calling me to come back home for the last hour. He won't let me be away from him for more than ten minutes at a time. Sorry, let me talk to him or he'll send someone in to get me." *Oh, Louis "The Caveman" Bruel,* I smile to myself at how some things never change.

"Yeah, of course, go talk to him. I have all the time in the world. I don't need to get back home to anybody. I don't have anybody to begin with and as of this morning, I don't even have a home. Ha-ha!" I try to be funny and lighten our mood, but hearing myself say those words out loud really hurts. I really am all alone, thirty years old and nothing to show for it.

Emily gets up and walks away from me. I can still hear her talking to Louis. Besides Lola, the tattooed bartender, and us, Pete's is empty. I've heard her say, "I love you" twice already. When she talks to him, her face softens and an unconscious smile takes residence. What would it feel like to have someone not want me away from them for more than ten minutes? What does being wanted in that way taste like, I wonder. Em must be nervous because she's playing with the diamond ring of her wedding set. I hear her telling Louis that I need her help and that she needs to spend some time with me to get me back on track … *Oh, she's good!* She looks my way and I see a big sly smile on her face. I think the little bitch just bought herself some freedom with a ticket on the "Let's Help Sara Train." God, I'm proud of her. That's my girl!

"Okay, good news. I have a few hours to spend with you before I need to go back and reattach myself to Louis. Let's go and get you settled in. I don't mind if you want to crash at The Plaza…I know it's your favorite. Just because I had my heart crushed in the lobby doesn't mean you can't go there anymore." It's a good try but I don't buy that pile of shit. I'm sure she wouldn't step foot in The Plaza even if she owned it.

"No, I'd honestly rather stay at The Pierre. I don't feel like running into anyone I know." It's a half-truth; everyone I know spends way too much time at The Plaza. And now with the new food court downstairs, the Bergdorf shoppers—AKA my mom, my sister-in-law, and all her friends—have all become permanent fixtures there. I don't want to run into anybody that knows Jeff or me.

*Jeff…*every time I say his name a chill seeps inside me. If I were only a few years older when we'd met, would I have been his wife? Would we be raising a family together? Will it ever stop hurting? I need to change my life around. I need to start fucking ASAP and get myself out of this depressive funk. After fifteen years of only letting one man inside me, isn't it time I make a change? Shouldn't I feel what it's like to have a careless fuck with someone I don't love? Maybe I should call Scott? He's been trying to get inside my panties for the past few months. I overheard his secretary tell my secretary in the bathroom that she had to blow him for thirty minutes until he finally came, but it was worth it because he ate her out like no one ever did. *Nah,* I'm not in the mood for oral—that's way too personal and then

I'll have to see him around the office. *Bad idea.* I'll just call Brian, my neighbor, or more accurately, my former neighbor from 8B. At last year's building holiday get together, when I asked what he does for a living, he answered, "putting a smile on women's faces" and handed me his number. I could use something to smile about. Tonight, I need to be happy. It's nice to be able to call people when you know exactly what you need.

"Sara, Sara…earth to Sara. Are you all right? Where did you go? You're spacing out on me. If you're ready, let's go." Yeah, I'm ready to start changing my life. I'm ready to start acting like that slut that everybody thinks I am.

"Yeah, I'm ready. I was just thinking about what I'd like to eat for dinner tonight." Or to be more precise, *who* I'd like for dinner. I should text Brian before I change my mind. "Em, give me a minute and let me send a text," I say, as I walk toward the bar to pay our tab and muster all my nerve to text Brian, whose last name I don't even know, and see how he plans to hopefully put a smile on my face tonight.

-Brian, this is Sara from 10P in your building. Do you remember me?-

-Kate Moss' doppelganger? How can anyone forget you, Sara? Are you out of sugar?-

His response makes me laugh, I haven't had anyone call me Kate's twin in many years, but in high school and college, I used to hear that at least twice a day. I think I look nothing like her.

-Are you available to eat tonight?-

It takes him less than a few seconds to answer me.

-I'm available to eat you tonight.-

I blush at his forwardness, but that's the exact response I needed.

-9PM at The Pierre Lobby Bar.-
-Are you trying to make this hard for me? You know I can just come up. But if you're into role-playing I'll be there and I'll bring my appetite.-
-I'll bring your main course.-

I type out, thrilled at my level of audacity.

-I'm getting hard just thinking about your main course.-
-Can't wait...come hungry.-
-Fuck, Sara...I may be upstairs earlier to get a sample.-
-Lol. See ya at The Pierre-

I have a big smile on my face as I walk back to our booth and look up to see Em studying me like a mother hen.

"What?"

"You know what. Did you just arrange a booty call?" Yeah, the first booty call of my life that's not with *him*.

"And what if I did? I don't have a hot husband to help me get myself off. Some of us need to fuck multiple people in our lifetime before we find someone we want to fuck until our vagina dries out." We laugh in unison. I need to laugh, pretend like I always do that everything is just peaches and cream. I always believed if I pretend hard enough then it was true.

"Can we talk about the man you fucked in St. Lucia? I know, I know; you didn't fuck him. You just woke up naked in his bed with no recollection of what the fuck happened the night before." My brazen potential booty call had momentarily side-tracked me from our main problem.

"I think I would know if I fucked someone. Don't you think? Why would he tell me nothing happened if it did?" That's a good point. Maybe the dude didn't take advantage of her?

"So, why do we care about this guy again?" My phone starts vibrating with a text. I look with a smile, sure that Brian is getting antsy about our date tonight.

-The realtor said you left some clothes at the apartment, where are you staying? I'll have them messengered over later today.-

It's Gavin.

-Have it delivered to The Pierre. I'm staying there for now-, I text back as another text comes in and this time, it's not Gavin.

-I love you...we need to talk-

It's him. I'm lightheaded and I can't breathe; I feel my heartbeat in my ears. He can't say those words to me. He doesn't know what they do to me. Em kneels at my side. Why am I on the floor? Am I crying?

"Sara, honey...what is it? What happen? Did Gavin text you?"

I shake my head. "No, it's him, Em. He'll never leave me alone. He'll never let me go."

Realization finally hits Emily as she yells at me, "Is it Jeff? Sara, you need to let Louis and Eddie talk to him. He needs to let you live and make a future with someone else. He can't keep popping up in your life. It's like he knows when you're weak and he preys on you. You know he can go to jail for statutory rape. Sara, sweetie, don't cry...please, I hate it when you cry." We're both on the floor of Pete's Tavern as Emily wraps her arms around me and kisses the side of my head. I hate crying. I don't want to cry. Only dumb cows cry. I'm a dumb cow. "Okay, no more tears," Emily announces as she wipes my wet cheeks with her designer T-shirt.

"You just flashed me," I say as we both smile again.

"Yes, yes, my boobs have magical power and I use them to heal the world."

"Is that what Louis, says?"

"Once a day and twice on Sunday."

"Maybe if I start sucking them all my problems will go away, too."

"If you start sucking them, you'll have Louis Bruel as a problem." She's right, that man is obsessed with my best friend and her magical boobs.

"What did he want? That stupid cock sucker," Emily barks out.

"I love it when you cuss. It really puts a smile on my face."

"Come here. You don't have to tell me what he says. But if any of us can help, just say the word." Nobody can help me because nobody but Jeff and I know the truth. Nobody knows what we promised and the decisions we've lived with for the past fifteen years.

"Thank you. Let's get me settled at The Pierre and I'll return you back to Louis before he sends the FBI, CIA, and Mossad after you." If I ever find a guy who wants me half as much as Louis wants my best friend I'll be the luckiest girl in the world.

"Come on, Louis already has you booked into the penthouse residential apartment at The Pierre for the next month. That triplex is bigger than my townhouse. Your best friend is married to a real estate big shot, that's got to yield some perks."

"Em, you guys didn't have to do that. I can just get a regular room that I can afford. I'm not your problem."

"Sara, you are my best friend in the whole wide world, my only real friend! When we stopped talking while you were married to that schmuck, I felt more alone than ever...I was lost. I would move you into my house if I thought you'd agree to it...trust me, having you a few blocks away at The Pierre is more for me than for you. And anyway, that apartment is on the market, why shouldn't someone enjoy it if it's empty? I hope you know that Louis and I would do anything for you."

Just when I think my life is total and utter shit, I get a reminder of how lucky I am to call Emily Bruel my best friend. Maybe my shit will fall into place one day. For now, I'll be licking my wounds in style at the top of the swankiest penthouse in all of New York City.

William

"Everybody Wants To Rule The World[6]" by Tears For Fears

These last few weeks have been the longest weeks of my bloody life. Even longer than having to wait for my sister at a restaurant to celebrate her birthday, only to find out she's never coming back. I miss my Isa; it just doesn't stop hurting knowing that he gets to live while she's long gone.

I've been trying to follow Emily and her worthless husband for weeks, and I don't know what to do with myself anymore. *Why hasn't she called me?* Did she not feel what I felt? How could a smart, kind, beautiful woman like her believe that lying, cheating, scumbag of a man? How did Isa fall for him, too? Why are all these women willing to give their love to him? If she were mine, I'd make her smile all day long. I'd spoil her and kiss the fucking ground she walks on. I know what that sick fucker is into and it's not being married and making one woman happy, that's for sure! The arsehole hasn't left Emily's side to let her goddamn piss on her own in the last few weeks. I just need to talk to her. She needs to know. I couldn't save my sister, but I need to save her. I need to save that beautiful woman who has crawled under my skin and set up camp from that monster if it's the last thing I do. That's what Isa would want me to do.

I hate staying in this hotel in this goddamn city. Everything my eyes touch brings me back to Isa. At least in St. Lucia I'm too busy to think about all the shit that makes up my life. How I went from having a family to being part of a broken team of strangers. I miss my life when my sister still lived at home. Maybe I should go back home. Emily clearly wasn't as affected by our encounter as I let myself imagine. I bring my fingers to my nose and I know it's crazy but I can still smell her on my skin. I've washed my hands a thousand times since that night and yet I bloody swear her scent is etched in my brain.

As much as my fucked-up head keeps telling me to get as far away from her and New York as humanly possible, my broken heart won't hear it. My heart wants what it wants and it wants Emily. I wouldn't even need that long with her, just a few hours to tell her the truth. To tell her all about the heartless monster she thinks she loves. She doesn't know what I know. I can't just leave her here with him. My sister trusted him, loved him, and he just tossed her out and married the first young innocent girl he met. Isa would've been thirty-five on Sunday. I can't leave, I won't leave, I won't let him destroy Emily; she needs me!

I have two hours before she's out to go running in the park with her trainer. Today, I'm going to talk to her. A loud banging brings me out of my thoughts. *Who's knocking on my door at seven in the morning?* I ordered breakfast for eight. *Strange.* I get up from the chair I've been sitting in for the last two hours, watching the sunrise over central park.

"Hold your face, I'm coming!" The banging actually gets louder. "Bloody hell, give me a minute," I yell as I walk across my suite to the door. I don't even ask or look to see who it is before opening the door. As soon as I open the door, my heart stops and then instantly jump-starts from the view. In front of me is the person I loathe most in the world. I would love to murder this animal and gladly spend the rest of my life in jail with the biggest smile on my face. *Why does he get to live while my sister lies dead?* I ask myself for the millionth time. "Look who came to visit. Louis 'The Wanker' Bruel, to what do I owe this revolting pleasure? Did your doctors say it was all right for you to leave the hospital?" How did he even know I was in New York? He looks older, less cocky. Maybe it's my imagination but he looks nervous. He doesn't answer, just looks at me and smiles. That sly smile that I need to wipe off his face.

"Nice place Willy boy, it's good to see Daddy's money is still paying for your lifestyle."

Daddy's money, that's rich coming from this hypocrite who only has a pot to piss in because his papa croaked and left him everything. "Louis, you should know a thing or two about spending Daddy's money." I love how his eyes just sharpened. Arrogant prick. People in glass houses should shut the bloody fuck up. "Why are you here and what do you want?"

"Thanks for inviting me in," he says as he pushes the door fully open and lets himself in. *Dickhead.* "Did you miss New York, William? You know I have a restraining order against you. So, don't forget to count to ten and think twice before you act out." He walks into my suite with his hands behind his back as he looks around, not sure what he's bloody looking for. He walks past me towards the huge window overlooking 5th Avenue and Central park. Louis Bruel thinks he's king of everything. But he can't fool me. I know what kind of scum he really is. I close the door and follow to stand behind him, and if I had a weapon, he'd probably be dead already. He sits in the same chair by the window that less than five minutes ago, I sat in while fantasizing about my gorgeous Emily. That thought brings a smile to my lips.

"You came to me. Take yourself the fuck out of here and I won't have to restrain myself from rearranging your mug." Maybe I'll finally have the chance to murder this wanker.

"Sit down, Liam, we need to talk. I've been very generous

with you," he says, pointing to a chair opposite him.

This whoreson is being generous with me? I snicker to myself. I loathe that he calls me Liam, it means Isa told him. "Oh, Master Louis, please, do tell why you're being so very generous with me. I won't be sucking your knob or kissing your dirty arse so drop the bureaucracies and let's take care of business like men—without calling the coppers. And don't you bloody call me Liam or dare and try to tell me what to do. I'm not some vulnerable girl you can manipulate and destroy." If I were older when Isa got mixed up with him, I would've slaughtered him.

"Liam, sit down. This is about Emily." Emily? Hearing her name come out of his mouth physically pains me. What happened to Emily? I should sit down and listen to what this arse has to say. I'm starved for any information about her. How is it possible to go from detesting the girl I thought contributed to my sister's death, to being hopelessly obsessed with that same woman? I haven't been able to get her out of my system in weeks.

"What about Emily?" Even hearing myself say her name out loud somehow feels painful. But his reaction to me saying her name is fucking priceless. *Possessive lowlife.*

"Did your dream come true when you drugged my wife and got her naked into your bed, Liam?" Stupid pig, I would never hurt Emily, and if he calls me Liam one more time, I'll kill him.

"Well, you're still breathing, so obviously my dreams haven't come true, yet." If he actually died, I'd be with Emily right now. I would get a chance to show her how a woman deserves to be treated and loved. Why do good people die while imbeciles like him and his friends get to live? "How many innocent women will you keep luring to their death? What do you promise them, anyway? Isa didn't need your money, why would she be with a person like you? Poor Emily, what have you put that sweet girl through?"

He looks mad. He's ready to pounce. "Don't talk about my wife like you know her," he says through gritted teeth. Stupid, arrogant prick; *I know your wife inside and out*, I think to myself with pride.

"I do know her. Better than you may be comfortable with, mate." A big smile spreads across my face when I let my head think back to our time together in St. Lucia. Emily came there alone, broken, and in pain, thanks to this cheating, lying monster. I helped her, I made her forget about him and smile again. She sang for me, danced for me, and I'm sure she felt it, too. How did an arsehole like Louis Bruel who probably fucked most of Manhattan find someone like her?

"Emily told me everything. I know she came to your father's resort accidently because she was running away from something she thought she saw. I also know you were very chivalrous and offered her half your room, and that you tried to get your revenge on me by getting her drunk and putting her to sleep naked in your bed. Did I miss anything, William?" Yeah, you missed the part where she drank to forget about the pain you caused her and how sweet those lips tasted while I made her moan, I think to myself.

"You forgot many intimate morsels that I'm sure Emily didn't think were any of your bloody business." Look at him—Louis is holding himself back. He really wants a piece of me. Come and get me, fucking oinker.

"Emily and I don't have secrets from each other. I'm here to tell you that it's time to stop waiting and spying on my wife. Willy-boy, go home before I call your father and have him come get you. Go stalk a nice girl back in London."

Funny, I haven't spoken to my parents in months. After Isa's death, our family just crumbled thanks to him. Everybody does his or her own business and nobody speaks. I don't even think my parents knew I was engaged a few months back. I wonder if my parents even talk to each other anymore? I get my instructions from their assistants and everybody is peachy. *Did she really send Louis here to tell me to leave?* Did he tell her I was using her? I snort to myself, thinking that perhaps she actually believed me when I said nothing happened that night. That morning, she didn't look like the confident woman that stripped for me the night before. She looked scared and embarrassed. I didn't want to add to her hurt; she looked on the verge of another massive panic attack. When she questioned me about what we did, what was I supposed to say? That I kissed those lips all night, and that I touched every inch of her body? That I'd hoped in the morning she would wake up and ask me to make love to her? I couldn't tell her that she was supposed to remember me kissing her and not moan out his name while I sucked her beautiful tits. I hate him so much, yet all I wanted that night was for my name to fucking be Louis. I have to talk to her; she can't think I would try to hurt her. If I tell her what kind of a monster he is and what he's capable of, surely she won't want to stay with him.

"I'll leave once I speak to her," I answer him. His eyes widen. The piece of rubbish is scared I'll tell her everything. "Louis, I'll only tell her a few stories from Isa's book."

He's up and in my face, breathing hard with veins popping out of his neck. "If that book...I swear to God, if it ever sees the light of day, it will cost you and your father every last penny you've got."

I laugh before saying, "But it will cost you Emily. I'm willing to give up a few quid to make that happen."

I don't have time to react before he has me on the floor. He puffs hard, frothing at the mouth, trying to choke me, and I'm laughing as I'm barely able to get him off of me. He's maybe a little taller than me, but I'm younger and in way better form. I push him off me, he stumbles backwards on his arse and I shove him further down and straddle his chest. I now have him under me and I can see he's battling to get me off. This fucker had a heart attack a month ago—this can't be good for him. "I can kill you, old man. It would be a fitting homage to my sister and a present for Emily." He has kids; I wouldn't do that to them or Emily, as much as I'd love to. I'm not an animal like him. I want Emily to pick me, not by default, but by choice. It's the reason I brought her back to him in the first place.

I get off the floor and walk over to the liquor cabinet trying to catch my breath while I fix myself a drink. I don't look behind, but I can hear him still huffing and puffing, gasping for air.

"How old were you when Isa died?" he asks me while still lying on the floor in the middle of my suite.

I hate hearing him call her Isa; I call her Isa. I don't want to discuss this with him—the man who brought my family nothing but pain. I will not desecrate my sister's memory by making conversation with this despicable excuse for a human. I look out at this beautiful city sprawled out before me, and I can't stop from wishing things would've turned out differently. What if Louis loved my sister like she wanted and needed him to, would Isa still be alive? Would Emily and I be together? We're almost the same age. Would she be my destiny? All I can think about is how beautiful and perfect we could be together. I ache to touch and caress every curve, every piece of her. I hear him moving on the floor and I come back from my daydream. I answer him, hoping to get him out of my suite before Emily goes on her morning run.

"I was seventeen when my father told me she tried killing herself for the first time because of you." Was it really that long ago? Twelve fucking years. It almost feels like time actually stood still from that point on. I've gotten older, but I haven't lived past that day. How could she try to hurt herself because of this scum? How can something as beautiful as my sister be gone and destroyed forever? Every goddamn day starts with me reliving my parents telling me two years ago that my beautiful Isa is gone to be with my baby brother. That Isabella and Thomas are together in heaven watching out for each other and me. I can still hear my mom crying, weeping like a baby as yet another one of her children gets ripped out of her hands. I remember my dad's dead eyes as he told me she was gone. I feel the guilt of her death every bloody day. I waited in that damn restaurant for over an hour and she didn't show, I called and she didn't pick up her phone. I just got fed up, threw her birthday cake in the bin, and left. I should've gone to her flat to look after her to make certain she was all right. Maybe I could've called the medics sooner. When they found her, it was too late.

I didn't understand back then that my brother and sister had been paying for my parents' sins. You don't get to have our wealth without being hated, envied, and cursed. Thomas was just a baby, I don't even remember when he was taken from us, but I grew up with Isa. She was beautiful, smart, kind, and had everything. She had herds of friends and every bloke in London wanted to take her out. Why would she let herself get involved with him and his friends? Why is he special? Why couldn't somebody stop it?

"I was thirty-eight," Louis says, bringing me out of my thoughts and back to our painful reality. "She called me that morning. I don't know how she got my number or why I picked up. I never answer numbers I don't recognize, but I did. She said she was sorry for hurting me and that she knows how much I love Emily. She'd heard we had another baby and that it was time to give up. I wanted to hang up on her, but I couldn't. I felt so bad for her...I failed her. We were friends a long time ago. I cared for her as a friend once, and yet I just stood there in the kitchen, watching my wife and listening to Isa say goodbye. She hung up and that was it. After everything she'd been through, with the failed suicide attempts and even after she got clearance from the hospital, I knew she was too sick to go on living a normal life."

I stand dejectedly and look out into Central Park, listening to Louis fucking Bruel tell me about my sister's last words. As he talks to me, all I can think is, why? Why would she call him and not me? It was her birthday and she didn't talk to me. Why would she waste her last breath on him? I feel a lump form in my throat and I know we need to end this rendezvous. I read her book. I know what he did to her. They weren't just friends. He used and abused her. Too much money, sex, and drugs. The way he talks, you'd think he actually cared about her. You'd think he wasn't the man that got off on seeing her mutilated by other men while he sat and watched. I feel bile rising and I want this jack-arse out of my sight.

"You need to get your fucking arse out of here. I'm done listening to your bullshit." He now sits on the floor in his hand-made whistle and flute, and for a split second I want to believe that he's not a monster. As much as I loathe him I want to pretend that Emily loves a good guy. But that second passes and I once again hear my sister's voice as she narrates his actions, and my heart turns to steel as I hate him even more.

"I'm leaving, but I need you to promise me that you'll leave my wife alone. I don't want you contacting her. It's just not safe for you to be around her. I don't know what kind of revenge you're after, but she didn't know about Isa when we met. If you have words, you know where to find me, but let's leave the women and children out of this." Did this cocksucker just say "not safe"?

"Mate, those drugs must be messing with your cognitive ability if you reckon me talking to Emily wouldn't be safe. I would never hurt her. I'm the one that brought her back home 'safe'! I would do anything to keep her safe, and if telling her the truth about her dirty husband will help keep her safe, I'll do that, too."

He gets up off the floor and goes to fix himself a drink.

"Help yourself," I say.

Louis turns around and replies, "I always do, Willy-Boy, I always do." He throws back a shot of whiskey and heads towards the door. "You have until nine AM to evacuate this hotel or security will help throw you out. This time, you happened to walk into my hotel, and I don't plan on sharing half my bed with you. New York is mine and so is my wife, remember that!"

Without another word, he leaves. "Cheerio, arsehole!" I call after him. Bloody marvelous, now I need to get to the bottom of his threat and I still need to find a way to speak to Emily. She needs to know! There is no way he owns this hotel. I would bloody know if he owned the goddamn Pierre! The fucker is bluffing, just trying to run me out of town. No chance, I'm talking to Emily if it's the last thing I do.

Sara

"Heaven Is A Place On Earth[7]" by Belinda Carlisle

It takes us over an hour to drive less than thirty-five blocks in New York City. Traffic is insane as usual and pulling up to a hotel on 5th Avenue is virtually impossible. The amount of tourists in this city is inconceivable at times. Em's driver finally lets us off on 61st Street, right in front of the hotel's main entrance. Security ushers the two of us inside like we own the joint. Emily and Louis are New York royalty and knowing them as just Emily, my best friend, and Louis, the guy who worships at her feet, is sometimes surreal. Seeing the girl you pee in front of on the cover of gossip magazines is still something I need to get used to.

Once we're inside the hotel, everything happens fast; we don't go anywhere near the check-in counter and we seamlessly follow a man that leads us to a waiting elevator where we're whisked off to the penthouse suite at The Pierre hotel. The elevator attendant greets Emily, obviously knowing exactly who she is. Emily introduces me and lets her know I'll be staying at their apartment for as long as I need. The elevator stops and we walk into a foyer that puts many of the top hotel lobbies in New York to shame. I know that once the mirrored doors open I will step foot into what only a handful of fortunate elites have ever seen. The middle set of doors part for us and it's hard to believe this kind of opulence exists.

Emily leads the way into the biggest ballroom I have ever seen. The sweeping staircase in the distance belongs in the grand library or a museum, definitely not a private residence on the forty-first floor on 5th Avenue. It's bigger than the Bruels' town-house, for crying out loud.

My family is very well off. I've never heard the word "No" when it came to buying clothes, shoes or taking trips. But what the Bruels have is something entirely different. Their type of wealth you only read about; it's the kind of money that will open any door. And believe it or not, Emily does not flaunt her status. Any other woman would be shopping day and night, surrounding herself with other wealthy snobby socialites, but not my Emily. I secretly love how my best friend only wants to spend time with her family and me. She doesn't let strangers into her inner circle. Besides her sister, Jenna, and me, Louis is her only other best friend. Their bubble is something to admire and strive for. Not that I could ever find someone that would only need my company the way her husband wants and needs to spend every breathing moment of his time with her. Anyway, Emily will never make another human question their worth in her presence. She's humble to a fault and couldn't be more down to earth if she tried.

She watches me take in this lavish suite we've entered and stands right next to me, taking it all in as well. Her eyes are dancing with excitement as though this isn't her lifestyle. I love that. We both smile at each other and I instantly think back to our slumber parties back when we were teenagers. She wasn't allowed to sleep anywhere but home, and my parents couldn't give a shit where I slept, so I would end up sleeping at her house almost every weekend. We would start off in separate rooms, but we always snuck in and ended up falling asleep in the same bed. *Oh, the good ol' days.* Where does the time go?

"What do you think?" she asks me with a ridiculous smile.

"'Heaven Is A Place On Earth[7]' by Belinda Carlisle," I answer with an expression I'm sure mirrors her own. Not sure why I'm so happy! I have more problems than God and I haven't figured out anything except that I won't be needing to crash at my brother's or my parents' or be alone at a hotel somewhere. "Tonight, will you fuck your husband extra hard for me?"

Her face drops before she starts smiling again. "If that statement came out of anybody else's mouth, I'd scratch their eyes out. Only you can say shit like that to me and it's actually comforting to hear." She smirks my way. She knows I wouldn't touch Louis if he were the last sperm donor on the planet. I may have slept with a married man my whole adult life, but Louis and Emily are family. It's like Eddie always said to me, *"you don't shit where you eat."*

We laugh as we continue to inspect my humble abode for the next month. I look over to a beautifully-set table and I swear it's like Pinkoulicious did the catering in honor of our arrival. Pink cupcakes, pink macaroons, pink mousse, pink lemonade, I think I even see pink tea sandwiches and wraps. I look over to see Emily holding her head in her hands and shaking it from side to side.

"Sara, I'm sorry! I told Louis we needed some girl bonding time and this is what he thinks women eat when they bond. He's not well, it's the drugs they have him on."

We both erupt into uncontrollable laughter. It's incredibly sweet how thoughtful her crazy husband is. To think that we're standing here, laughing, when only a month ago, Louis had been fighting for his life. If something would've happened to him, I don't know how Em would go on. He really is her whole life, her first real kiss, her first love, her first everything...*hopefully, first and last*, I think sadly to myself.

I always thought the boy I first kissed would turn into the person that I'd get the privilege of kissing for the rest of my days. Em must think that I lost count of how many men I've kissed in my life, but I can count them all on one hand with three fingers: Jeffery, Phillip, and Gavin. I don't even know if Gavin really counts as a kiss since we never actually kissed in private or exchanged spit. *What a sad life I've lived.* I wish I could tell Em the truth. How did I manage to lie and fool her for so long? I think I even fooled myself into believing that I can pick up any guy and just fuck his brains out and walk away. I think I'm the girl that can have one-night stands and never look back. If they only knew. Only I get to carry the burden of my lies and suffer the aftermath. I could've had a life, but I chose, and continue to choose to keep the charade going.

Emily is already directing my luggage upstairs; she orders us some sushi instead of her husband's food choices, and makes sure it's not pink. She walks over to me with a flute of pink champagne and says, "'Girls Just Wanna Have Fun[8]' by Cindy Lauper." Clinking our glasses, she adds, "What happens at The Pierre stays at The Pierre," and winks her baby blues at me.

"Here's to you telling me all about sleeping with someone other than Louis. And to 'Little Lies[9]' by Fleetwood Mac," I reply and wink right back at her. "Louis doesn't have this place bugged, right?" I ask, almost choking on my champagne as that thought hits my brain mid-sip.

"I'd rip his balls out. He hasn't given me a moment of privacy since we got back home. If he's listening in on our conversation, I'll kill him."

Yeah, he wouldn't go that far, I think reassuringly to myself as I go to plant my ass on the comfy-looking cream-colored couch that's calling my name. The staff is starting to leave one by one. I was adamant on our ride over that I don't want a guard or a nanny to watch over me. I'm a nobody and I only plan to use one room and eat out or order in; therefore, I don't need more than bi-weekly housekeeping services. The Bruels will obviously not let me pay for any of this shit, so I don't plan on taking advantage of their generosity.

"Can we talk about why your hair is so dark? I can't even see any of your blond," Em, states matter-of-factly, picking up a pink olive from our smorgasbord of pink treats. She lifts her eyes at me, pinning me with a stare. *Fuck, do I really have to tell her why my hair is almost black?* "Sara, what's up? You've been completely not my Sara ever since you married that asshole, whose name I won't even mention because I'm not trying to upset you or me. But Eddie did mention to Louis that he's worried about you. And you know I am as well. If you have something to say, you'd tell me, right? You know I would never judge you. I'm here for you—good or bad."

I nod as I look down, and once again, that feeling of shame and sadness spreads through my body like cold, liquid fire.

I need her to stop focusing on me and start telling me what's got her out of sorts. "Can we please go back to why you've called this meeting today? We need to talk about your mystery lover and why he's here," I say with exaggerated hand gestures. Em rolls her eyes and flops down on the identical couch facing mine. "Spill the beans, Emily Marcus."

She smiles when I call her by her maiden name. "He was a nice guy. I thought he genuinely felt bad for me and just wanted to help me out. You know I'm a naïve dimwit, Sara, I get fooled too easily," Em says in a small voice with her eyes closed.

I think of how I've lied to her our whole friendship and how spot-on her statement truly is. She is in many ways incredibly naïve and gullible. Emily has always accepted any stupid story I've told her over the years without requiring much proof or asking millions of questions. She has never doubted my tales and I guess it's one of the reasons I love her so much; she accepts me as I am, even if she really has no idea who her best friend really is. She wants to believe people are good and that whatever comes out of their mouth is the actual God's honest truth. She wants to believe that all men love their wives unconditionally the way her dad, husband, and brother-in-law love their wives. We couldn't be more opposite on our views about love and marriage. I've seen my parents in action so I know firsthand that fairytale love stories are exactly that, they're fairy tales that our parents tell us until we know better. Knowing Emily and her perspective on relationships I understand how broken she got when she saw Louis walk out of that hotel with another woman. It was nothing she could've ever imagined, and rightfully so. Just like she would never think that her best friend is the world's best liar.

"Em, babes, I'm still confused about what happened in St. Lucia, so I need you to give me the details and then we'll figure out how to deal." I look over at the window behind where Emily is laying down and I think to myself, where is he? He already texted me his daily *I love you* text, is he thinking of me right now? Does he know that I'm not okay?

"So, I should probably start by telling you how I got to St. Lucia in the first place," Emily finally says to me. "This conversation is long overdue, but I first need for you to understand how it all happened. The morning before I ran away, I was at The Plaza with Jenna, and Louis and I had already been fighting for weeks. We hadn't made love in months. He was the biggest dick to me that morning after I told him about a bad dream I had, so I think you get the picture of my overall frame of mind that day. Then I saw him walk out of the elevator with a beautiful woman by his side and I had a complete and utter meltdown. I don't re-member leaving Jenna, walking home, or how I even got home; it's just one big mush in my head. I remember sitting in my clos-et thinking that my world was over—lights out, bye-bye. How could I live knowing that Louis, *my* Louis, was somewhere lov-ing another woman, touching her, kissing her, making love to her? How could I go on when he is my whole heart, not just half my heart? Sara, I wanted to kill myself. I wanted to get hit by a car and just stop the pain. We haven't been intimate in months. Us! Can you imagine? The man who couldn't let me pass him by without somehow touching me, the man who sent me at least four messages and texts a day telling me what he wants to do to me once he gets home, that same man just checked out and slowly started to withdraw from any intimacy with me whatsoever." She takes a deep breath and I see the tears running down her face. I get up off my couch and come lie next to her, nestling her close to me. She takes a few more deep breaths and continues.

"I couldn't tell Jenna, I've never involved anybody in our personal issues. I mean, you know how it is, married couples fight and then they make up and everything goes back to normal. Why involve more people for no reason? I didn't say anything to her or Mike because they were happy, they just had a baby. You know how much my parents love Louis; I didn't feel right complaining to them and making them worry. I truly believed he was too busy at work to make time for me. You and I weren't talking, who could I have told about this? I was completely alone."

I was a selfish bitch when I stopped talking to Em after Gavin and I got married. She was the only one smart enough to question our phony relationship and I was too scared she'd know the truth and ruin my master plan. Those were the hardest years of my life. And now, hearing her tell me that she had no one to turn to is gut wrenching. I didn't think it was possible, but I'm even more disgusted with myself.

"All I remember is crying for hours and then I decided that I needed to get my shit together. I knew that I needed some alone time to clear my head and fight through the paralyzing fear of ending up alone and without him. I'm a mother, I have kids to worry about, and whether my husband decided to find a new lover or a new wife, I still needed to be Rose and Eric's mother. I picked myself up and left as far away from him and his city as I physically could. Before I got to the airport, I made a deal with myself in the cab that I would take the first non-domestic flight that I could get on. St. Lucia was my destiny and off I went." Emily untangles herself from our canoodling and goes in search of a tissue and some water, I think. I hear her blow her nose before she climbs back to her spot on the couch and cuddles into me again.

"Sara, you'd be proud of how drunk I got on that flight. When I got off that plane, my brain was too fucked up to function and I just fell asleep on a bench outside the airport." She raises her hand in the air as if swearing, letting me know she's serious.

"Shut-the-fuck-up! You slept outside on a dirty bench, alone? You stupid cow, you could've been raped or killed."

She nods her head; wow, she must've been so far gone. "My phone was dead, I didn't have a charger, and I was having a mental crisis on a wooden bench in the middle of the night in a goddamn Caribbean Island that I've never been to."

"I'm sorry." Now it was my turn to cry. "When I got your text 'It Must've Been Love[10]' by Roxette, I thought you were talking about me and my divorce. I told Eddie it was okay to tell you, and I was hoping you'd call me once you knew that Gavin and I were over. I'm sorry. I was sure it was meant for me. I should've called you! I should've answered your text but I was embarrassed after the way I left things off in London...I didn't even invite you to our stupid wedding dinner in New York." Emily wipes my tears with her used napkin. "Does that tissue have your shnats?" I ask her as we both laugh.

"Only my tears, I threw the booger tissue out. We can be tear sisters; two twats crying for no good reason. Don't worry about not inviting me, I told Louis that I wouldn't have gone even if you did. He was awful, Sara. Anyway, back to my story. In the morning, I asked a random luggage porter at the airport to recommend a hotel. He said Le Spa. I got on a helicopter and got myself there in less than half hour. So, listen to this part," Em says as she sits up to start employing hand gestures to continue her destructive tale. We're New Yorkers, I love how we talk with our hands.

"When I get there, I find out that the hotel is completely sold out. Zero rooms. The guy at the reception calls over his manager to try and help me arrange another hotel. The manager showed up and was looking at me like he's seen me before. But people sometimes look at me that way because they may have seen my picture by Louis' side in magazines. I never pay any attention to it, but then he said my name without me offering it to him, which once again, I chalked up to him reading *Fortune* or *Money* magazine, which Louis always gives interviews for." A knock sounds at the door and Em stops her story to go retrieve our sushi delivery.

A few minutes later, with a full spread of spicy Tuna and California rolls in front of us, she continues her sordid tale. "Sara, this perfect stranger was ridiculously nice to me. I was a mess, crying at the idea of calling Louis my ex-husband. This guy was trying to make me laugh and saying sweet things. He offered to give me his room. I refused at first but I was so out of it. My brain, body, and especially my heart were on life support. I needed a break and he was it."

"Why didn't you call or check your messages to make sure everything was okay at home?" I ask, knowing that it would be the natural thing for her to do. Emily is always responsible. Her not calling to check in is not her style.

"Remember I told you my phone was dead? Will was nice enough to offer me his phone and when I called home, Pam picked up."

"Who's Pam?" *I really know nothing about her life anymore*, I think sadly to myself.

"Pam is my housekeeper. She picked up and told me my parents slept over that night at my house. When I asked her where Louis was, she said he didn't come home. I asked if the kids were okay and then I hung up. I had it all figured out; Louis left me and didn't come home. My parents came to stay with the kids because Louis was MIA. At that point, I just wanted my life to end on that beach in St. Lucia."

Em tells me this whole story without looking at me. Her eyes are closed and I know she's beating herself up inside. She no doubt blames herself for Louis' heart attack, and I'm not sure what I need to say to her to make it better.

So, I decide the best thing is for me to be me, and say what Em expects me to say, "Where is the part about you ending up in bed with the manager of that hotel?"

She finally opens her tear-filled eyes and smirks. At that moment I know she needs me to be me. "Will actually owns that hotel. He gave me his room and I agreed only because he explained that he would be staying at his parents' Villa a few miles from the hotel grounds. His family owns half the properties in St. Lucia."

This Will manager-owner-dude is starting to sound very appealing. Not so much for me, but I can see how he could woo Em into spending the night with him on some remote island while she thinks her husband left her.

"I'm still waiting for the bed part. You really are milking this shit. What have you done? Spill it!"

She lays on her side, facing me, and we're finally eye to eye. When she looks at me, I know she will tell me everything. This girl couldn't lie if her life depended on it. When you look into Em's eyes, you see right through to her heart.

"He was a stranger and I needed someone to pour all the crap that was clogging my head. I was holding things in for months. I told him everything that happened with Louis in the past four months leading up to how I caught him cheating, and as I was telling him all this, he was getting all worked up. He then told me that his fiancée cheated on him with one of his friends, so here I go again, thinking that his reaction to Louis' actions made perfect sense. I thought that the cheating thing hit close to home for him. I was still crying and he decided that liquor would be the cure for my broken heart. Sara, I got obliterated to the point that I can't remember a whole entire day." Emily! Drunk! This story sounded so far-fetched...my best friend plastered to the point of no recollection is something I'd pay big money to see.

"Everything you're telling me is very hard for me to swallow. I can't believe you had the balls to get on a plane—wait, a commercial flight!—and just leave. Then you slept outside on a dirty bench, then you tell your business to a perfect stranger, and then you get piss drunk with the same complete stranger to the point of amnesia."

"I know, it sounds like one of your stories, but it's really mine. I woke up the next day in a room I've never seen, in a huge bed I don't remember going to sleep in, half naked, and I hear Will's voice next to me. Relax! He told me we didn't have sex and I think if we did, I would've remembered. Yes, you don't have to ask, you already know he was naked. He offered to help me forget about Louis and I said 'N.O. No!' I explained to him that I'm madly in love with my husband, even if he's *not* in love with me anymore. He kept saying that he gives Louis two days and then he'll show me how a man should treat a woman. It was all very sweet and chivalrous, but I had no intentions of being intimate with him, I swear! Yes, he was cute but he wasn't Louis."

I listen to Emily, but we're still in wonderland with this story that sounds nothing like the girl I grew up with. "So that's it? No hanky panky, no playing with his peen, no naughty secrets you'd like to share with Sara?" I ask, knowing full well that she just told me everything she thinks she knows. I wouldn't mind getting Will's side of the story, which I'm sure is juicier and probably more X-rated. I wonder if he remembers more from that night? *Of course he remembers more.* I'm positive something sexual took place in St. Lucia whether Em remembers it or not.

"He tried to kiss me, but I wouldn't let him. I was mad at

myself at how aroused I had gotten around him in the first place. Just getting wet felt like I was cheating on Louis." She offers me that little intriguing morsel of information and I eat it up and enjoy it immensely.

"When did you find out Louis had a heart attack?" I know she was by his side when he regained consciousness. She must've somehow got her little ass back home from paradise.

"Will saw the news and brought me back home without telling me what really happened. When I got home, Jenna and my mom were waiting for me at home, crying. I thought something happened to the kids, and then Jenna said that Louis had a heart attack and I fainted. I knew that he'd died. I swear, Sara, I thought one hundred percent that it was all over and that I'd lost him again, but this time forever. I kept thinking about Rose and Eric growing up without their father and it was all too much for me." Tears stream down her face again and my heart breaks for her. I cry with her, and as much as I know I should be strong, I can't help it. I know what it feels like to be alone without the person you love most. Having the love of your life ripped away by fate is something I know all too well. We all think we know what our life should look like, but when our real life materializes, sometimes the truth is too much to handle.

"Stop blaming yourself for what happened. Everything is okay; Rose, Eric, and you will never have to worry about being without Louis. Please stop crying, you still didn't get to the part of why Will is here!"

She wipes her tears with her T-shirt and tries to compose herself. "Yeah, well, a few weeks ago, I decided that I didn't want any secrets between Louis and me anymore. The reason we were in that mess to begin with was because he kept me in the dark. He didn't want me to know that Bruel Industries was heading toward bankruptcy and that he invested his money with the wrong people. To save his company, he had to pay debts with money he no longer possessed. He needed to sell our properties and he thought that he was failing me. Sara, how the fuck could he think that he could fail me by selling bricks and stones? You know how I feel about our wealth. At the end of the day, I just need him and our babies healthy, together, and all in one place, and I'd be the richest woman on the planet."

"I know, babe, you are as far away from someone that needs or cares about material things that I know." That, I can tell you, is three thousand percent true. Emily has it all, but never flaunts it and never asked for it. Her parents raised their daughters right. Her nana would be proud of her. I'm sure if Louis would've given her the choice, she'd have finished school and had a career, but that man couldn't share her with anybody. *Always the caveman,* I think.

"Once I saw that Louis was feeling a little better, and once we finally got a chance to make love, I told him that something happened in St. Lucia while I was running away from my overactive imagination. I couldn't tell him before because in some way, I felt like I actually did cheat on him with Will; maybe not physically, but emotionally and mentally. I knew how important it was for him to finally have our sexual bond back after everything that had happened. You know how alpha-ape he is when it comes to making sure everybody knows he's pollinating me." We both start laughing uncontrollably until we're crying once again. I bet guys don't cry happy and sad tears within a span of minutes like crazy, hormonal women do.

"Okay stop cracking me up and tell me what you told him. Was he freaking out? Remember when my brother and I first met him in Central Park and he thought Eddie wanted to fuck you? Did he have that deranged look on his face? Did he stand a little taller?" I don't think I will ever forget the way Louis and my brother's relationship first started. Louis is one of my brother's best friends today, but back then, Louis looked at him with a murderous stare. Who would've thought they would be such close friends after their initial encounter?

"He wasn't happy; he wanted to know if I was trying to kill him, again. But you need to hear this. I go into all the details I've just told you about meeting Will, blah blah blah, and then I say the name of the hotel that Will owns—Le Spa, the place I chose accidently—and Louis goes ballistic until he comes down long enough to ask me if it was William Knight who came to my rescue!"

My eyes enlarge to the size of melons as I start to smell the scandal. "Wait one fucking minute! Are you telling me that your husband knows this guy Will, William whatever his name is?" This is no good.

"Sara, he doesn't just know him, they hate each other. I-wanna-cut-your-throat kind of hate."

"What?! Why? Are they business enemies? Em, shit, is this Will guy trying to find you and hurt you?" Suddenly, it isn't funny anymore, and a cold chill spreads through my body as I think of somebody trying to get revenge on Louis by hurting Emily.

We both sit up as I try to make sense of all the details Emily's been telling me since this morning.

"I have to talk to you about something we've never discussed before." *Fuck! There's more shit!* I may need to get a pad and start writing crap down. Emily may need a lawyer, not just a friend. "When you and Eddie came to see Louis and I after we had gotten engaged at *The Blue Lagoon* in Turks and Caicos twelve years ago, do you remember that?"

"How could I forget?"

"Well, that day I walked in on Louis having a very disturbing conversation on the phone with another woman."

I may help Will kill Louis if she starts telling me that he hurt her back then, too.

"Sara, wipe that look off your face. It's not what you think. He was talking to a girl that he used to be good friends with. He told me that he slept with her once before he and I met and that she wanted more. She wasn't all there mentally and didn't take his rejection very well. She was a spoiled rich socialite with a drug habit and a penchant for wild sex." *She sounds like every guy's wet dream.* "After she heard about Louis being off the market and with me, or probably before that as well, she wrote a memoir. A freaking tell-all book about her fucked-up life!"

I'm about to say *"who cares"* when Emily stops me from talking.

"The book was about her and Louis. How she loved him, what she did for him, and what he did to her. She was going to publish a book of lies to ruin his career and probably try to break us up as well. Thank God that book never made it anywhere. Louis, with an army of lawyers and your brother's help I'm sure, stopped the publishers and I believe Louis bought the rights to that book and won a judgment stating that if any illegal copies of it ever see the light of day, it would cost her father everything he's worth...which I heard is a lot."

I grow confused with her story and this strange detour about some woman and her book. "Em, I think I need to start writing down some information because I'm getting confused and I don't want to get to the point of negative returns, where my brain starts subtracting facts. Sit tight, let me go get my writing pad." I start getting up as Em jerks me back down.

"I don't need a lawyer, I spoke to ten already, I just need one friend."

She's right, I need to turn my attorney radar off and just listen as if we're teenagers. "Sorry, keep going. You were up to the part where the book was never printed and I suspect they have her father's assets tied into their lawsuit, which I'm sure included defamation of character."

She nods and continues. "Louis also had video footage of this girl saying that if he doesn't continue having a sexual relationship with her, she will ruin him. I know that video played a big part in the trial, too. I should also tell you that she tried to kill herself unsuccessfully before and after we got married." Em's eyes fall to her hands as she plays with her engagement ring. I see them glaze over with tears once again.

"What is it? Do you think he loved her? Is she a threat to you guys now? I can't even believe that this is something you were dealing with at age eighteen and I'm only hearing about it now." I guess we both have secrets.

"Sara, she's dead. Third time's the charm. She managed to successfully kill herself about two years ago. Her name was Isabella Knight."

I listen and it takes my brain a few minutes to connect the dots. But once the lines have been drawn, it all makes sense. "Will Knight and Isabella Knight are husband and wife?"

She shakes her head. "No, Will is her little brother," she tells me, and alarm bells suddenly go off in my head, one by one. "He blames Louis for Isabella's death. He even tried to have it out with him many years ago, and the police got involved in their altercation. So, in short, I walked into Isabella's family's hotel in St. Lucia and right into Will's arms—or his bed, as Louis keeps reminding me."

I'm speechless! Just speechless!

"I don't think he was trying to hurt me like Louis believes. He brought me back home safe on a private jet. He drove me to my house, and he was the one who caught me when I fainted on my front porch when I heard Jenna's news about Louis. He only left my side once I regained consciousness. He mentioned that we should talk. I have his number and I truly would like to talk to him without feeling like a traitor. Louis doesn't let me out of his sight. He works from home, he even escorts me to the bathroom," she says, rolling her eyes. I totally believe it; that sounds exactly like Louis!

"I think you should talk to him and get his perspective from that night. Find out why he didn't tell you that he knew exactly who you were. What was his motive for lying?" I feel like a hypocrite saying those words; what was—or is—my motive for lying my whole life? Some people are just liars, no ifs ands or buts about it. "Do you know where he's staying?"

Em shakes her head. "I just have his number, and he mentioned that he's staying at a hotel not too far from my house. But I don't know which exactly. I'm not even sure he's still in New York, but he said that he'll wait until we talk before he goes back home."

"Do you want me to do a check and see which hotel he's at? You know, if you want, I could go meet him for you and ask him shit on your behalf?" I'm sure I'll get more information than Emily from this guy. I'm good at getting men to talk, that's why my clients keep me.

"Do you think we could do that? Maybe we can send him a text and you could even meet him downstairs in the lobby. You can interrogate him and see what he wanted to tell me? You could explain that due to the ongoing lawsuit Louis has with his family it would be unwise for us to meet. Sara, I didn't even think about you going to meet him, but that's a great idea! I need answers without going behind Louis' back and you can get those answers for me. God, I love you," she squeals and lunges herself at me.

Sara

"Call Me[11]" by Blondie

An hour later, we've finished composing our first text to Will to see if he's still hanging around the city waiting for Emily to call. The way we're conspiring has a very *Pinky and The Brain* quality about it; you'd think we were trying to take over the world. We also have a list of questions we need answers to that only Will Knight would know.

-Hi William, it's Emily Bruel from St. Lucia. Please let me know if you're still in NYC and if you're available to meet. I have a few things I'd like to discuss with you.-

His response comes in almost instantaneously.

-Emily is that really you?-

Em and I look at each other and start giggling immediately; this really does feel like we're back in high school prank-calling a poor fool. This even reminds me of Emily at eighteen trying to stalk Louis before they officially met. I remember her telling me how she would pass his office a few times a day hoping she'd run into him. I even helped pick out the dildo version of Louis back in the good ol' days.

"Wait, do you think we're doing the right thing? You know, he'll think that he's coming to meet me. Sara, I don't want him getting angry with you. I don't exactly know if he's mentally sound or even dangerous," she says as the real Emily starts making an appearance. Truthfully, I didn't even think she'd take it this far. But I'm not worried about Will; I deal with deranged asswipes for a living. From all she's told me about him, he seems ninety percent saner than most of the men I get paid to deal with.

"Let's not get ahead of ourselves. We don't even know if he's here. It's been what? Over a month! I can't imagine he would just hang out and wait until you finally decided to call him."

Emily's phone rings and we both jump up like the guilty schemers that we are. She looks down and, of course, it's her parole officer slash husband; it's like he can smell trouble.

"Let me talk to him, I don't want him getting worried. Sara, *do not* answer his text until I get back. Promise me!" she warns me with her version of the look of death. Emily has yet to scare me or anybody else.

"Yeah, sure, I promise. Go stroke your man's ego and tell him that you'll let him pollinate you later," I yell after her as she sticks her tongue out at me and proceeds upstairs to talk to her neurotic husband. Well, he's crazy, but at least he's crazy about her. At least she never has to share his craziness with anybody. I'd give anything to have a crazy to call my own.

As soon as she's out of sight, I look back down at my phone and think nothing will happen if I just answer him a *yes*—he wants to know if it's really Emily, so why should we keep him waiting?

-Yes, it's me.-

His response comes in even faster this time.

-I need to see you. I'm in New York, not too far from you. I'll meet you anywhere, anytime. I have much to tell you. Don't believe anything you hear about me. I would never harm you. You don't know how happy I am to finally be able to talk to you.-

I read his reply five times before I type back

- Can we meet at The Pierre tonight? It's on 5th Ave between 60th and 61st street. I have a suite reserved and I think it's better if we meet privately away from the paparazzi or anyone that could recognize me.-

I don't feel out of line and have no qualms about texting this poor schmuck. Isn't this what Emily wanted, closure, for me to meet him and get answers?

-I know exactly where it is. What time should I come?-

I do a quick calculation in my head and figure I can get rid of Em by six this evening and be showered, rested, and ready to meet this fool by ten.

-10PM. I'll leave you a key at reception under the name Jeffery Rossi.-

I'm pleased with my quick thinking; if Louis ever decided to check the guest list seeing Jeff's name won't raise any alarms.

-I'll be there.-

As the adrenaline starts dissipating, I realize that Emily is about to have a shit attack when she finds out I made arrangements to meet Will without her consent. The woman is an anal control freak and that five-minute interaction would've taken her two hours at least. I decide that it's better if I erase my conversation with Will and give her info on a need-to-know basis. I finish erasing all our texts just before she makes it back down the stairs.

"Oh Lord, I just spoke to Louis and he told me that he heard from a friend of his that Will is in New York trying to have Isabella's book published. He's upset and he begged me to be careful, and that if Will tries to make any contact whatsoever to avoid him at all costs. Louis is freaking out, Sara. He's afraid Will may have pictures of me from St. Lucia and that he'll try to use that against Louis. Oh God, thank goodness we didn't make any plans to meet him. Let's forget about this whole stupid idea. I need to let Louis deal with him, especially since it involves Bruel Industries. That was a close one, huh?"

I'm a little speechless, but since lying comes natural to me, I just smile and say, "Saved by the bell. We just won't answer him. I'll block his number so he won't be able to text or call me back, or well, he thinks it's you." *Oh Lord, what have I done?*

"Perfect, I'm sure he was just trying to use me to get back at Louis for his sister's sake anyway. I must have it stamped on my forehead: 'I'm a gullible fool, lie to me.' I don't need that kind of book about my husband floating around. Can you imagine if Rose were to find out about it? You know how mean kids can be, I'm sure they would make fun of her and it would be all over the news. And if Will has pictures of me naked in bed with him from St. Lucia, that would be catastrophic. I think Louis would definitely murder him." She falls back on the couch and covers her face with her hands in horror. No doubt imagining Louis' face if naked pictures of her hit the tabloids.

This Will guy is starting to sound like a big douche, and suddenly, a plan started materializing in my head of chaining him to the bed until he signs a few legal documents that I'm itching to draw-up, making sure he won't try to hurt Louis by dragging Emily and those beautiful kids through the gutter...*son of a bitch*. The only way to hurt Louis Bruel is by hurting what he loves most in the world, and I believe that Will probably worked that out for himself by now. I will most definitely keep our meeting, but my goal now needs to be ensuring that my best friend and her children will not be used as a pawn by Will Knight, in his sister's grand scheme of revenge.

Emily finally leaves to go back home and I'm left all alone in my new, beautiful, temporary abode until I figure out where the fuck I want to start building a new worthless life for my lonely self. I mean, the path my life is on right now is pure crap, how much worse could it possibly get? Gavin and I are done, we used each other to the max and there is nothing left to our relationship, not even a friendship. I need to somehow rewire my brain and my heart to forget about the only man that ever mattered. I know he loves me, but it's not enough. I need to start a life, a family; I've waited too long. I have no one to blame but myself and I accept it, and I'm moving on. I hear my phone buzzing with a text message, but I need to shower quickly and get ready to meet Will the asshole and set him straight once and for all. No one messes with my girl and lies to her...well, I lie to her, but I do it for her own good. She needed to have an adventurous friend that she lived vicariously through and that was me. None of the lies I've ever told Emily were meant to hurt her. The only person that pays and got hurt by all those stories was and is me.

The shower at my new penthouse is incredible. The hot water cascades down from the ceiling with at least ten jets pounding at my sad limbs. I look at my reflection through the thick glass shower door and wonder to myself what is it about me that is not quite desirable enough? What is it about me that he can't seem to let go of and yet not quite adequate to be his everything? Maybe I need to get my boobs done? I'm tall, I could use bigger boobs to look sexier. Who am I kidding? I would never alter my body for a man, especially since he's never once mentioned a need for my breasts to be fuller. He loves me as I am; it's just that in our case, love is not always enough.

An hour later I'm out of the shower with steam still coming off my body. Jeff and I could never shower together because I only bathe in scalding-hot water. Last time he joined me in the shower, he said he got second-degree burns on his back. *Stop thinking about him, Sara,* I mentally yell at myself, no good ever comes out of thinking about him.

I lay on my big, beautiful bed and look at the clock on the wall. It's almost seven. I need to stop daydreaming and come up with a kickass plan of attack for when I meet this bastard, Will. I should've asked more details about him from Em. Unless he takes his drawers off, I really have no clue what the fucker looks like. *Maybe I should ask him to send me a picture to refresh my memory,* I think as I start giggling. He'd know for sure that someone who's not Emily is fucking with him behind those texts. I'm an attorney, I'm sure I can figure this out. How hard can it be to spot a poor fool looking for a woman?

I decide that it's better for me to wait for him at the lobby cafe, and watch to see who enters. I will leave Jeff's name and a key at the check-in counter. My plan seems solid; if he looks too mental, I'll just call security and abort the mission. He has no idea who I am and what I look like. No one will know and we'll all live miserably ever after. The End.

I decide this undercover rendezvous calls for my black Gucci one shoulder cocktail dress paired with the black Louboutin Pigalle heels. I finger dry my hair, add a little blush, gloss, perfume, and off I go to help my best friend rid herself of

Will "The Problem Intruder" Knight. I was there when Emily fell in love with Louis Bruel. I know what he means to her and what those two have; it's not something that a stranger from St. Lucia is going to ruin with a book and some photos. My best friend almost lost her husband a month ago. I will not let this parasite try to destroy them. I will make sure he leaves Emily and Louis Bruel alone if it's the last thing I do. I owe her that...

William

"Karma Chameleon[12]" by Culture Club

The pompous fucker is some kind of shareholder in this bloody hotel. Maybe he bought stock in the hotel when he found out I was staying here. I don't have many belongings with me, I didn't even pack an overnight bag when I got on the jet to bring Emily back home to her dying husband. I've been waiting for her to call me, text me, bloody anything for the past forty-one days. I've been this close to speaking with her twice. She's just always either with him or her children. *Stupid idiot, she has children, go home!* my head keeps nagging at me. He's alive, she loves him, she chose him, and I need to let her live her life. If she thinks he's good to her, why am I still bloody here? Maybe people change. I try to convince myself of that, knowing just how false the notion is. I wish Isa had found a guy that was good to her, that wanted to change for her. I swallow the big lump in my throat that my thoughts have conjured up.

I sit on a lonely bench by the main entrance of The Pierre Hotel while I wait for my car to arrive, attempting to map out a plan. I should just arrange a flight back home and call it a day. Forget New York, forget Emily, forget Louis and just let sleeping dogs lie. I haven't officially been back to London since Isa's funeral. I did come back unofficially for a few hours to announce my engagement to my parents only to find out my fiancée has been sucking off my best mate on a daily basis for years, therefore ending our silly engagement before anyone even knew. Serves me right for going after his fit secretary. Jason always bragged how Brandy is a godsend and helps him think clearer. Bullocks, to think I almost married a woman that works on her knees for someone other than me. Can a bloke's life be any more fucked up? I snicker at my pathetic existence. I actually feel nothing for Brandy, we had nothing but good sex, really good sex. I don't need to marry someone for good sex; I can pay for that. I want what money can't buy. If I had one wish right now, and the choice to bring Isa back wasn't available, I'd wish for a fair shot with Emily. I would make her so happy, she would never have a reason for that hopeless look she had on her face when she came to me. If I had her, I would be the luckiest man in the world. You can't buy that.

I get a text from my driver letting me know he's outside. I stand up to leave the hotel to find my ride when my eyes register what my mind has dreamt up for weeks. I see her walk through the hotel's main entrance. I'm certain that it's her in the revolving doors, and it's hard for me to breathe. She's here and she's walking towards me. I walk towards Emily in utter and complete disbelief. This is a dream, my prayers have been answered and she bloody came to me. Then, suddenly, like in one of my nightmares, she passes by me as though I'm invisible and abruptly makes a sharp right turn and enters one of the waiting elevators. Boom—she vanishes. As soon as the elevator closes I feel lightheaded and I let out the breath I must've been holding. *Well fuck me, Lucy.* Emily, *my* Emily, is at The Pierre! Maybe they fought? Maybe she left him? Maybe she's looking for me?

I walk over to reception and try to charm the knickers off the cute Asian bird working behind the desk. "Would you be kind enough to check and see if my friend checked in already?"

She gives me a smile and answers, "Do you know what room your friend is staying in?"

I have no clue but nobody needs to know that. I decide that Louis wouldn't go through the trouble of coming to see me this morning unless he was trying to avoid me running into Emily this afternoon. And if Emily were my wife, I would have her booked at the best suite this hotel has to offer.

"I believe it's one of the suites, maybe the Tata Suite or perhaps the Penthouse," I tell her with a smile that I think women find sexy.

She smiles and blushes, confirming my earlier assessment. She starts typing into her computer before she asks me. "What is your friend's name?" Another easy one, I think to myself. What would the fucker use?

"Louis Bruel." I say without hesitation.

The woman looks at me and tells me without missing a beat, "Yes, your friend has arrived. Should I call up and let him know you're here?" My heart starts beating again. Fate leads the way. Just like she walked into my hotel forty-five days ago, she just walked into my arms once again, and no matter what Louis is trying to pull by having me escorted out of New York and far away from Emily, I will get my chance to see her again. I thank the receptionist and ensure her that I'll call my friend on his cell to come fetch me.

I dial my chauffeur and cancel my ride. I sit myself down at the café and wait until my heart starts beating regularly again and until I come up with a way to see Emily. If she only knew how I want to run up and see her, but I don't have a way to make it past security and the elevator attenders know I've checked out. But I can wait, I have all the time in the bloody world to let destiny bring us back together again.

I try to keep calm and act busy, check my emails and Instagram accounts repeatedly when I get my first text from Emily, a text that I've patiently waited for over forty long days to finally receive.

- Hi William, it's Emily Bruel from St. Lucia. Please let me know if you're still in NYC and if you're available to meet. I have a few things I'd like to discuss with you.-

I start typing quickly before this somehow proves to be a mirage or a figment of my imagination. The first thing I need to make sure is that this is, in fact, real.

-Emily is that really you?-

I wait breathlessly for her response. Who else can it be? Why is she being so formal with me? 'This is Emily Bruel from St. Lucia'…does she really think I wouldn't know who she was? Does she really not know that I haven't thought about anything or anybody but her in the past forty-five days? I can't even think back to a time where she wasn't a permanent occupant in my mind. I take a few deep breaths but I can't halt the panic from spreading because she still hasn't answered my text.

-Yes, it's me.-

Her reply comes in almost ten minutes later. I smile like a loon as I eagerly press send to the message I already had written out.

- I need to see you. I'm in New York, not too far from you. I'll meet you anywhere, anytime. I have much to tell you. Don't believe anything you hear about me. I would never harm you. You don't know how happy I am to finally be able to talk to you.-

I hope and pray she'll want to meet now, today or tonight, because I have no intention of leaving this hotel without seeing her. I need for us to talk. I need to touch her, feel her, or just be close to her. I bring my fingers to my nose again and try to remember her scent. The way she let me make her come was the sexiest thing I've ever experienced. The only thing that mars that crazy wild night was when she screamed *his* name once she finally let go and detonated around my fingers. How could she not remember anything? Am I that unremarkable compared to him? Maybe she does remember, perhaps she's embarrassed that she let me make her forget him and the pain he caused her. How could he have neglected her and then cheated on her? Louis fucking Bruel was and always will be an animal. When you give a pig a diamond, he doesn't know better and still treats it like rubbish. Fucking dirty cheater. I feel bile coming up every time I think of all the things he did to my sister.

I look down at my phone and see another text from her.

- Can we meet at The Pierre tonight? It's on 5th Ave between 60th and 61st street. I have a suite reserved and I think it's better if we meet privately away from the paparazzi or anyone that could recognize me.-

Amazing, not only did her stupid husband not succeed in driving me out of his so-called city, he probably helped fate once again by bringing us together. Thank bloody God that Karma is a brilliant bitch.

-I know exactly where it is. What time should I come?-

I find myself smiling so hard my face starts to hurt. I haven't smiled like this since that time we spent together. My cock springs to life just thinking about that night.

-10PM. I'll leave you a key at reception under the name Jeffery Rossi.-

Perfect, I've been called worse before, Jeffery will do just fine. I'm sure her stupid husband made sure I was banned from having access to any of the rooms at this hotel. *But you can't keep us apart, Louis,* I think as the permanent smile spread across my face widens. I'm euphoric and my giddiness won't subside. It's only four in the afternoon, but I don't mind waiting another six short hours if it means seeing her. I quickly leave the café and walk towards the hidden restaurant away from inquisitive eyes as I type back, *-I'll be there-* and patiently wait for the fair chance Emily and I never got.

Sara

"It's Raining Men[13]" by The Weather Girls

I take the elevator down to the lobby bar at The Pierre hotel feeling for the first time in weeks like a woman. I've really kept to myself and my work after the whole Gavin breakup. Besides my pajamas and business suits, I haven't worn anything remotely as feminine as this slinky black dress. I wonder what this Will guy looks like? In my head, I picture him looking more like Gavin—black hair, handsome, tall with big balls. I smile to myself, remembering Emily's vivid description of his package. I wonder for the hundredth time if anything happened that night between those two. What a scandal that would be for the Bruels! Louis might have to start peeing on Em to re-mark her. I am full-on laughing to myself, making the elevator attendant smile; if she only knew what mental image I have dancing around in my mind of Louis peeing on Emily. *Men.*

I walk over to the receptionist and hand him one of my room keys. Em had given me two keys just in case I misplace one.

"Hi, I'm Sara Klein, I'm a guest of Emily and Louis Bruel, I'll be staying at The Penthouse for a little while. Can I leave this key with you to pass along to a friend whom I'd like to have access to my suite? His name is Jeffery Rossi. He will be arriving tonight around ten. Could you please give him this key and send him up?" I ask the man at the desk.

"Sure thing. We'll just add him to your approved guest list and send him right up with the key. Mr. Jeffery Rossi, correct?"

I smile, nod, and walk away.

My goal is to find a quiet little nook to do some thinking. I decide that the little restaurant tucked past the iconic Pierre rotunda will be perfect. As I step into the famous rotunda I look up at the blue-domed ceiling, I smile remembering the great debate Em and I always had about where the best place in the city was to have our weddings. Emily was firm on The Plaza and I always had a soft spot for The Pierre because of this stunning room. After all these years, I still feel like I'm inside a fairytale surrounded by the neo-Renaissance murals. I enter Sirio, the small Italian restaurant, and find a seat at the bar to try and figure out what my approach to Will "The Problem" Knight should be. It's only eight in the evening so I have plenty of time to eat and construct a killer plan of attack.

I look around and see only a handful of people. I'm actually the only one sitting by the bar. This place is cozy with soft, boring, old-fart music streaming in. I take out my pad, order a French martini, and start writing down some notes about my line of questioning.

"Is this seat taken?" I hear someone ask as I lift my gaze to find Brian looking sexy and edible, smirking down at me. *Fuck!* I forgot to cancel my "booty call" with him. *NO! NO! NO!* My insides scream. *What the fuck do I do now?* I start looking frantically around to try and figure out how to get myself out of this disaster. I see a good-looking, light-haired man sitting at a table studying his phone. I get up and give Brain a hello kiss, looking at the stranger on my left again. This time he's smiling down at his phone and I decide that he will do just fine for what I'm about to use him for.

"Brian, shit, I can't believe you came all the way here!"

"You don't make it easy. I was looking for you at the lounge by the entrance. You weren't answering my texts; I thought you'd bailed on me. Sara, this dress and you, I'm excited about this. I haven't been able to stop thinking about you. I knew this would happen one day," he says with downcast bedroom eyes as he runs his fingers down my bare arms.

"Brian, this is going to sound really shitty but I shouldn't have texted you earlier. I was just mad and fighting with my boyfriend," I say and point to the oblivious handsome stranger sitting just far enough away to not hear what I'm saying. Brian looks over at my fake stand-in boyfriend and sure enough, the handsome stranger smiles at us and nods his hello. *Perfect!*

He lowers his head in disappointment before lifting it up with a sly smile and says, "Okay, I don't want to cause any trouble, unless you're looking to spice up your relationship. I actually thought you were married, but if you and your boyfriend are cool with me joining in, I don't mind sharing you tonight." He lowers his head and whispers in my ear, "I've been dreaming of fucking you for a while and my dreams usually come true. Or I can always wait until the next time you have a fight with him." He waves to my fake boyfriend once again, who is now sitting back and watching us intently. "Would you like that? Do you want me to join you guys? We can both enjoy you, and I am very hungry!" Brain whispers with a smirk and a wink, making me regret wearing panties because they're drenched.

I shake my head and smile, thinking how amazing it would be if the first time I had sex with someone other than Jeff would be with two gorgeous men. *Yeah, right. Ha!* Maybe "The Sara" would be up for that kind of adventure, but I'm too much of a pussy to have sex with anyone other than Jeff, let alone two men at the same time. It's especially funny when one of those men in question doesn't even know what he's not going to be part of … funny and sad, simultaneously.

Brian gives me a kiss on the cheek, waves goodbye to our ignorant stranger and leaves. As soon as he's gone I let out a big breath and sit back down at my spot by the bar. Thank God that's over; it almost ruined my grand scheme. I go back to writing notes when I'm interrupted once again. *For the love of God, what now?*

"Can I buy you a drink, sweetheart?" some weird-looking guy with a thick southern accent and a beer belly asks, standing way too close for comfort.

I roll my eyes, raising my hand to say *no thanks.* Old tourist man doesn't understand my hand gesture and sits his old ass at the empty seat right next to me.

"Thank you for the offer but I already have a drink. I'm waiting for someone and I'd like to get some work done...*on my own,*" I say, emphasizing the last part. He nods his head and remains seated at my side. I try to ignore him but his BO and cheap cologne is fucking with my concentration. He also keeps looking at me every couple of seconds. Some men have so much confidence it's utterly bewildering. I can't imagine having the balls to come up to a guy I find attractive and offer to buy him a drink, and when he refuses, just sit right down next to him and fucking stare. What the fuck? Where do they get this self-assurance? It can't be the mirror. The urge to scream starts to surface.

I've made zero progress with my plan of attack. This red-neck at my side has got me so off track that I forgot my train of thought altogether. I don't have much time, and as I try to find a document on my phone, the rude weirdo slides his hand up my thigh and sends shock waves of creepy crawlers up my body.

This cannot be happening to me!

William

"We Don't Need Another Hero[14]" by Tina Turner

I've been killing time at the little Italian restaurant located inside the hotel for hours. I've only left my post once to piss and I'm attempting to stay away from the manager who escorted me out of my suite this morning. I need to stay out of his sight until I meet Emily later tonight. I try to compose my excitement and my scattered thoughts. I ought to be sharp about this chance and figure out how to tell her about her dog of a husband and yet not seem like a jealous hater. I don't know what he's already told her about me. She may think I tried to hurt her in St. Lucia.

I go over the events of that night in St. Lucia in my head. I didn't harm her. I never forced her to do anything she didn't ask me to do. We were both a little zonked...well, she was very hammered. I can bet my left nut that half the things she told me about herself she'd probably never uttered out loud. I think back to the way she begged me to come back to her room, well, it was really my room, but I moved my rubbish out of there for her. She asked me to rub her feet, but then she removed her top and bra and sat in my lap, presented her bare back for me to massage instead of her feet. I remember rubbing her shoulders and thinking that in my wildest dreams I'd never see this, us interacting like this. After walking in on Brandy sucking Jason's knob, I truly had no desire to even talk to another woman. Emily came out of nowhere and I'm still reeling at my level of infatuation with her. Maybe it's because I've followed their lives for years. Maybe it felt like I knew her because in some creepy-stalker way I really did, even before we'd officially met.

After Isa got discharged from the hospital for trying to harm herself for the second time, my parents asked her to move in with them. She refused so I moved in with her to make sure she'd never feel alone. I recall her crying for days, begging me to explain what some ordinary, young, stupid, American girl named Emily had that she didn't. Demanding to know why Louis treated Emily like a queen yet disposed of Isa like yesterday's rubbish. My heart bleeds every time I think back to what Isa wrote in that book. I wonder if Louis ever did those things with Emily, too. *God, I can't think this way.* Emily would never watch as her husband fucked other women in front of her like Isa did with him. Emily bloody ran away from him when she saw him at a hotel with one of his whores. He would never allow his dirty pack of mates to do the things he let them do to Isa in front of him. My sister vividly described what kind of events he orchestrated to get himself off. Acid rises, burning at my throat as I get myself all worked up yet again. Isa let him do anything he wanted in the hopes of being the chosen one, and in the end, he chose Emily, a young, innocent girl who'd never even had a boyfriend before him. He no doubt tainted every inch of her. I wish I could go back in time and save them both from the fucking devil known as Louis Bruel.

I'm so lost in thought that I don't even notice how the hours are passing me by. I look down at my phone and it's almost seven PM. I stand up to stretch out before sitting back down. I've had two bloody salads already. *In three short hours, I will see her again.* My emotions are all over the place today. I'm afraid that when we do finally see each other, face-to-face, it won't be what I've let myself imagine. I'm worried that maybe it was all one-sided. Perhaps only I felt the intense connection we had that night. Lord, what will I do with myself if she tells me to piss off and leave her alone? What if she's waiting for me with him to try and make a fool out of me? Maybe Louis will try to humiliate me by having Emily reject me in front of him. That scenario tauntingly plays out in my mind, and yet I know with certainty that I am willing to take that chance, for at least I will go down knowing I've told her everything he's been keeping away from her for years.

I've been staring at my phone and at her texts for over an hour. I can't help but open my photo folder on my iPhone to look through the dozens of pictures we took together that one night. I have one shot that I've been wanking off to for the last three weeks. Emily is squeezing her big tits together with her mouth slightly ajar. My fingers are pinching her pink nipples and I can't stop myself from smiling like a loon. I look up to make sure no one but me is privy to my exclusive Emily show when I see a couple looking right at me. I nod my head and shut my phone at once. I have a full-on boner that I may need to go take care of somewhere privately. I look for the loo when the guy and girl from before look straight at me once again. This time the bloke raises his hand and waves at me, I wave back. *That's a bit odd*, I ponder to myself. The bird at his side smiles my way before kissing him on the cheek. The fella glances back my way as he leaves, giving me two thumbs up. *What in the bloody hell was that all about?* I think as my erection still strains at my trousers.

I try to calm my thoughts about Emily and her tits when a little while later I see another man approach that same poor bird at the bar. Maybe she's a call girl, I reckon, which does nothing to calm down my dick. I sit back and watch how this beastly old man sits down and watches over her as she writes on her pad. He moves back and checks out her fit arse and then the bloody fool slides his dirty paw up her thigh. The poor girls jumps up in horror and that's my cue.

I take a few steps towards her and once I'm close enough, I slide my arm around her waist as if I've done it millions of times before. She's tall and seems a bit fragile in my arm as I pull her in close. I lower my head and she smells nice. When she looks up at me, she seems familiar. I bring my other hand to her cheek and slightly brush the back of my hand over her über white skin. I whisper loud enough for the arsehole that just helped himself to a feel to hear, "Are you ready to go, love? You look lovely tonight." She's cute up close, I think. She's definitely not a prostitute; I smile to myself at my earlier assessment.

The rude yank that I almost forgot all about gets up and leaves without a word as I disentangle myself from the helpless young woman in my arm. "He's gone, I'm letting you go, I think it's safe unless you have more blokes coming your way," I say. She still hasn't said a word to me and I hope I haven't crossed the line. I was just trying to help her out. I don't need to get myself into a brawl before meeting Emily. *Emily!* I remember as alarm bells start going off in my mind and I look down at my watch. "Do you usually need to ward off men when you go out? I'm meeting someone later tonight, but let me know if you need my services in the next half an hour."

She slowly looks away from me and says, "Yes, I-I-I'm meeting someone, too. Thank you for helping me with those two guys." I helped her twice? Interesting, I wonder how I helped with the first fella. I reckon that I may need to stop saving girls. This superhero complex I have going hasn't been working out for me lately.

I watch her as she starts putting away her belongings into her purse. She really is a pretty girl. If I didn't just hear her strong New York accent, I would think she was European. I smile as I take in her appearance. I begin walking back to my table and just before I sit down, I turn and ask her, "Out of curiosity, what did you tell the first fella?"

"I told him you're my boyfriend and that you and I are back together and that I won't be able to hang out with him tonight. It's my fault, I just forgot I made plans with him and I scheduled an important meeting instead." She's doesn't look at me anymore as she finishes the rest of her drink with one swig.

Why is she here alone anyway? I reckon that girls shouldn't be in pubs alone; even in swanky hotel pubs. What if I wasn't here to help her? That creeper could've gotten aggressive with her. I watch her delicate body move. I want her to look at me again. Not sure why, but I guess I need someone to talk to other than the demons inside my head. "As your boyfriend, do I at least get to hear what the poor bloke said when you gave him the brush off?" *Am I flirting with this poor girl?* Nah, I'm just being proper and making conversation.

She finally looks up. She really is very pretty. Not my type, but pretty. My knob sprouts to life once again. *Look away from her and concentrate on how you're going to convince Emily to leave her husband for you.*

"He asked me if you'd be okay if he joined us in a three-some." She smiles and winks before turning her back on me to sit down, leaving me speechless. My dick is at full staff as though this pretty bird were talking straight at it. I look down to assess how obvious my bulge is and how long before I can get the fuck out of this pub and go up to see Emily.

Sara

"Wake Me Up Before You Go-Go[15]" by Wham

I've pissed away my whole interrogation prep time and now it's almost ten fucking PM. My head is total mush, thanks to seeing Brian, slimy hillbilly, and sexy Brit attack. I need to go back up in case Will Knight decides to come see Em early. I should probably go wait for him upstairs.

As I head toward the elevators, I ask one of the receptionists if they let anyone up to my suite while I was playing Inspector Clouseau at the bar.

"Hi, I just wanted to see if my friend Jeffery Rossi stopped by to gain access to my suite. I'm staying at the Penthouse," I ask, although I'm sure Will won't come up before ten. I wish I asked Em more questions pertaining to his appearance as opposed to his cock.

The woman behind the counter types and then sweetly answers, "Oh, yes, your friend is waiting at your suite. We've sent him up about half an hour ago."

My heart rate picks up as a cold chill passes through my body. How could I have stayed down at the bar for so long? Then I think back to the two disasters I got distracted by and roll my eyes at how amateurish I've handled this whole fucked-up evening. I run quickly to the elevator to finally go meet Will "The Problem" Knight.

As I exit the elevator into the lavish foyer of my suite, common sense finally rears its head. This guy Will could be dangerous. I know nothing about him except that he's trying to avenge his sister's suicide through the people I love most in this world. When he sees me instead of Em, he won't be a happy camper. I need to come up with a plan of action, pronto. The truth is, if he hurts me, no one will even know he did it because Jeff's name is on the record for visiting me. I've erased all our earlier text messages... *I'm screwed*; there is zero evidence that Will and I ever met.

"Sara! Where have you been?" I'm startled as I look to the left and at the top of the stairs where his voice is coming from. "I've been going crazy. Why aren't you answering your phone?" he barks my way.

I look at Jeff who's standing right there, looking at me as if he's right where he belongs. As if he has the right to question my whereabouts. My heart clenches and bleeds as I look at him, wishing that he did have the right to question me. I don't want to act strong anymore. We can't keep doing this! I want him, I need him and yet he's not mine to want or need. I made decisions that I had no right making, and I've been paying the consequences ever since. I close my eyes, drop my head and belt out a wail at how much I want to rewind and be able to redo it all over again.

He is at my side instantly as I sink to the floor and try to forget everything. How do I stop this...us...him and me? He should be mine, he's already the reason I open my eyes each day. How can I deny myself the only thing I've ever wanted?

"Baby, come on, don't do this. I don't want to see you cry," he whispers as he lifts me off the ground and walks us up the stairs to my bedroom. "I called Gavin when I couldn't reach you for hours and my key to your place wouldn't work. I was worried, Sara, and rightfully so." He lays me down on the big bed, props a few pillows behind my head, removes my shoes, and kisses the top of my feet before covering my legs with a throw. He walks over to the under-counter beverage fridge and brings me a bottle of water.

I've known this perfect man for fifteen years, and in those fifteen years, nothing between us has changed. He always took care of me, even when he wasn't supposed to. Even when I wasn't his problem or his business, he always made sure I knew just what I meant to him. If it weren't for me, he would probably just go on living a perfectly normal life with his wife, whom he's known even before we met. I've always pretended that he's the one that ruined my life, but the reality is, I've ruined his. I've done more damage to him and his family than he ever did to me. Why can't we let each other go? What is it about us that nothing or no one can stop us from loving one another?

"Drink, calm down, and talk to me. I still don't understand for the life of me why you wouldn't call me, or come to me! Didn't you know he sold the place and that you'd have to evacuate?" he asks with confusion and anger mixed in his harsh tone. If he only knew it took me almost every shred of willpower to not dial his number. Every day I try to stop being his problem. We made a mistake that has turned into a lifelong syndrome that neither one of us knows how to cure.

I nod my head. I'm too tired to talk to him or anybody else. This day has drained me and all that's left are my aching, heavy bones. I close my eyes as he removes his shoes and climbs into bed beside me. He pulls me close as I breathe him in like a deprived addict. He doesn't smell of a particular cologne or after-shave, but his scent is calming. It's the familiar scent of promise and hope. It's the scent of home that I've always imagined we'd have. I smile as I feel him breathe me in, too. Look at us—two pathetic individuals who can't seem to get it right.

"If I don't touch you at least once a day, my whole day feels like a waste," he whispers, already kissing down the side of my face. My limp body starts to respond to his soft lips. "I wish you would let me see you every day. It's not good for us to be apart." I do see him every day, he just doesn't know it. He doesn't know that I can't start my day without seeing him. I know what suit he chooses, how he styles his hair, I even know which car picks him up. But he gets to have a family while I get to watch, so he doesn't have the privilege of having it all.

"Why didn't you come to our apartment? I've been working from there all day hoping you'd turn up. It's our place and yet you haven't been there in years."

I will never go back to that place. I stiffen as my resolve hardens. He knows what that space means to me. He knows what that place means to us. Everything I've ever wished, imagined, and prayed for was ripped away from me there. I'd rather live on the street than go back there. He stops kissing down my neck when he feels my body tense up at the mere mention of our place. I'm not stupid, I know there is no "*our.*" I push away from him as I turn toward the window.

"Jeff, when will you let me go?" I ask, knowing that the answer is never.

"Why would you want me to let you go? You are my life, Sara, our time will come, and then we will never have to be apart again, baby." I wonder if he means when we die and then our poor lost souls can finally be together like Romeo and Juliet.

He moves my hair to the side and kisses my exposed neck. His touch feels right as he lowers my dress strap and kisses my shoulder. I can feel him tracing my freckles first with his fingers and then with his tongue. I lower my head back and let out my first moan at the feel of having him with me. He releases a deep groan, pulling me flush against his chest as I mold my body to his. I can feel his erection straining as he slowly starts moving up and down into me. We're both undulating and breathing hard as our bodies gain traction. He pulls up my dress and slides his hand past my panties right into my crotch. He stops gyrating as he slowly slips his middle finger inside me. It feels like heaven and I don't want to think of the consequences or the guilt, but just of how good his touch is. I'm dripping as he pumps his wet finger into me slowly.

"I can do this all day," he chokes out into my neck. "You, only you, baby."

My eyes are closed and my body begins to melt into his. When he touches me, everything in the world is right again. I would never let or want anyone but him to touch me like this. I'm petrified that if I let someone else touch me—this, him, us, will just disappear and cease to exist.

He withdraws his drenched finger from between my folds and brings it up and starts massaging my clit. It's slow and lazy at first, but as my breathing becomes notched and my muscles begin to tense, Jeff recognizes how close I am to seeing stars and begins rubbing my clit at a rapid pace. He knows after not seeing me for a whole day, he won't last long once he finally penetrates me. He wants me on the verge and ready to go, and I am, I'm close…I want him to stop teasing me with his hands and make me his the only way he can, even if it's a momentary illusion.

He's still fully dressed, as am I. My thousand-dollar dress is a heap of fabric around my waist; my panties are pulled to the side like a two-dollar whore's. Liars and cheaters like us don't always have the luxury of undressing and taking our time. I know I get him for a couple of hours before I have to give him back and turn into somebody he didn't choose.

"I'm close, don't stop." I yell out, knowing he's aware of when I'm about to come before me. He knows my body better than I do, and I only know his body and no one else's. I feel him unbuttoning his pants. He pulls his underwear down to grab his cock and enters me quickly before he has his usual sobering re-action.

"Fuck, I forgot the rubber. Hold on!" He fishes in his pants, now around his knees, for the condom he replenishes daily and resumes his position. I'm used to this move, I sometimes believe he just wants to feel me barebacked for a few seconds before the harsh reality of making sure I never get pregnant sobers him up.

"Get out of your head, Sara. I want you in the moment with me, okay?"

I smile and sadly think what I wouldn't give to be with him for millions of moments. *Why can't it be easy for us?* "I'm right here, JJ, nowhere else," I say reassuringly to the love of my life and offer him my lips. I can see him smile as he lowers himself to kiss me. His lips and my lips fit perfectly together. He and I have a rhythm to our kissing that's hypnotizing. I love the taste of him, all of him. He playfully sucks my tongue before sinking lower to my breasts. He flickers his tongue until my nipple is as hard as his cock and my whole body is covered in goose bumps. When he hears me start to beg for him to stop, only then does he finally take my whole nipple in and suck it like a pro.

He unlatches and looks up at me. "I need to be inside you. I've been going crazy trying to find you all day. Please don't keep me away and don't ever ask me to go. You know what you are to me."

I'm nothing, I chime in my brain.

I run my hands into his soft, wavy hair, outlining with my thumbs his thick eyebrows before nodding and saying, "No more talking, I just want you to love me one more night. I won't ask you to go or stay anymore, I promise." He's suspended above me and since his dick is as stiff as a rock, I doubt he understands anything I'm saying to him at this moment. He doesn't have enough blood in his brain to recognize that this is goodbye. To-morrow morning, I won't see him off to work. Tomorrow, I'll be gone and all the hurt and lies will finally stop. I take hold of his dick and help guide him toward my aching pussy. Tonight, we fuck, and tomorrow, I pay the piper.

"Fuck, I'm coming, Sara…I'm not gonna last…oh, I'm fucking coming." I've decided that tonight I won't let him make me come, because I don't want to remember this night at all. I won't visit today in my mind and think of how he made me orgasm for the last time. This night doesn't deserve to be remembered. My tears are running down my face again, but these are silent, calm tears. These are goodbye tears. "Oh, I love you, baby. Don't ever question that. What you and I have doesn't go away. Nothing would make me stop loving you." He's still inside me as I try to stay awake. I'm not sure if he actually said that or if it's already part of my dream. He'll probably fuck me again before he goes home, I think, lingering on the verge of sleep, but I have this feeling that I've forgotten something. *Did I lock the door?* It's okay, I'm sure Jeff will lock it when he leaves.

I wake up in the morning and I'm in bed alone. Jeffery is gone, back home to have breakfast with his real family as he always does. The family I can only dream of, the family that reminds me of what I'll never have. Karma, I've met her, she knows me well and she hates me. I lay on my side, looking out the window at the sunrise over the city that I both love and hate. I still have my dress wrapped around my waist and I feel alone and dirty.

The realization that I forgot and missed my meeting with Will Knight hits me like a car crash. *Fuck!* Jeff—the real Jeff—must've taken the key I left for Will, which means he obviously had no way of gaining access to the suite without that fucking key. *Fuck! Fuck! Fuck!* I botched everything up. I need to go find my phone and see if Will texted me. I hear a stirring in my room and see movement in the corner of my eye. I look over the edge of the bed to spot someone curled up in a ball on a small loveseat by the wall. My heart clenches in fear, as I know by the clothing and hair color it's not Jeff. *It can't be Will! He had no way of getting in.* I try to stay calm and rationalize my situation, but I can't. I'm scared. The terror begins to quickly spread across my body and gags me into silence. I open my mouth but no sound comes out. I'm paralyzed with fear as my brain tries and fails to convince me that I'm not gonna die. *I need to run before it's too late. Oh my God, who the fuck is in my room?*

The voices inside my head scream for me to do something. My nonexistent self-preservation mode suddenly kicks in as I slowly try to move off the bed without making any noise and quietly get the fuck out of this room and call security. *Who is this predator? What if he wakes up and tries to kill me? Why hasn't he killed or raped me yet? What was he waiting for?* The non-stop questions collide and blur in my head as I struggle to glide out soundlessly. I haven't looked away from him while I attempt to find footing. As luck would have it, I step directly on my discarded heels and stumble off the bed, making a racket. I close my eyes knowing that it's all over. I fucked up and I'm about to confront my subjugator and have my self-destruction prophecy fulfilled earlier than originally anticipated.

William

"Look Away[16]" by Chicago

I reckon I won't go up to meet Emily exactly at ten. I will go up to her suite around quarter past ten; this way I don't seem like an eager eejit, which I really am. It's almost time to go up as I walk over to the smiling, dark-haired receptionist that I've seen once or twice before. *Time to lay on the charm.*

"Good evening, my name is Jeffery Rossi, my mate is occupying the penthouse and was to leave instructions on granting me access to the suite," I nervously say as the thought of them asking for my ID pops in my head. The prospect of seeing her again finally feels close enough to taste, the last thing I need is for our meeting to go tits up because I can't show proper documentation for this Jeffery fella.

The woman is looking at me funny. She gets up and walks over to a short bald man standing at the far right of the check-in counter. They're chatting and looking my way. *Bollocks!* I don't want any issues. I just need to see Emily for the love of God. It bloody feels like I need to jump through hoops of fire to see her again.

I spy the receptionist returning with less of a smile on her face. All I can think is that I bloody must charm this woman into forgetting to ask me to show any valid form of identification. I smile my fake "I like you" smile and try to telepathically convince her that I am indeed Jeffery Rossi. She smiles warmly at me and says, "Sorry, sir, I just had to check with my manager since it states in our system that we've already given you the key earlier tonight. We've also had your ID checked and placed on file. Have you misplaced your key?"

I have no clue what this dimwit is talking about. I try to give off an air of confidence as I nod before saying, "Yes, I may have misplaced the bloody thing." *Oh, God why is it so hard for me to see you, Emily?*

"Not a problem, Mr. Rossi. We have an extra key that we can use to let you up. Or we can just call your friend to let her know you're coming."

"Yes, if I could borrow your key, I'll be certain to bring both keys back. I wouldn't want you disturbing my friend this late; she may be sleeping already." I say as calmly as I can. *Sweetheart, please go get me the bloody key without attracting too much attention or alerting that manager who escorted me out this morning and let me see the woman that has been dancing naked in my mind for weeks.* My facial features are starting to hurt from the ridiculous smile I've been wearing.

"Right away, sir," she answers as she walks away, hopefully fetching me a key. *Whose ID do they have on file and who has access to Emily's suite?* I start to ponder and worry as the thought of someone else going up to see Emily makes me slightly uneasy. I'm still, however, smiling as I finally thank the woman at the counter, grab the key before somebody changes his or her fucking mind or starts asking me more questions, and run with it.

As soon as the doors to the elevator finally shut I let out a breath and hope for the love of anything holy that Emily is waiting for me upstairs and will listen to me. I pray she won't be cross with me for not telling her who I was and just how well I know her and her cheating husband.

The elevator stops moving as the attendant welcomes me to the forty-first floor. The lights come on as soon as I step into the foyer and I make my way to the mirrored doors ahead of me, key in hand. Once I easily unlock the entrance I take a deep breath before walking through those doors, knowing that she's on the other side waiting for me. I enter a huge room that feels more like a ballroom than a living room in a hotel suite. I look around and it seems quiet. This place is extravagant, beautiful, and probably the nicest piece of real estate in all of Manhattan. This little residence must cost a bomb, nothing but the best in Louis' world. I walk a few more steps inside and still I don't see or hear anybody. *Odd.* I want to call out her name, but I first need to assess the situation I'm in before I start beckoning her to me. I decide that the best thing for me to do is sit on one of the many chesterfields like a good lad and wait for her to show herself. *Maybe she's changing*, I think as I look toward the monstrous staircase leading to a well-lit second floor. Maybe she's showering for me; the notion makes my lips curve and my knob twitch. Maybe she does remember how good I made her feel that night and that's why she wanted to finally see me. My heart accelerates as I get myself even more excited. Her stupid husband probably doesn't know how to make her moan or give her any pleasure, but he sure knows how to give her pain. I walk over and choose a couch and situate myself facing the staircase. I've had a nutty day today, starting with Louis and now ending with Emily. I look at my watch and it's half past ten. *I hope she doesn't keep me waiting for too long.*

I open my eyes and I'm in total darkness. It takes me a minute or so to realize that I'm still at The Pierre and I dozed off waiting for Emily. I look at my phone before I get up and realize it's well past midnight. *She never came down!* I check my messages, she never called or texted, either. Maybe something happened! Louis probably found out and locked her up at home. Or maybe she's upstairs and also fell asleep waiting for me.

I decide to go up. I walk quietly up the massive stone stairs and make a right into a dark hallway lined with doors on one side. One of the doors to the left is completely open and I reckon to start looking for her there.

The bedroom is dark but I can still make out its palatial size with huge windows overlooking New York City giving off a bit of light. I suddenly hear sounds and see movement on the bed. I step to the side of the door to make sure nobody sees me. My eyes adjust to the dark and I start to make out two people in bed probably fucking by the sounds they're making. My heart stops beating once my stupid brain receives the message of what's actually going on and what I just walked in on.

It takes me less than a minute to feel like an unwelcomed intruder. I'm hurt and confused. I'm all out of sorts to even begin to fathom anything going on with my life lately. Why would she ask me to come meet her? She wanted to humiliate me! She wanted me to walk in on her and Louis fucking! *Maybe it wasn't even her texting me, it was him!* It just dawned on me that on the same day he comes to see me I finally get a text from her, the woman I've been waiting for over a month to form any bloody communication with decided to reach out to me today of all days.

I close my eyes as the need to scream and hurt someone slowly chokes me. I should get out of here and not give him the satisfaction of knowing I saw him sleeping with my Emily. I start to walk away slowly as Louis groans out his release and shifts off of Emily. I should go, I should run, but I'm paralyzed with disbelief like a bystander in a car that's caught on the tracks, watching a train approach, knowing he's about to be wrecked. It's over, I lost, and yet I'm still standing, waiting to see her one more time. I think I see her face in the light illuminating from the window. I try to make out her features in this darkness, features that I've spent the last month tracing and stroking in my dreams.

I can't move, I'm transfixed as I finally see her lying in bed. I'm so dazed and confused I don't even know my own name, but I most definitely know that this girl lying in bed is not my Emily. She looks familiar and it takes me a few seconds to recognize her from the pub earlier. This was the fit bird I rescued from those two blokes. Why is she in Emily's room? Why is she in bed with Louis? Louis starts moving as I instinctively move and hide myself in the dark, open closet. I need to find out what in bloody hell this rubbish is all about, because everything in my mind is spinning out of control.

I move to stand behind the closet door as I see movement. Louis gets up off the bed and a few minutes later, leaves. Adrenaline pumps through my veins as millions of scenarios flood my brain. That pretty girl at the pub said she was meeting someone; it must've been Louis. She was meeting him and they naturally fucked because he's an animal and bangs everything that moves. I hear the sound of the elevator arrive and then the doors close, which means he left. I slowly walk out of my hiding quarters and back into the dark colossal room. I bravely get close to the bed just to make sure that the woman lying there is in fact not my Emily. I edge closer as I ensure for certain it's the American girl from before. She's half naked with her tits out and her dress around her waist. She stirs and moves her head towards me. I notice her closed eyes and the marred black mascara on her cheeks. She was crying! *Of course she was crying, Louis makes every woman cry, it's his signature touch,* I reflect with disgust. I hope he didn't hurt her.

I move away from the bed and decide to stay here until morning to talk to this poor girl, because I need answers. I'll make sure she's okay and perhaps warn her off Louis fucking Bruel, too. It would actually work quite nicely in my favor if Louis chose his mistress over Emily, but I truthfully wouldn't wish him on bloody anybody, not even a whore.

I sit on a chair by the closet for a bit, watching this strange girl. She's moving about quite a bit in her sleep and making pained sounds every once in a while. This day has been increasingly tiring and I'm buggered, my eyes slowly close, and my head falls to my chest as the jolt wakes me. I spy a comfy-looking tufted divan and move my confused, tired arse to let my head rest for a few while I wait for this poor girl to wake up.

William

"Welcome To The Jungle[17]" by Guns N' Roses

I wake up with a shudder to a crashing sound. I look over at the bed and she's not there. I spring up and see her body tangled on the floor and it looks like she's trembling. I hope she's not drunk or high. I need her capable of answering questions. I take a few steps towards her with my heart lodged in my throat.

"Please don't hurt me!" she cries out. "Just take what you want, just take it all and go," she cries as I kneel down beside her, confused, and try to help her up. She's rocking and sobbing. I take hold of her arms to help lift her back into bed and our eyes connect. Hers are so expressive; I register fear, shock, relief, and then anger in them.

"Get your filthy hands off of me. It's you! You! From … from the bar? What the fuck are you doing in my room? Who let you in here?" She's getting herself all worked up as she covers her breasts by pulling her dress back on and struggling to get as far away from me as possible, situating herself on the other side of the massive, four-poster bed. I still have not uttered a word. I just look at her and aim to work out how to handle her.

"I'm Jeffery Rossi," I say as her eyes enlarge in shock and her hand flies to her open mouth.

"*You're* Will Knight?" she asks and once again, I'm as baffled as ever.

I nod my head. "Yeah, that would be me. So, who does that make you? You're surely not Emily."

She closes her eyes and falls face first on the bed before erupting into uncontrollable laughter, which I know from experience will only end in more tears. I fold my arms over my chest and wait for this nutty girl to simmer down and tell me how she knows my name and what in the bloody hell makes this situation a rib-tickler. It takes her a full ten minutes to stop laughing and snorting like a farm animal, which, as I predicted, turned into crying. Now she's at the hiccup stage. I can see her brain working as she laughs and then starts to cry. Something is off with this bird. Did Louis put her up to this? Maybe he's using his whore to keep me away from Emily. He does like to share women.

I walk over to a small beverage fridge and fish out a bottle of water. I set it on the bedside table and go into the en suite bathroom to fetch her a paper napkin or a wet cloth to help get herself together so that she can illuminate me with her knowledge. I come back as she sits up against the headboard in the middle of the big, stark bed. I hand over the warm cloth and the water bottle. She takes both and just looks at me. I'm a gentleman; therefore, I make the first move.

"Tell me who you are, since you already seem to know who I am," I say as seriously as I can. She wipes her face and takes a few sips of water before answering.

"I'm Sara, Sara Klein," she says and then looks at me with amazement, waiting to hear what I want to know next.

Her name resonates in my head like déjà vu, making this feel familiar, which is peculiar since I've only seen her last night at the pub and hadn't gotten her name. "Sara, why are you here? Where is Emily? Was it you who sent me those texts yesterday?" We're still staring one another down. My heart breaks for this poor girl with her sad-looking eyes trying to read me. She was pleasing yesterday at the pub, but today, I don't proper fancy her one bit. Never would I think her to be American and my first thought last night at the pub—that she's a prostitute—starts to make more sense.

She nods and finally replies, "Yes, I sent those texts…with Emily, at first, but she doesn't know I made arrangements to meet you." With that, she breaks our stare and looks down at her hands.

When she mentions Emily's name, my heart literally clenches as a hundred more questions materialize and beg to come out. This bird Sara then covers her bare legs with a blanket, which I think is odd—her trying to fake modesty. I bloody saw her get banged last night, and her tits were hanging out a few minutes ago. Her covering her legs is quite amusing.

"Sara, why is Emily not here?" My voice betrays me and cracks into a plea. Her eyes dart up as she registers how pathetic and hurt I just sounded. I'm being played, I'm just not sure by whom!

"Will, you need to leave Emily alone! Whatever issues you have with Louis and his involvement with your sister, don't take them out on her!"

As I chew over her word choice, my blood begins to boil. That fucking bastard sent his whore to tell me to stay away from Emily. I look at her with disgust. I don't plan to dignify her daft outburst with an answer. *I don't take orders from scum or sluts*, I turn and walk away. I'm done with this pile of crap. I'm halfway down the stairs when I hear her yelling after me.

"If you hurt them, you will have me to answer to, you hear me, Will?" she yells from the top of the stairs.

I turn around and take two steps at a time to reach her. She's tall but I'm still a good head taller. I glare down at her and she can try and act as brave as she wants, but I know she's scared of me. She should be, she doesn't know what I'm capable of.

"I don't take empty threats from whores," I answer as her eyes enlarge and sharpen right before I feel the sting of her hand across my face. I haven't been hit on the face in a while and it actually feels good...sobering. I wish it were Louis standing here before me so I could finally help him meet his maker. She spits in my face and tries storming away. *Oh, we're not finished yet, sweetheart*, I grab her arms and pull her towards me.

"Why don't you explain to me why one of Louis' whores would tell me to stay away from Emily? How much is he paying you for this? I can pay you double if you give me a plausible explanation as to what in bloody fucking hell is going on here!"

"Why did you just call me Louis' whore? How did you even come up with that?" she asks as she stops trying to pull herself away from my grip. She shakes her head from side to side as if what I said to her is highly offensive and muddling.

I let go of her arms and instinctively push her away; she flies back and falls on her bum on the carpeted floor. I immediately feel like a jackarse for treating her callously, even if she is his whore; she's still a girl, a sad girl. She looks up with surprise at my brutality and I have this unexplainable need to wipe that disappointed look off her face. *Don't look at me like that, Sara, I'm the good guy.*

"Sorry, I didn't mean for you to fall."

She fumes and rolls her eyes with disgust; she looks away from me and I feel like the biggest arse on God's green earth. I lower myself to my knees and inch closer to sit next to her on the floor. This girl is my only ticket to Emily, I shouldn't let my pride lose the plot.

"I don't know why you think I'm Louis' whore, but I'll have you know that Emily Bruel is one of the most important people in my life. I will do whatever it takes to protect her and her beautiful family." As she says this within a yard of my face, she starts crying again. This bird is an emotional rollercoaster.

Tread with caution.

"So why are you banging her husband?" I ask bluntly, and the emotions that pass on Sara's face are quite priceless. She wants to laugh and yet looks cross simultaneously, and I see her battling and talking herself off that ledge.

"William fucking Knight, if you refer to my relationship with my best friend's husband as sexual one more time, I swear I will claw your pretty little blue eyes out and shove them up your stupid British ass. Is that understood?"

I smile at her descriptive dismemberment warning. She's a cheeky American, my favorite kind.

"Sara, I came up last night per *your* request! I saw you and Louis boning in this bed. I was hiding in the closet when he left. I know you must be lying to your best friend and I'm not here to tell you what to do, I just want to talk to Emily. I don't know what kind of magic Louis keeps weaving to lure all of you women to him, but I just need to talk to Emily and she needs to listen. She owes me that much."

Sara smirks to herself before pinning me with her beautiful, sad gaze. "Yes, I was having sex with someone last night, but it wasn't my best friend's husband, you idiot. Louis is more of a brother to me than someone I'd ever want to sleep with; his magic only works on Emily."

I was here, I saw with my own eyes the man she had in bed; he was tall and broad with black hair. It had to be Louis, I'm certain of it. "Who were you with, then? I came up here, per your instructions, and it was quiet. I sat down to wait for Emily and I dozed off. I woke up and came up here to check and make sure she wasn't in bed waiting for me. I saw you in bed with him! Was it some kind of setup? Was I supposed to see you two in bed together and think it was Emily and Louis and just leave?" My head is a mess and nothing makes sense anymore.

"You need to stop talking. It wasn't Louis Bruel in bed with me last night, it was Jeffery Rossi," she says and closes her beautiful eyes. The way she just uttered his name reminds me of the way I say Emily's name. It's an unconscious submission and I recognize it immediately. I'm silent, patiently waiting because I know she has more to say. "I came up last night to meet you and talk to you. Emily told me you were in New York waiting to speak to her. She isn't legally permitted to have any contact with you, so we decided that it would be best if I spoke to you instead. I came upstairs and Jeff was here waiting for me and I tend to just forget the world when he's around." Her lip is trembling and I reckon more tears are coming.

"Why did you tell me to use his name to gain access to this suite? Did you not know he would be coming to see you?"

She shakes her head. "I gave the hotel staff and you his name so Emily, or more importantly Louis, wouldn't know I had you up here. I just wanted to talk to you and explain that Emily doesn't want any problems for her family. I'm hoping to convince you to leave her alone. She wanted to thank you for bringing her back home to her family safely and she just wants some answers." She says all this very calmly and professionally. She sounds like an attorney but looks like a broken ballerina.

"Who is this Jeffery fella to you?" I ask, somehow knowing that my simple question doesn't have a simple answer.

"He's everything and nothing," she replies and it takes all of my restraint to not pull her in and try to soothe her. *She's a nobody, don't you bloody touch her,* I keep repeating to myself. She's trying to be strong. I can see the moment that she hears the words she just uttered out loud sink in. Jeff and Louis must be best mates. Louis fancies being surrounded by bastards that enjoy hurting women.

I need to change the subject and have this fragile girl talk to me about my Emily. If they're best mates, maybe I can convince her to arrange a meeting. I have things that must be said that Emily must know. "Sara, tell me what I must do to see Emily. I would never hurt her or her children. I just want her to be safe and aware as to whom she married. There are things she ought to know about him. I have a book that Emily should see for herself."

"I don't think I can help you with seeing her, but I can listen and pass along your information to her."

I don't like the sound of that. I have no guarantee that what I tell Sara will ever make it to Emily's ears. And besides, I need to see her again. I can't carry on with this unfinished business hanging over my heart.

"Sara, I have information about Louis that I can't share with you for legal reasons. I'm willing to lose everything as long as I get to tell Emily the truth about her lying, cheating husband."

Sara does not like what I'm saying. "Listen to me. Louis is not cheating on Emily! She ran away to St. Lucia because she thought he was cheating on her but he wasn't! He was trying to save his company from bankruptcy and had just closed an important deal with a woman from Russia. Louis was not sleeping with that woman; Emily misunderstood. When she ran away, he was looking for her all night around New York City like a deranged lunatic. He had a heart attack and almost died looking for her. You keep saying things about him that make me very uncomfortable. You don't know what they have. That man loves her and his kids more than life. If someone loved me one percent as much as Louis loves my best friend, I would be the luckiest girl in the world. Don't you dare say anything bad about Louis! He is a great son, a loyal friend, a loving father, and the best husband any woman could ask for. I don't know what happened with him and your sister, but what he and Emily have is bulletproof."

Her words are making me bleed inside and I won't hear any more of her rubbish. He is not a good husband—he's a fake, a liar, and a cheat. If Sara read my sister's book, she wouldn't have such a high opinion of Louis fucking Bruel.

"Do you want to tell me what evidence you have confirming that Louis committed the heinous misconducts you speak of? I think your opinion of him is based on hearsay. You accused him of sleeping with me a few moments ago while the truth of the matter is he wasn't even here. Don't you think he deserves a fair trial before you go accusing him without any proof of acts he's never been a part of?"

This girl is most definitely a solicitor, and she may look fragile and weak, but I'm starting to think that she's as strong as they come.

"I'll tell you what, Mr. Knight, how about you go make us some coffee while I go shower and change. You and I can sit down and talk like two adults. I promise to listen to everything you think you know about Mr. Bruel, and if I feel your information has merit, I will immediately convey your concerns to Mrs. Bruel."

Her stoic tone and her formal mention of Emily and Louis' names are meant to draw the line in the sand between us, and yet I feel like we're about to cross lines I didn't even know existed. I smile and nod. I know I don't have any choice; if there's any chance of seeing and getting through to Emily I need this bird to help me. I get up and quickly offer Sara my hand. She accepts it easily and waits for me to properly answer her back and accept her proposal. "How do you take your coffee, Sara?"

She smiles, which makes me smile. She's such a conundrum; she appears fragile, almost breakable, but I have this hunch she's tougher than I am. I can't explain how I know, but I just know it in my gut.

"I take my coffee in the form of tea with milk and two sugars, please," she says while walking towards her room.

I yell back after her, "Are you sure you're American? I don't know any tea-with-milk-drinking American girls under the age of one hundred."

She pops her head out while smiling and says, "Well, you do now, Liam."

Liam! How did she know to call me Liam?

Sara

"Things Can Only Get Better[18]" by Howard Jones

The hot shower helps me wash Jeffery from my mind and body. I have the urge to yell and cry but I'm calm, I'm used to this. After all, I wake up every morning with only his old grey T-shirt around my body instead of his arms. But today feels worse because I'm not there to see them all leave. I feel physical pain that is slowly turning into a massive, silent panic attack. Starting a day without seeing him off is almost as hard as knowing that my time with him is finally up. A thought crosses my mind: *If people ever knew the truth, would they hate me?* At least he'll know the truth even if no one else does. Today was supposed to be about me coming up with a plan to start fresh and escape this pathetic existence I've staged and orchestrated for myself. I shouldn't have made love to him last night, but in a selfish way, I'm glad I got to be with him one last time. I may pretend, but inside, I know that there is no us—never was and never will be. I've been as strong as I could be for as long as I possibly could without going crazy. I've waited, prayed, believed, lied to the world and myself, and ultimately...I lost. The tears run down my face but the water washes everything away...even him, and hopefully, one day, the pain.

I know—William fucking Knight is downstairs and I'll have to figure out a way to deal with him without Emily or Louis knowing I did this. This will be my gift to her. After being the shittiest friend any girl could ever have, I owe her this. She may never find out that I took care of Will "The Problem" Knight for her and Louis, but I will know and that's enough.

The shock hasn't worn off yet as I think that this stranger was in my room last night watching Jeff and I make love. The thought of him spying on us causes my body to respond in a very unprofessional way. I need to be Sara Klein, attorney at law, not Sara Klein, slut extraordinaire. How could that stupid man think I was fucking my best friend's husband? I mean, yes, I'm fucking somebody's husband, but that's a different story. What Jeff and I share is not some transient secret office affair. Ours is a heartbreaking love story that spans half my life.

I dress casually in comfy shorts and a soft sweatshirt, fighting the urge to wear Jeff's old T-shirt under my loose top. That old grey T-shirt is one of my most prized earthly possessions and I handle it with tender loving care. I head downstairs to try and make the British fool understand that he needs to go back home to Mother England and stop dreaming about breaking up my best friend's marriage. I saw the look in his eyes when he said her name. The only other man who has the right to have that look in his eyes is her husband, and he does!

My new guest is in the kitchen. He's removed his light jacket and stands in a wrinkled white T-shirt. The boy obviously lives in the gym; his biceps are on display as he expertly pours our tea. I look away from his arms and catch him eyeballing and assessing me as well. He knows I'm his only meal ticket to Em and

I'm sure he's about to try and milk me. I need to use his weakness for that woman and extricate every shred of information needed to help send him packing.

I give him a small smile as I pick a seat at the round kitchen table. He walks over and places my hot cup of tea in front of me, and smiles back. "Tea. Should I have poured the milk prior to your tea?" he asks.

"No, I like adding it after and watching the milk disperse and hide the tea," I say, not sure why I'm offering him any explanations about my tea preferences. He nods and smiles and he's sorta handsome in that carefree, Australian surfer kind of way. When I was a teen, he would have been exactly what I'd lust over. His eye color looks Photoshopped and those disheveled blond locks would have made him the perfect candidate in my childish fantasies. I wonder how far he and Em really got in St. Lucia. The way she described his dick and blushed really was a Kodak moment.

As I add the milk and take my first sip of tea, I can't help but close my eyes and hold back a sigh, trying to savor the comforting flavor. If this were my last cup of tea on earth, I'd be okay with that—it's that good. I don't think anybody, not even my mom, has ever made me a cup of tea. Jeffery probably makes Jacqueline tea all the time.

"Nice shower?" he asks me as I return back from my mini tea-induced orgasm to the here and now.

"The best shower of my life," I answer sarcastically, thinking that telling him I just washed the love of my life's scent off my body forever probably wouldn't be wise.

"Really? That good? Well, I may have to give it a go myself," he says with a smile and a wink. I want to hate him, but I don't think I can. I kinda see how Emily could've given into him and his British charm, he is slightly sexy. I don't think he's a bad guy, just confused and very misinformed. He and Emily are very similar and, in an interesting way, remind me of one another.

They both seem to believe everything at face value. How do people not know that things are not always as they seem? Even if we think our loved ones are telling us the truth, sometimes they're not. I'm not sure what he thinks he knows about Louis, but I've known Louis Bruel for almost twelve years and his only fault is loving my best friend too much. "I made tea and ordered us some breakfast, now why don't you tell me how you knew to call me Liam?"

His question catches me off guard. *Did I call him Liam?* I called him Liam because he doesn't look like a Will or a William; he looks like a Liam. I don't even remember saying or calling him Liam outside my head. "Sorry, it was a slip of the tongue. It won't happen again, Will, William, or Mr. Knight. I'll call you whatever you tell me to call you." He looks down and that carefree, smiling, winking Liam—I mean Will—is gone.

"No, it's quite all right, it's just that only a handful of people call me that. I...I just miss being called Liam." He swallows and almost looks as if he may start to cry. I suddenly need to know who used to call him Liam and why they stopped.

"Why don't you just tell people your name is Liam and not Will if you like it?" That's not the real question I want to ask, but I don't think he's comfortable enough to tell me the truth yet; therefore, I just do what I do best and fish around for information.

"Leave it, it doesn't matter. You just rattled me a bit by calling me Liam. Let's talk about Emily. You mentioned she wanted to ask me some questions." And he's back to the smiling, winking British boy from the bar last night. I need to know more about him before I offer him any information on Emily. I need to gain his trust and understand his motives to be able to diffuse him and send him packing.

"Liam—I mean Will...fuck. Argh, I'm sorry." *Stop calling him Liam!*

He smiles placing his hand on my knee to assure me it's all

good. "No worries, love. I like you calling me Liam."

I look up at him and for a split second, I see my life in a completely different light than the hell I orchestrated for myself. For a moment, I feel hope. As soon as he removes his hand from my knee, that spark is gone and I'm hopeless once again. I don't remember if I asked him, or he asked me something. I must look as confused as I feel because he's looking at me with pity. I don't fucking need his pity, I just want to get him out of my friend's life and figure out a way for me to disappear where surely no one will notice or get a heart attack over my absence.

"Tell me about this book. Is there a way I can get my hands on it? I'd like to read it for myself and perhaps understand if, in fact, it's non-fiction or fantasy." I take another sip of my delicious tea and think back to my time in London—the Brits really do make the best cup of tea.

"I have the book, but I'm not sure you reading it is best. You seem to be on guard when it comes to Louis Bruel. Are you and he related?" he asks.

I laugh at his ridiculous statement. "You think I'm defensive when it comes to Louis, who's my friend-in law? What kind of reaction are you hoping to get from Emily once you start slandering her husband?"

"Sara, I'm not slandering the holy Louis Bruel! I'm just stating facts."

"Facts? Liam, did someone disclose these facts to you? Were you there in person to witness these alleged acts between Louis and someone else? How are you certain that the information in that book is the truth and not a concocted tale your sister fabricated?"

He stands up without breaking eye contact. I can see I've just pressed the center of the wound. If he could kill me with a look, I'd already be dead.

"You seem to be very knowledgeable about my sister. Are you calling her a liar?"

"No, I'm calling her an author! She wrote a tale like many authors do. It may have some truth to it, but it may also be laced with lies. Liam, I know it must be hard to read a book about someone you love that isn't here anymore for you to ask questions about. She's not here to defend herself and tell us what really happened, but Louis is. Don't you think you should at least hear what he has to say about this?" I can see that I can't reason with him. He wants to believe whatever his sister wrote in that stupid book and then he wants a living, breathing punching bag to punish for what happened to her.

"If my sister had never met him, if he hadn't ruined her by introducing her to drugs and orgies, she would've had a normal life. You don't know him; you don't understand what makes him happy. If you think he's been a perfect husband to Emily, then you're just as blind and naïve as she is. He's a liar and a cheat. My sister loved him; she did anything and everything he asked of her, and when he got bored with her, he simply discarded her like yesterday's rubbish. I was there to pick up the pieces until there was nothing left of my sister!"

My heart breaks for him as I see the unshed tears pooling in his eyes. "I'm sorry," I say, because I truly don't know what else to say.

"I don't need your bloody sorry. I'm here to save Emily from him. It was too late to save my sister, but I can still save Emily." So this is it, he feels guilty for his sister's suicide and wants to be somebody's hero.

"She doesn't need saving. She has a fantastic life with the *love* of her life. If something were to happen to Louis, I don't think she'd be able to move on." He listens to me and nods, like he agrees although he clearly doesn't. When I mention Emily and Louis' life together, it just goes right over his head.

"She had no problem moving on with me in St. Lucia."

Okay, we're getting somewhere; good boy, keep talking. "Yeah, I know. She told me about the night you two spent together when she ran away."

His eyes actually light up. He's happy that Emily told me about him. "What did she tell you happened that night?" He raises his eyebrows at me with what can only be described as a glimmer of hope.

"You know what she told me, but I'd like to hear your recollection of that night's events. She feels a tremendous amount of guilt over the situation and because of all the alcohol involved and you informing her that nothing happened, she's worried that you don't remember what transpired between the two of you." As I tell him my interpretation of what Emily recalls about that night, he closes his eyes and sighs almost as if he feels relieved. I knew that something happened and his facial expression and body language just confirmed it.

"I'm really pleased she remembers. I was afraid I wasn't memorable," he says with a sheepish smile. "That night was everything to me. She had to have felt it, too. I could never imagine feeling the things I felt and still feel for her, knowing who she is. Sara, I've hated her for so long. I thought that if it wasn't for her, my sister would be with that bastard, but at least she would be happy and alive. When I'd spy those two in magazines, my blood would boil. I couldn't look at her. But when she came to me that morning, she looked fragile, lost, scared, like she was alone in the world. She wasn't this gold-digging bitch I've let my head believe; she's sweet and innocent and doesn't have a bad bone in her body. It's him who's the monster, and I owe it to my sister to save Emily."

I want to ask him if they had sex, but if I ask and they did then he'll know that I don't know shit. Instead, I ask, "Emily wanted to know why you told her that nothing happened that night. She said that in the morning when she woke up she didn't remember much and that you assured her that you two didn't fuck." As soon as that word leaves my mouth, I cringe; it was too harsh. I can tell by the way his eyes digest my comment.

"I didn't falsify a thing to her. It's just that when we woke up she was different. The liquid courage from the day before was gone and she was a mess again. She was looking at me with her enormous blue eyes and I felt awful and guilty for remembering everything from the night before. She'd been in shock and just clueless. I told her we didn't shag and I saw how relieved she was, which made me feel like a bloody bastard for how intimate we were." He says this while staring at the window behind me.

"So, you just lied to her to make her happy?" I ask, still struggling to assess just *how* intimate those two actually got.

"She didn't ask me what we did, she just wanted to know if we had sex and we didn't, so technically, the court would accept my answer as the truth. As a lawyer, I'm sure you would agree," he says, pinning me with a cocky stare. He just called me out as an attorney, so perhaps he's not as stupid as I imagine him to be.

"Yes, you would, however, be liable for your omission of the truth, Mr. Knight. We should also address why you elected to not disclose to Emily at that point in time that you knew exactly who she and her husband were." He gets up and walks over to the window. He puts both hands in his pockets and I no longer think I'm getting my answer; my witness just closed off. "Liam, when you first saw Emily that morning at your hotel and when you realized who she was, did you want to make her pay for what you think she and Louis did to your sister?"

He drops his head and I'm not sure if I nailed his motives or if I just offended him.

I wish I could figure him out and enlighten him as to what kind of man my best friend's husband truly is. Em did mention a video, I remember, as I try to work through all the info from our conversations yesterday. I need to figure out what this video has on it and perhaps show it to him. I should call my brother; Eddie heads Bruel Industry's legal division and Em also alluded that he was one of the prosecutors on the case back then. The case that made sure Isabella's book never got published.

I practically jump out of my seat when the doorbell to the suite rings, startling me. Liam turns around and we both feel like two conspiring thieves. *Fuck, what if it's Emily? What if it's Louis?*

"Sara, answer the door," he commands.

"Okay. Yeah, just maybe go wait for me upstairs. In case it's Emily, I'd like to explain why you're here." He nods and makes his way down the corridor and toward the stairs.

I answer the door and it's room service; our food has arrived and is waiting to be brought in. *Thank fucking God.* If Emily or Louis showed up before I had a chance to deal with Liam, I'd be in deep smelly shit.

Liam

"When Doves Cry[19]" by Prince and the Revolution

This feisty lawyer is just as confused as every other bird that thinks she knows who Louis Bruel really is. Isa didn't have to tell me anything; I know that if even half of what that book says is true, then he is a worthless excuse for a human being. The scene that I always come back to, and the scene that has forever changed what turns me on sexually, is a party my sister described. The party took place at Louis' friend's club—a guy named Phillip Dashell. The first time I read that chapter, I remember having an out-of-body experience: my head read, my body responded, and yet I wasn't able to fully comprehend the information as a whole person. A brother should never have to read about his sister being raped by ten men, including the man she supposedly loved. What normal boyfriend would let his friends and strangers take turns and then all at once rape his girlfriend? How could she have allowed it? What kind of hold did he have on her? Did he get her so drunk and high that she didn't care what was being done to her? You'd think she was doing it for the money. Isabella Knight had more money and recognition than Louis and all his scummy mates combined. *Why?* Why would he do this to her? How could he have allowed it? What did she ever do to him? All she wanted was to be loved!

If Emily doesn't want to see me and wants to believe her husband is a saint, then maybe I should just leave her alone and allow her to keep living a lie. They clearly all think that my sister is some kind of fibber and that Louis had no hand in her tragedy. I only fancy telling Emily the truth; what she bloody does with it shouldn't be any of my concern.

Standing by this window, looking down on New York City, I wish I were anywhere but here. I want to go home, but I don't know where home is anymore. My home doesn't feel like home without my sister there, but it's the closest thing I have to a place where I belong. It's sad to think I can't walk down the streets of London without being recognized, and yet I don't even recognize myself. Who will I call when I miss her? *Nobody!* Who will I call when I feel alone? *Nobody!* How could she have left me behind?

"Liam."

I hear my name and for a second, I let myself imagine it's Isa, but I know my head will ruin it for my heart. I know it's just Sara, the sad girl with haunted demons in her own eyes. The girl that schools her face so that the world doesn't see the sadness hiding inside. It takes sad to know sad and that little bird is as sad as they come. Perhaps she, too, is with a man she thinks is a saint like Louis. Maybe she is as deliriously happy as Emily is, so delirious that she cries herself to sleep every night. I turn to see her carrying a tray of food; our breakfast has arrived. I walk over and take the tray and set it down at a table set for two by the window. She doesn't say a word or even look at me. She's studying the rumpled bed sheets and there it is...Jeffery Rossi. I don't know him, but I could bet my left nut he's a bastard. Haven't made up my mind if I want to know their story, but there's definitely a story. By the look on her face, it's not one with a happy ending...not for her, anyway.

"We should eat, I'm famished. Thank God you ordered

breakfast," she says, already starting on the chocolate croissant.

"I wasn't sure what you'd fancy, you threw me off with your beverage choice, so I ordered every pastry on the menu. I've been living at this hotel for over a month. Their pastries are stellar."

She looks up from her half-eaten croissant and smiles. "Thanks, I only eat chocolate croissants for breakfast, so you hit the nail on the head. You've been staying here at The Pierre for over a month...why?"

Why? Because I may be in love with a married woman who's the wife of the man who helped kill my sister. "I've been waiting to talk to Emily. At first, I wasn't sure what Louis' state of health would be and I couldn't just abandon her. If something were to happen to him, I wanted to be close, in case she needed me. I also owed her an explanation for my 'omissions of truth,' as you previously referred to my unwillingness to offer my true identity at first. I wanted a chance to talk to her, to tell her in person. I promised her that I'd wait in New York until she rang or came around to chat with me."

Sara sits with her long legs stretched out on the windowsill, wearing grey shorts and a sweatshirt that says *"NY is for Lovers."* She has her dark, damp locks arranged in a bun at the top of her head. She and Emily both look like schoolgirls. I haven't sat down yet; I decide to lurk and enjoy the view, still trying to figure this bird out.

"Why are you here, Sara? Isn't this suite under Louis' name? Did you know I was leaving yesterday and then organize being here to meet me? I truly am enchanted as to the coincidence of having Louis throw me out of The Pierre, only to have his wife and her mate break me back in."

"Why were you leaving?" she asks with sudden interest. "Did you change your mind about talking to Emily?"

"No, I haven't changed my bloody mind. Louis paid me a lovely visit yesterday morning and threw me out, informing me he now owns this hotel."

This must be news to her, because she sits straighter and sobers up. This must mean that Emily had no idea I was here, or that Louis came to see me.

"I still need to understand why you're here. I saw Emily here yesterday, too. That's why when you texted me to meet you at The Pierre, I had no doubt I'd be meeting Emily."

"When did you see Emily? Were you at the hotel when we came yesterday?"

I nod. "Yeah, I was waiting for my driver when I saw her enter and I decided to stay and wait. I had hoped to see her." She's quiet, just drinking her tea. What's running through that nutty head of hers? "Why were you here, you and Emily?"

"It's not important why we're here. It's just an interesting coincidence that we've all ended up at the same hotel." She's back to scoping the city line outside the window.

I finally sit down and say, "It's important to me. I'd like to know why you're here. I'll talk to you about things you want to know, but I'm not interested in a one-way interrogation. I'd like us to understand each other and maybe you'll help me." *Perhaps if you need me to listen, I could help you, too, Sara.*

She tears her eyes from the window to look at me and says, "I wouldn't even know where to start." She takes a sip of her tea before looking away again and I believe I actually felt her anguish in those few words.

"Go back to where it doesn't hurt to talk about it. Tell me how you got to a point in your life where you spend a passionate night with a lover at the most exquisite penthouse in New York City, but it doesn't end with chocolate croissants and tea with milk and two sugars?"

She shakes her head but then her whole body trembles and tea spills on the floor. Her head sinks into her hands and the tears flow freely again.

I think I just found the one other person in New York who's perhaps even more broken than me.

Sara

"The Promise[20]" by When In Rome

I feel myself being carried somewhere. I try to stop drowning in my tears and open my eyes and tell him to put me down. Liam carries my trembling body out of my room. "Where are you taking me?" I ask as we enter a bedroom I didn't even know existed on the same floor.

"We need to sort your issues out before we get to mine, and if you start bawling on me every time you get a whiff of that arse from last night, we won't get very far." He lowers me onto a clean, crisp bed in a room I've never seen in this penthouse. "This is the last time I'm bringing you a wet cloth to clean your pretty face, got that, Sara?" I smile because he is kinda sorta being sweet.

"Okay, but Jeff is not an ass," I say back to him in a small voice that's not very convincing even to my own ears. He just shakes his head and goes into the bathroom for yet another stupid towel to dry my stupid tears.

I clean my face and blot my puffy eyes. I look over to see him sitting at the edge of the bed, watching me with a frown, probably dying to know why I'm endeavoring to help Emily with her issues when, clearly, I'm the one that needs all the help.

"Am I finally gonna hear who this Jeffery Rossi is to you? And everything and nothing are not valid responses. I accept full sentences that include profanity. I've already concluded that he's an arse by the way he left you in the middle of the night after he finished wanking off inside you. Don't tell me he didn't because I was here to see it with my own eyes, your honor. Your eyes are disturbingly sad and you haven't stopped crying since we've officially met. And FYI, blokes who are not arseholes don't put the women they care about in hotels to bang whenever they please and then go home when they're done."

I attempt to be strong and not look away from his knowing eyes after everything he just said to me. It feels shameful knowing that he really was here last night, watching Jeff and me. And I know that everything he's saying is factually true, he just has no idea the role I've played in my own misfortune. I did this! I allowed my life to spin out of control and get to this fucked up point, and I have no one to blame but Sara. I'm the asshole, the bastard, and the lowlife ruining perfectly good lives, not Jeff!

"Is it the money?" he asks, momentarily shocking me with his question.

"Really, Liam? Did you just ask me if my relationship with Jeffery is about the money? Does it always come down to money in your privileged world?" What an arrogant piece of shit this British fucker really is!

"Well, why else would you be made to feel this way and carry on? Why would you let some stag leave you in the middle of the night with tears dried on your cheeks?"

"It's none of your business, that's why. Get the fuck out of my life. I don't owe you an explanation. Don't stick your nose where it doesn't belong," I bark at him.

He gets up from his perch at the foot of the bed and comes over to me, towering over while I'm still half-lying in bed. "Well that's bleeding rich coming from you. I didn't ask to be here watching you fuck that tosser. Don't go forgetting who summoned whom here pretending to be Emily, sticking her nose in my business...so imitating a self-righteous bitch won't do you any good, sweetheart."

Up until now, he seemed nice, I could even pretend to understand what Emily saw in him and how he lured her into his bed. But seeing the way he's frothing at the mouth and trying to intimidate me shows me his true ugly British colors. He's come here to hurt Louis, and Emily is just part of his game. *Not if I have anything to do with it, asshole.*

"Stop trying to psychoanalyze me, Sara. I say what I feel, no disrespect. I'm bloody clueless as to why you and Emily and my sister would want or need men like that in your lives. It's driving me bonkers and I don't have any answers. I'm hoping that you'll tell me it has to do with money. Money I know, money I can understand. But if you're not with that knobhead because of his loot, and seeing your current state and knowing it's because of him...I'm lost. Sara, make me understand." He sits down on the bed by my side, looking at his hands.

"Liam, you and everybody else have no idea what being me feels like. You wouldn't understand and I couldn't explain it to you if I tried. This is my life and nobody but Jeff and I can understand our choices." He looks away from his hands and back into my eyes.

"Make me understand. I don't know anything about you besides that you and Emily are best mates and you're a lawyer. You have sad eyes and I've just decided that I want to know why and who's responsible. I don't think you'll get a better deal today than a stranger wanting to hear your story. What are you frightened of? There is no way I could cause you more pain than him. I have nowhere to go, no one is waiting for me or looking for me. I'm all yours, Sara. Let's talk and try to work your problems out. I won't hurt you...I promise."

He hasn't looked away from me and I don't want him to. His eyes are clear, baring his own loneliness and desperation. I'd like to have eyes like that look at me without the pity and judgment. I wish I had someone besides Jeff who'd understand my choices and my mistakes. "Liam, do you really need for me to tell you about my fucked-up life? You're just trying to get on my good side so I can help you find your way to Emily." There, I said it. I'm not playing games with him; he has no reason to care about me or who Jeff is to me. His only motives are to gain my trust and access to Emily and somehow discredit Louis in the process.

He gets up from his seat and kneels on the floor beside the bed, quietly observing me. He reaches out his hand to fix a lock of hair that fell into my eyes and places it behind my ear. I have my head on a pillow and his face is so close I can see his pores. He is kinda sorta good looking. *If something were to happen to Louis, he's not a bad plan B for Em*; the silly thought pops into my head.

"You're going through something and you're sad. It's nice that you're trying to help your mate and deal with me on her behalf, but I don't think you have anybody to help you. I'm not here to pass judgment on you; I'm no saint. I won't hold anything you tell me against you in a court of law, so help me God, nor do I need to repeat our conversations to anybody. But talking to someone, even a stranger like me, must be better than bleeding yourself to death on the inside. You need a friend and I'd like to be your mate, Sara, unless you plan on going back down to the pub to find that red-nosed wanker from last night. I come cheap, all I ask is for you to shuffle over and share this comfy bed with me and I'll listen to you for as long as you want. And I make a wicked cup of tea with milk and two sugars."

This guy is unbelievable! I don't understand what his angle is and why he's bothering with me. I shouldn't be talking to anybody other than Jeff, and he's a goddamn stranger, the enemy. I can't just tell him my life story; nobody but Jeff and I know the truth. But how nice would it be to say the truth out loud, to not have to lie. Maybe I could tell him a little bit if he promises me something. "I need you to promise me a few things and then you and I can upgrade our relationship status to pain buddies."

"Sure thing, what kind of deal am I about to make with an American lawyer?" he says with a big smile, still kneeling by my side.

"You need to promise me, that a) you will not terrorize the Bruels by trying to get your sister's book published, and b) whatever information I divulge about my life will never leave this room." I have my hand out for him to shake on it. He's looking at my hand and contemplating my deal, no doubt trying to figure out what he gets out of our agreement except a crazy story and a big headache. I add before he tells me and my deal to go fuck ourselves, "I also have information about your sister that you may not be privy to; if I can successfully get my hands on it, we can both see it." This seems to pique his interest.

"Can I add something to our pact?" he asks and I nod. "Will you promise to tell Emily that I never meant to harm her in any way? I'd like you to tell her that she means a lot to me and if she wants me to leave her alone, I most certainly will. But she needs to give me the chance to tell her about Isa and Louis." As he says those words, I know one hundred percent that I don't need him to sign any stupid piece of paper ensuring that he never hurts Em. I know with confidence that he would in no way do anything but love her if ever given the chance.

"I will, Liam, I promise." And with that we shake hands and form the Lonely Broken Hearts Club that has its first official meeting atop the Pierre Hotel.

Liam

"In Your Eyes[21]" by Peter Gabriel

Sara slides over on the bed and makes room for me. I toe off my shoes and climb in, jeans and all. It feels quite nice to lie down after spending the night hunkered down on that wretched bench. We're both facing each other on our sides, and in a juvenile way, I'm a wee bit excited at the prospect of becoming better acquainted with this sad little bird.

I only now see that her dark green eyes shine with tiny flecks of gold; they seem clearer, less clouded than before. She looks very sweet, like a human China doll with delicate features. She looks almost breakable. I catch myself before I fix her hair again. *She's not mine to touch,* I need the reminder. I know I've seen her tits, but I must make sure I only fancy her in a neighborly mate sort of way. I must remember this is about her opening up and letting go of some of her sadness. I'll try and be her pal for a few hours and then arrange to go back home—wherever I decide home bloody is!

My stupid fantasies ought to stop. If Emily truly wanted to see me, she would've found a way. I've been here for over a month waiting like a loon. Perhaps she truly reckoned it was Louis in her bed that night and not me. The thought makes my stomach churn. I felt more that night than I'd felt in my whole life. I had more chemistry with her than every woman I've ever known combined. On the other hand, she was pissed and did call out his name numerous times, but she felt perfect in my bloody arms. How could I have misread that? I get out of my head and forget that night to try and be present for Sara. I must stop thinking about Emily and think about Sara for now. She's a lost sort and I suspect alone, emotionally at least.

"Tell me, Sara, tell me how you got here. I think if you're honest and allow yourself to trust me, we can discuss what's been troubling you and perhaps make it better before we talk about my predicament."

She snorts out a laugh, which makes me smile and is probably the sweetest thing I've ever heard. Well, second sweetest thing I've ever heard, after Emily singing to me naked.

"Okay, but you have to promise to not feel troubled once you understand that nothing you can say or do will help make my problems better. And you have to promise not to hate me after you hear my sordid tale...I hate me enough." She must think that she's the only one with baggage. I know what it feels like when nothing or no one can fix your pain. It doesn't matter how much money I've got, or who my parents are, I will never have a sister. I became an only child two years ago and I don't suppose anyone can fix that kind of pain.

"I promise not to hate you and I will try to see things from your viewpoint. I'm sure you're being much harder on yourself than you deserve." I fail to restrain myself this time and fix that dark renegade lock that keeps falling into her eyes. She doesn't say anything and lets me show her this small measure of affection. God, she's lovely. I almost want to tuck her into me and tell her that everything is gonna be all right, one day. *She's not yours to touch.* I can't bloody wait to hear who it is this pretty broken bird actually belongs to.

Sara

"Total Eclipse Of The Heart[22]" by Bonnie Tyler

I can't do this, but I need to do this. I can't just leave everything and everybody and disappear without anybody but Jeffery and I ever knowing the fucking truth. It would be unfair to tell Emily that everything she thinks she knows about her best friend is a fabricated lie. How selfish would I be if I piled all my shit on her? She has her own issues to figure out, her own crap to dig through. Hopefully, Liam will not be one of her problems. I mean, how could he? He really is a nice guy; I honestly believe he kinda sorta cares for her, in his own silly way. Emily will be okay without me, she'll be better off, for fuck's sake. What kind of friend am I if all I've ever done is lie to her about everything anyway? She has so many people that genuinely care about her, and most importantly, she has Louis and her kids. It hurts when I think about how much I lack in all aspects of my life compared to Em. Are my choices ever going to stop hurting me? Where is my happily ever after?

I take a look at this stranger who just crawled into bed with me, fully dressed. He is handsome and sexy and *The* Sara would have him naked and riding his cock by now, but *this* Sara is just happy to have someone who wants to listen. I feel a physical relief at the possibility of having another human to talk to that isn't Jeffery Rossi. If I admit the truth to myself, Jeff and I haven't really talked since I agreed to marry Gavin. When I left for London, he finally got the message loud and clear that we're not meant to be, and that things will never happen for us the way we've imagined and longed for. After my move to London, we finally stopped making empty promises that neither one of us could keep, so in essence, we stopped lying, at least to each other.

Liam reaches out and moves my hair away from my face; it's the second time he's done this today. It's not a big deal and it's not sexual or anything, since I'm betting the farm he's madly in love with Emily, but I still like it. He accidently brushes my cheek with the back of his fingers tucking my hair behind my ear, and I can't pretend it doesn't feel nice. Why couldn't I meet a guy who was available for me back then? I've wasted half of my life pretending, chasing a promise that has amounted to nothing but lies. I don't want to pretend anymore, I don't want to lie...

The prospect of telling this perfect stranger my past is making my heart pound at a horror-movie pace. I should tell him that I never do this, and how terrified and unprepared I am to talk about my life and its level of fucked-upness. "Liam, I don't talk about my life with anybody. I'm not sure I can do this."

"You've told your best mate! Right?"

I shake my head and feel the shame spread like wildfire. "I will lose my best friend if she ever finds out, and Jeffery will have lots of problems if the truth was to ever surface. I probably shouldn't be talking to you about this at all. You will try to use this information to get to Emily. The only way you and I can talk is if I get some kind of non-verbal assurance from you. Like, you surrendering the files containing your sister's book to me. I need to know I'm not a pawn in your game of revenge. I haven't known you long enough to make any assumptions. You should know that Louis is under the impression that you've been trying to get that book published and humiliate his family as payback. Is that what all this is about?" I ask him point blank.

Liam is silent, just watching me, and then suddenly, he

springs off the bed and storms the room without a second glace or even a word to me. My heart drops at his sudden exit. I pushed him too far. The only person who ever pretended to want to talk to me, hear my problems and maybe make them better just left! This is my life in a nutshell. Everybody leaves me. I turn toward the mirror on the wall and look at my reflection as the tears roll down my face, yet again. This is my life, a perpetual state of tears. I would have thought by now I'd be used to rejection and pain, but surprisingly, it still hurts. I do my best to never let anybody close enough to hurt me. I've only bestowed that honor on one person. I close my eyes as I try to escape in my mind to a time before everything hurt, when every day was an adventure and the future had promise. It's hard for me to find that place all those years ago; every disappointing year takes me further away from it.

"Sara!"

I hear Liam call me from somewhere in the room. I don't even want to open my eyes and see if he changed his mind and came back. I just want to drown in a happy memory.

"Sara, why are you bloody crying again? Oh fuck, love, no, no, I'm sorry, you didn't think that...I just ran out to go get something. Sweetheart, please don't cry—I wasn't leaving you."

His words make me want to cry even more. I feel pathetic and worthless; it would be better if he actually did leave. I could go inside my head and find that happy moment and live there for a day or two. I feel him slide back into bed behind me and pull me against him. He wraps his arms around me and tucks his head into my neck whispering, "Sorry" over and over. My brain knows this is a friendly gesture meant to calm the crazy bitch he needs to deal with. However, his presence, his scent makes me feel things I haven't felt in years. My stomach feels like the breeding ground for a butterfly farm. He shifts closer behind me and we're completely flush, his body now touching every part of mine. The sensation causes every neuron in my body to fire and

I'm starting to hyperventilate and overheat at the same time. What's happening? What is he doing to me?

"I want to be your mate, Sara; you and I need each other, and we shouldn't be alone," he murmurs into my neck.

The feel of his breath on my skin warms me even more. I don't like this; well, no, that's a lie, I like this a lot, but he needs to stop touching me like this. We shouldn't be this close, he should leave, it's not right. *How did this become about us?* I wonder as Liam slides his hand lower to my butterfly-filled stomach and forces my body into his even closer. This needs to stop now! I'm sure that it's his dick I'm feeling through my shorts...*this is crazy, what is he doing?* The panic and excitement are growing.

"Liam," I say, and it comes out sounding more like a moan then a stop command. I can't fucking trust my voice not to sound like a horny twat, so I try to stop this by placing my hand on top of his, which lingers over my lower stomach. He doesn't interpret my hand on his as asking him to stop—he simply moves his hand and places it over my hand. His lips are still at the curve of my neck and I'm not sure what's happening or if it's my imagination, but I swear I feel him ever so slightly grinding into me. It's either that or The Pierre is shaking.

"Liam!" I try again, but I sound like a woman who hasn't been laid in months. *I just had sex last night with Jeff, why am I not stopping him?* Alarm bells go off inside my mind, my body is ready to go to war with my brain. This man probably has feelings for my best friend; he's trying to find a way to talk to her, so why are we dry humping each other? *Am I also grinding into him? Fuck! I can't stop. I'm a whore.* He guides both of our hands up my body, using my hand to touch me, and it feels wrong, but I don't want him to stop. I've never been sexual with another man besides Jeffery. I feel like I'm cheating on him and it's fucking ludicrous because he's freaking married! This, this is what's wrong with me. I feel loyal to a man with whom, in the eyes of society, I've been cheating with for over a decade. That thought makes me laugh out loud.

"Are you taking a piss out of me, Sara?" he says as he stops driving his hips into me.

I turn to look at him, thankful for this moment of clarity. Once I calm my head and pinpoint those gorgeous blue eyes of his, I know that Liam Knight is about to become the catalyst I need to leave my old ways and JJ behind. Maybe fate threw me a bone by bringing this British dude to help me. He doesn't need to know about my epiphany, but I'm about to use him. I should let him fuck me until I'm strong enough to leave Jeff. I've tried everything else, but I've never tried to be the person I always pretend to be. Being loyal and waiting hasn't gotten me anywhere in life. All I've managed to do is invent a life and lie for the sake of everyone else while fading to nothing on the inside. Why shouldn't I fuck someone else? I gave Jeff everything: my life, loyalty, and my love, but now I will do whatever I can to give myself to someone else.

"Are you sure about this?" I ask him.

He smirks and shakes his head. "Forgive me for being a wanker. I don't know where this came from. We should stop, if you want. I truly have no bloody excuse. I...I simply got carried away with your fit bum so close to my knob and you smell perfect. I shouldn't be in bed with Emily's best mate. I don't even know who that bloke is to you from last night. It's just...you're truly lovely, and I reckon it a bit odd but I fancy being close to you, and it may sound strange, but I want to be the one to help mend you. I just don't know you very well. The only thing I'm certain of is how my chest hurts every time you cry and I don't want a pretty girl like you to cry. I want to know that I can make you smile."

I'm the one that moves his hair off his handsome face this time; it's an unconscious act, but we both feel the intimacy of my gesture. We are a fucked-up pair, the two of us. When I tuck his blond lock behind his ear, he closes his eyes like a puppy getting attention from his owner. I suddenly have this pang in my chest, a feeling I can't even explain. *No fucking feelings, Sara.* I just need to let this beautiful stranger fuck me and break the hold Jeff has had on me my whole adult life.

I've never summoned *The* Sara in a real-life situation; I've just lied about her countless times. However, I need her now and she needs to emerge. "Liam, could you and I fuck, please?" His eyes spring open and I can see him attempt to figure out if this is a trap or a joke. "Relax, there's no catch. This will be just between us. You have nothing to worry about because no one will ever know. I need you to do this, it's important to me." I aim to be semi-businesslike with my proposition because I need a willing participant. He, however, doesn't take me very seriously and starts cracking up. I mean, full-on laughing with his mouth open and all. Great, this is the first man besides Jeff that I truly want a sexual relationship with and he laughs at me. "I can be on my stomach or my side, you don't have to see my face. I just need for us to do this." *I need this!*

He stops laughing and shakes his head from side to side. "This Jeffery fucker did a real number on you! Why in bloody hell wouldn't I want to see your beautiful face if we were to have sex?" he questions. I can't tell if he's mad or disgusted with me. "I'm not interested in banging a faceless girl or having you pretend I'm someone else. I'm lucid and you're not plastered; therefore, I, Liam, want to fuck you, Sara, so help me God."

"Is that the vow for fucking these days?" I ask with a smirk.

"Yes, my cock just wrote you a vow to make it official, isn't that romantic?"

"No, it's most definitely not romantic, but I'm not looking for romance and neither are you. It seems we both need to get laid for different reasons. I'm a realist and I'm cool with that." I truly believe it.

"Well, I'm not! Yes, it would be fantastic to bang and I very much find you beautiful and sexy, but don't you find it a bit odd that I've been intimate with your best mate? I find it a bit odd that you probably want to pretend that I'm this Jeffery bloke. I prefer women calling *my* name when I fuck them. Sorry, my ego can't take you moaning out his name. Just bloody thinking about it made me go soft. Here, feel." He takes my hand and places it on his semi-hard cock. He's holding my hand over his jeans as I mold my fingers around his "knob" as he keeps referring to it.

This feels wrong on so many levels, and yet my fingers have no shame in helping themselves to a feel and are already working this man into a full straining hard on. I can see him fight to keep those clear blue eyes focused and open.

"Sara, please promise to not pretend I'm someone else when we do this." He cups my face and I feel myself completely melting. He gets closer and says right into my mouth, "Don't stop looking at me. I'm going to kiss you now and I just can't chance you closing your eyes and imagining I'm him."

"I promise I won't. I need this with you, Liam. I hope you won't fantasize that I'm Emily, either. We must only fuck each other and not ghosts. Deal?"

He nods as he brings his lips to mine for a kiss. I've never kissed anybody with my eyes open before, and it feels awkward at first being this close to someone, especially someone I just met. It's weird, different, and so much more intimate than any kiss I've ever had. I still have my hand on his dick as I continue to massage him, and I can feel him grow harder with each stroke, which is doing crazy things to my insides. His hand is at the base of my neck as he slowly kisses my trembling lips and watches me intently. I try to pretend I'm not nervous as if I know what I'm doing, but I'm shitless and even my hands start to shake. I want to close my eyes and enjoy what he's making me feel, but he's right—if I close my eyes, I will be with Jeff and he will probably be with Emily. What we are to each other is a quick fix, a type of superficial physical diversion. In my professional opinion, we're both in great need of some major therapy.

Liam

"In The Air Tonight[23]" by Phil Collins

The sounds that come out of her mouth are fantastic making my balls twitch with excitement. She outright asked me to close the deal and "fuck" her, and I'm not sure who's taking advantage of whom, but I don't bloody care. Sara feels nice in my arms and against my body, and as dirty as it may seem, I swear she smells of sex and it's driving me bonkers. I really am a sick fucker; I don't have any bleeding clue as to how involved this bird is with that tosser from last night. I shouldn't be kissing her, itching to touch every inch of her, or driving my cock into her, but fuck me if she doesn't seem perfect. I haven't touched anybody since meeting Emily. I don't even reckon wanting to, up until this crazy brilliant moment. All I have to do is lower her shorts and bury myself between her long legs and it'll be epic. She wants this, I want this, and there's no other place my dick wants to be than inside of her cunt...

I keep replaying in my mind the way she says my name; it's out of this world. When she fixed and tucked my hair behind my ear, I knew it was just a small gesture and yet it felt intimate and different with her. What would it be like to have a woman want me, take care of me in ways only a true lover could? How sweet would it be if she shouted my name over and over as I pound the sadness out of her? She makes me outrageously hard. I start to drown in my illusions of us fucking, but I could easily continue just kissing her all day. I mean, how long can this lust bubble last before it all disappears?

My conscience, which is buried somewhere deep beneath my lust, is explaining to my enthused knob that what this beautifully broken ballerina and I are doing means there will be no going back. I can't touch Sara like this and hope to have a shot with Emily again. Am I banging Emily's best mate to get Emily out of my system? *Probably.* Am I all over this poor girl as a way of sabotaging any chance I may have with the one girl I know I can't have? *No doubt.* I need to stop thinking about Emily; she made her choice and it's not me. She wants Louis, everybody wants Louis. Sara, she's my choice and I need to be a good choice for her, right now. I want to be somebody's bloody choice. Isa didn't choose me, Brandy didn't choose me, and Emily certainly didn't choose me...I need to make sure Sara chooses me!

As I kiss her lips slowly, she almost stops stroking my rod and just watches me without blinking. I see how every kiss affects her, it's different—not bad different but nice different. People should only kiss with their eyes open, otherwise they'd miss this. I fancy how my kisses are making her smile and blush. She's quite exquisite when she smiles. She needs to find a good fella that will only make her smile and often. I can't help but mirror her giddiness as I try to get my fill of her by slowly and tentatively kissing those swollen lips. Her stupid bloke from last night, he did this. He made her question her worth. How could she think I wouldn't want to see her lovely face as I fuck her? Does she not know that any man who gets to touch her should consider himself blessed? She's beautiful and smart, why would she think someone would not fancy her? I just pray that her proposing we fuck is not just her way of pretending I'm him. I'm

best friend; that alone should be enough of a reason to stop this. I don't even know how far those two got and now I'm letting him kiss me. I love his lips, they're spectacular lips. I don't think I've ever seen a man with such perfect lips; these lips belong on a girl. His kisses feel like heaven and I don't deserve heaven. This is why my life is shit; I allow myself to be put in impossible situations. He will just be another lie I'll have to tell Emily to explain my fucked-up current affairs. It's sad that the truth, in my case, is always too painful to say out loud. It's a good thing I stick to lies; they hurt the people around me less.

I haven't looked away from him or closed my eyes since we started kissing. I have no idea how long we've been sucking each other's lips, but honestly, I don't want it to stop. I'm aware of how selfish I'm acting, using him for pleasure while I should be trying to get rid of him for everybody's sake. But the way he looks at me while cupping my face and licking into my mouth makes me feel okay for being a selfish bitch. He makes me feel naked and wanted, and I need that!

"I don't want to stop kissing you, Sara," he whispers between kisses.

"Then don't," I answer and feel my cheeks blush when he smiles back.

He fixes my hair and moves to whisper in my ear, "This would be much better for both of us if we got to know each other first. I'd like to know what I'm getting myself into with you, love."

"You'd be getting into my pussy and perhaps my mouth and other warm, wet places if you'd stop talking," I say with a mischievous smile, glad that *The* Sara got the memo that her attendance was required at the pathetic lonely club meeting atop the swankiest penthouse in all of Manhattan.

He pulls away after giving my lips another peck. "Oh, lovely, I didn't know I'd be shagging a funny lawyer." His face splits into a grin from ear to ear. The way his eyes catch the light from the window and glisten is exquisite. I need to stop looking in his eyes and come up with a plan. I push him away in jest and lie down on my back. My body hums with excitement as though electric currents zing through me, making everything tingle. I haven't had these kinds of feelings in years; I almost feel like a teenager, not a thirty-year-old anything. If I had to describe this moment to Em, I'd say "What A Feeling²⁴" by Irene Cara.

"Do you also like to sing '80s songs and dance naked?" he asks, practically reading my mind until the second part of his question registers in my head. I feel a screech, halt, and stop from his words. *Sara, you dumbass!* This dude has been with Emily, my best friend. Emily, the one I'm supposed to be helping make this British ass go away, not make him stay and convince him to come inside me. My excitement is extinguished, my smile has died, and I'm back to the real Sara Klein, attorney at law.

I try to sit up as Liam lowers himself on top of me, sensing the mood change. "I'm sorry! Forgive me! I shouldn't have said that out loud. I shouldn't be bringing Emily up since she's your mate. I assure you, I'm not an arse that just bangs everything he meets. I haven't been with anybody since Emily." He kisses the tip of my nose as he rolls off me and spreads out by my side. He takes my hand and laces his fingers with mine. "Maybe we should start over. What if we could have a go at meeting again like perfect strangers?"

"Do strangers lie in bed holding hands?" I ask, trying but failing to sound sarcastic; I'm just stating a fact.

"It's our world, Sara. In this world, strangers actually meet in bed. Holding hands is a special kind of handshake. They kiss each other for a bit with their eyes wide open and they talk about what makes them sad, and then they touch each other for a bit longer and talk some more. If they fancy holding hands, kissing, talking, and touching, they sometimes proceed to the next stage of their courtship and make love."

I like his level of delusion, it almost sounds made-up and pain free. It sounds easy, with very little expectations or broken promises. "Sorry, Liam, your world only exists in books. What happens when the real world catches up to our made-up world?" I ask him, not expecting an answer. I close my eyes and try to imagine a new world I desperately need to find for myself.

"We don't let it. Only we can make it real and then nobody can take it away. It will be our world. We just have to want it badly enough and choose each other." I look over at him and he's also lying on his back with his eyes closed, no doubt wishing he were somewhere, anywhere but here with me. We're still holding hands, and suddenly, as I look at our joined hands, I admit to myself that I do want to be a chosen part of someone's world more than anything...but who and what will that new world cost me?

Liam

"To Be With You[25]" by Mr. Big

I used to believe that tits and knobs could be mates, but *nope*, that is complete made-up dribble. If knob and tits fancy one another, even a tiny wee bit, they will find a way to play naked together. Yesterday, I made eye contact with an American girl at a pub, I later rescued her from a drunken wanker only to see that same bird in bed with a bloke I could bet my left nut was Louis Bruel. I am now in a different bed with that same American chick, offering companionship when all my cock and I really want is a chance to play naked. Like I always say, tits and knobs can't be mates; they can try, they can pretend, but most of the time, they will find a way to play naked.

I am well aware of the sort of arse I seem to be for wanting to be with her and mentioning Emily in the same breath. She actually needs me to calm my balls and be her pal. She requires a stag who only fancies being with her and no other. The way her eyes go from clear to cloudy is uncanny. I truly can't stop looking at her, and just when I think I can see through those troubled, lonely eyes, she closes them. It did feel glorious when I made her smile for those few times. If only that world I just described actually existed, and Sara and I didn't have loads of baggage between us. What if we could begin fresh? It would be ace to live in a world where your family stands by you and doesn't forsake you, and your heart only fancies the things it's allowed to keep. No ghosts or demons clouding our eyes…just this feeling of hope and warmth and of being wanted and chosen from amongst all others. I'd give anything to live in that kind of world.

As much as I long to kiss her all day and bang her all night, I know it's not the square thing to do. I shouldn't even put my tongue inside her without knowing what kind of pain her insides are filled with. I can't become the cause of more hurt for this sad bird. We ought to have words, but not here. Suppose that tosser, Rossi, comes back to bang her again? I'm almost certain that he doesn't frequent her bed during the day, but what if he does? I'd kill him. *Enough!* Why do I even care if he bloody touches her? This is about working Emily out of my system and hopefully convincing Sara I'm trustworthy enough to be able to meet up with her mate, which will help me move on with my fucking life. Therefore, I don't have a right to care who touches her—she's not mine, but brother do I hope she's not Jeffery's, either.

I close my eyes, too, as I lay beside her, holding her delicate hand and trying to think about the "real world," my fucked-up worthless life, and how alone I truly am. Yesterday, all I wanted was a chance to talk to Emily, to perhaps touch her again, and now, suddenly, I fancy making her best mate, a sort I have no business knowing, a bird I only just met and who's proving to be the perfect distraction, I suddenly have a need to make her smile. Fucked up is too light of a term to describe how confused I am. The only thing I know for certain is that if we leave our real worlds behind, perhaps one day we'll have an opportunity to be happy.

"We don't let it. Only we can make it real and then nobody can take it away. It will be our world. We just have to want it badly enough and choose each other." *Our world…* I roll that combination of words in my mind and it sounds so far-fetched.

Did I just ask her to choose me out loud? Am I a total fucking loon? Why am I wishing she would tell me we're not crazy for going down this blasphemous road and that this is where we ought to be? *Sara, choose me,* I whisper again in my mind, and then I feel her squeeze my hand a little tighter…and that's all I need.

Sara

"No One Is To Blame[26]" by Howard Jones

Liam and I need to have words before we upgrade our relationship from strangers who lick into each other's mouths to strangers who get naked and lick into each other's mouths. He can't go around building imaginary worlds for us when there is no us! He's nothing to me! I just need him to fuck me hard and fast so I can let go of this stupid idea that I belong to Jeffery. I don't belong to anybody. But first, we both need to be in agreement on one very important truth. "Liam, you—I mean, we need to talk about your feelings for Emily."

He opens his eyes and looks at me, and just before he starts opening his mouth to try and talk, I hold my finger up to shut him up. I need to say my piece first.

"I need for you to understand what Emily shares with her husband. Don't roll your eyes or yes me, I need to make you understand that what those two have is a once-in-a-lifetime kind of love. I'm allowed to say that because I was there from day one. From the moment their eyes locked, their futures were sealed. You get that, right?" It's a funny thing trying to describe Em and Louis to someone who hasn't witnessed their love affair in person. If I hadn't been there from its inception, I may not believe it, either.

I'm in the midst of verbalizing the greatest love story I've ever had the privilege of witnessing first-hand and I can sense Liam's withdrawal; he isn't looking at me, I'm not even sure he's listening. "Liam!" I want him to keep looking at me as I try and make him understand. He opens his blue eyes but he stares straight up at the ceiling. "Liam, if Emily were your sister, you would sleep well at night knowing that Louis Bruel loves her, only her. I'm sorry about your own sister. I don't know what happened exactly and neither do you, but she did what she did to herself, and you can't blame yourself or Louis for causing any of it. She made that choice to take her own life.

"I can't do this with you if somewhere in the back of your mind or in your heart you believe that you and Emily have a future. I won't stand for it as her best friend and I won't stand for it as your next lay. She and Louis are happy together; they have two gorgeous children and enough memories and good times to fill books. I won't let you try to hurt them to avenge the death of your sister. That's my deal breaker, if you have feelings for Emily as more than a friend then you need to leave." His response will tell me everything I need to know; his words will decide our involvement. He doesn't answer me. It's a bit eerie just waiting for him to say something. "Liam, if there was even a one percent chance in my mind that you and Em could one day end up together, I would never in a million years be kissing you or having anything resembling sex with you. Do you understand that?" He nods his head but continues to look away. "Can you tell me what happened that night in St. Lucia? I need to know."

He turns his head to look at me and I can't decipher his look—is he mad, sad, or just defeated? "I know she loves him," he whispers in a hoarse voice that sounds broken.

"So, why are you so hell-bent on seeing her?" That's a logical question; if he knows she's with the man she loves, why would he try to cause trouble and rip them apart?

"Isa loved him, too. I was worried that he was treating Emily the way Isa described him treating her," he mumbles, suddenly appearing nervous.

"I don't know what your sister described in that book, but I can assure you Louis has never physically hurt Emily, not even accidently. He treats her like a precious heirloom. And those kids are the luckiest kids in the world, you couldn't design a better father than Louis if you tried." I know my words are hurting him. If Louis is suddenly a good guy and hate is out of the equation, Liam will have no one to blame for his sister's death.

He starts biting his nails, illustrating his nervousness. "He had parties, where sometimes he invited ten men to have their way with my beautiful sister, right in front of him. He got off on seeing her raped and humiliated in front of him. He would sit and watch while his friends tied her up and did things that I can't even say or I'll start crying like a fucking baby." He puts his arm over his eyes as if trying to block out his imagination that no doubt paints a horrible, vivid scene. It's hard for me to imagine his sister writing and describing such events, let alone living though them, if they actually happened. I've only ever had sex with one guy, so having ten men fuck me in every hole while my boyfriend watches doesn't sound like a treat. I squeeze his hand, knowing that what he just told me must hurt like hell.

"I'm sorry, that sounds disgusting and horrible and I can't believe you had to read that, but I'm sure he doesn't do things like that with Em if you're worried. Em wouldn't allow it."

He nods his head with his arm still draping his eyes.

"Liam, look at me." I don't know what he's going through unless he looks at me. I need to gauge his state before I try to question him further or offer my two cents. "Don't shut me out. I know it wasn't easy for you to say that out loud, but all we have is this small window of escape, we can help each other work the past out of our heads, but you need to look at me and let me in."

"Sara, you can't help make her pain go away. It's my job to

keep hurting for her because she wasn't strong enough to keep living with the pain." He finally looks at me. His eyes are red-rimmed, making the blue in his irises even bluer. He suddenly seems like a hurt little boy and nothing like the carefree sexy man that has been driving my insides crazy. He needs a hug, he needs someone to understand him and love him. The reason I know what he needs is because I need the same thing.

He continues. "I didn't fix her and she couldn't fix herself, and now she's gone. He and his friends had a hand in her downfall. I also had a hand in her suffering because I didn't do enough to save her." The guilt pours out of him and makes his anguish almost palpable.

"What could you have done? Murdered Louis? Slayed all his friends? If you could go back in time, what could you have changed so that she would stop hurting? Nothing, Liam! Absolutely nothing!"

His eyes close at my words, and there is a good possibility I've pushed him away and he'll most likely leave. But I have to make him understand that his sister's choices and actions had nothing to do with him. "You loved her, she made the decision to stop loving herself, not you. You can't be held accountable for other people's choices. Liam, she was sick." I watch as tears run down his cheeks, and everything inside me starts to ache. I don't even know this guy, but I just want him to stop hurting.

I let go of his hand and move closer to burrow my body into his side. I place my head on his chest and my hand on his heart. His hand covers mine as he looks down at me, and it's weird but it feels like there is no one in the world but us right now. I have this unexplainable instinctual reaction to him that almost feels like this is where I belong, and I cannot be held accountable for what I know is inevitable...even if it's wrong.

Liam

"I Melt With You[27]" by Modern English

"**I**'ve changed my mind. No more talking," I say as I lower my lips to give the broken ballerina at my side another kiss. I don't want to talk, knowing that between the two of us loons we have enough problems to talk for years. I just need to be somewhere else, I want something to stop the pain that I feel from the guilt I can never escape. I want her and I want her now. No more words—they won't help anyway.

She nods her head and pulls herself up to straddle me. She takes hold of my face and brings her lips down to lightly kiss my cheeks. She kisses the trail my tears left, and I'm aware that I promised to not close my eyes, but if I keep them open, I'm afraid the tears will start to fall again. I don't feel as manly as I ought to.

"It's okay to close your eyes, Liam, only for this one time... I will be whoever you want me to be. Maybe I can help make it hurt less," she says into my ear on the verge of tears herself.

I love that she cares, but her words slice me open and this is not how this is going to go down. I flip us over to change positions and our depressing moods. Right now I want her, only her, and I won't let her think she needs to be anybody else but Sara, my broken ballerina. "I don't need to close my eyes because it's you I fancy. I want us both to escape; we just need to drown out everything else around us. I, Liam, want to fuck you, Sara, so help me God."

She smiles. Yes, yes, this is what I want! That bloody smile is glorious, it's brilliant and it lights up her eyes like pure magic. For the next few hours, I will make her smile and laugh and be so deliriously happy that she will forget how to cry and who her heart longs for.

"Thank you," she says with tears in her beautiful green eyes.

"What are you thanking me for? I haven't done a bloody thing to you, yet. Hold your thank yous and applause until after my stellar performance," I add with a wink. This, her and I, right now, is going to be anything but sad. It's going to be bloody ace and she will be wearing the smile I instigated long after I've left, and so will I. We don't need to talk; we need to fuck, hard, and forget the world and every last bastard inhabiting it.

I reckon the speaking portion of our day has just ended and the best part is about to commence. The expression and the smile on her face are doing funny things to my brain. I'm getting high on Sara and there are no drugs involved. We ought to start subtracting some coverings and let the fun begin. Talking and trying to sort out our rubbish, I'm not very good at, but fucking her in this bed will be my pleasure, and with any luck, hers too.

I go back to kissing her, enjoying how the bright room illuminates every piece of her. It feels like we're inside a thick fog operating at slow motion. I'm holding myself up on my forearms, letting just my hard tool touch her lower stomach and I feel her trying to gain more traction with our only point of contact. She wants this—my horny, broken ballerina wants me. *Not yet, baby, let's see what makes you squirm first.* My cock will wait. My eyes need to get their fill of seeing her enjoying my touch.

I sit back on my knees and remove my T-shirt. I see the way she takes me in. She zeroes in on my tattoo and sits up to get a closer look. She traces the letters of my sister's name and it feels odd as I normally wouldn't allow somebody to touch it, but there is no way I'd tell her to stop. The way she traces the tiny scripted letters, you'd think they were written in braille. She slides her legs from under me and also sits up, mirroring me on her knees. She explores my body with her gaze, and I can't stop looking back. She touches my chest and runs her delicate fingers down my arms, making everything flex and come to life. We're not looking away from one another and I don't reckon I could if I tried.

I slide my hands under her loose top and slowly remove it. I want to look down at her chest. I want to lower my head and give her breasts a taste, and yet I can't bloody look away from Sara, my Sara. I'm fully aware that I keep calling her mine in my head, but nobody can hear me and she is mine, for right now.

Sara

"Listen To Your Heart[28]" by Roxette

I feel beautiful when he won't look away from me. For the first time in my life, I feel like the only girl in somebody's world, which is preposterous, since I'm sure he wishes I were Emily. I don't blame him; I wish I were Emily half the time, too. When Jeff and I make love, or fuck or whatever it is we've been doing for years, I never see his eyes open and it's almost always dark. Liam hasn't looked away from me or closed his eyes once and I'm turned on without him even touching me. My head is telling me how stupid I am, but I won't listen. I've listened to my head for fifteen years. If I had listened to my weak, worthless heart, I wouldn't be here today. I wouldn't have let the only man I've ever loved agree to do what's right and fair in the eyes of society. I would've been selfish and demanded things that my immature, helpless heart couldn't ask for back then. Is it too much to want to be loved above all others, above reason, above common sense, and above what's expected? Shouldn't every girl be with someone who only wants to be with her?

I need Mr. Knight in Shining Armor to keep looking at me as if I really am the only girl in the world. Because right here, right now, it's just us. This will be exactly what we both need; I

Liam

"Englishman In New York[31]" by Sting

I recall Emily naming off all these songs from the '80s while she was three sheets to the wind. I fancy some of those songs; I recall my mum playing them by the pool and Isa singing along. Emily even wrote a page full of songs and asked me to study and use them based on their lyrical meaning instead of words to tell her how I feel. We were so zonked that it was nonsensical. I'll never forget her reaction to me using those old corny songs during our conversations that night, quite hysterical. She asked if I fancy any of the songs on her cheat sheet and I pointed to one I recalled from childhood, which made her squeal and start jumping on the bed like a child. She said it was her best mate's favorite song and she then went on to sing it for me as if she were Beyoncé on stage giving the performance of her life. That was the moment she shed the remainder of her clothing and started her full monty '80s concert. I was gobsmacked; seeing her beautiful blond hair and knockers bouncing up and down while she sang happily was epic.

But now, Sara also mentions some song from the '80s and I answer her back like Emily taught me, and her reaction to my song choice is brilliant. Everything begins to happen at lightning speed; she pushes me down on the bed and kisses me like an animal. It's not like before, this is intense and rough and it's incredible. Her breathing is hard and the look in her eyes reveals a pure, desperate need, a kind of longing that's strangling me and driving me mad. I don't think I've ever felt this wanted or needed by another human being. I plan on giving her everything she wants; I understand what she needs and I don't know what more I can do to get closer to her.

We're full-on getting off and she is already working on my trousers. I can hardly wait to feel those delicate, soft hands of hers wrapped around my dick. I hope she pulls hard, squeezes me tight, and strokes me to fucking happiness. The sounds she makes should be illegal. *Oh fuck,* she just slipped her hand into my pants. When her fingers finally make contact with my cock, she must see something in my eyes that tells her she just bloody sent me to heaven.

We've stopped kissing, trying to catch our breaths, but she won't stop rubbing me. Goddamn, she's beautiful; every inch of her is smashing. She nods her head and I nod back, not sure what I've just agreed to, but there is very little I wouldn't agree to at this junction. She lowers her head and starts kissing down my chest; she licks and flickers her tongue at each of my nipples, stopping to slowly kiss the tattoo over my heart, which causes my heart to explode, too. I have never had anybody touch my tattoo before, let alone kiss it. I don't know what I fucking feel, but it's like someone set my insides on fire and I'm willing to let them burn. Please God, don't let her stop. I don't even want her to look away; this moment needs to go on forever.

Her lips continue down my stomach, slowly teasing me along the way, her eyes not once abandoning me and it's the closest I've ever been to baring my soul to a girl. She is with me, not with Louis Bruel, not with Jeffery Rossi, she is with me— Liam Knight, by choice. She moves lower, positioning herself at my crotch. My cock looks enormous in her hands and it feels surreal doing this with her. She pumps and rubs my tip over her closed lips, spreading my pre-cum, in the perfect position to take me in. *Open your mouth and taste me*, I beg her telepathically because I don't reckon myself capable of actually speaking. The tip of my shaft touches her smooth skin and I know she's about to taste me. I'm about to shatter.

How did we get here? How did I manage to get this beautiful woman I've just met under the worst possible circumstances to allow me to ram my dick in her mouth? All I can think is *God bless America*; this girl is going to make me see stars today.

Sara

"Hungry Eyes[32]" by Eric Carmen

I'm in the middle of an out-of-body experience and I can't stop, or even slow it down. The hunger that this man has unleashed inside of me will not be satisfied until we're both passed out cold.

His dick feels perfect, I'm acting like a complete slut, and it feels even more perfect. I shouldn't think of Emily right now, but she wasn't kidding about his balls. I don't have much to go on from personal experience, but I have yet to see anything resembling Liam's balls attached to a human. I have an unexplained animalistic need to taste him and smell him and make out with his impressive penis. I play with his tip and spread the moisture around my lips like lip gloss, failing to play it cool and dying to taste every part of him. I know I shouldn't be comparing him to anybody or even letting my mind think of anything but him and us and this, but I can't help it. This is my first sexual experience with somebody other than Jeff. I've never seen or touched another man's privates besides his and I'm kinda sorta nervous. I've had plenty of practice with silicone dildos, but never with anybody other than Jeffery.

Besides being scared, euphoric, and beyond aroused by this

guy that has invaded my life and is turning everything upside down, I'm also trying to put this whole thing into perspective. Once we're finished, I need to make sure my brain files this encounter and places it on the right shelf. To him, I'm just a quick lay, but he is my key to freedom. This means more to me than Liam will ever know. If I can do this with him, then I can do this with anybody, not just Jeffery Rossi.

He won't take his eyes off me, and we haven't said a word to each other since he named that damn song that he had no right knowing, let alone uttering it as I literally attacked him. I've never had this kind of connection, this type of understanding, a silent bond with another person, except Emily. I never even knew it was possible to have someone other than Emily get me.

I need to calm my feelings because I know this stranger doesn't know me and how fucked up I am on the inside. He's just sexually frustrated and I'm a willing participant, but since I'm also a liar, my heart has already convinced my head that he loves me, that he can't take his eyes off of me, and that there is no one on earth he would rather be fucking and loving right now but me.

I thought when I first asked him to fuck me that I would be wishing and dreaming for him to be Jeff, but I'm not. This experience belongs to Liam and me and no one else. I can't wait to see his eyes when he finally enters me. Just thinking about him being inside me makes me dizzy with lust. I don't know much about him, but I do know that it won't be the usual regret or sadness in his eyes that I always see in Jeff's.

I've teased him enough. I open my mouth to finally have my first taste of Liam fucking Knight and I love how he watches me, waiting, holding his breath. I grip him with both hands and lick him from root to tip like a skilled slut, swirling my tongue from side to side. He sits up a bit to move all my hair off my face, making sure he gets a full view of both my mouth and my eyes as I attempt to suck his cock whole. I like the pained sounds that come out of his mouth; I can tell he's trying hard not to make any noise. I stop the root-to-tip licking and open my mouth to take him in, to have my first fill of him. I'm only a few inches in before he jerks my head up by my hair with some force.

"I know I shouldn't be talking, but I want you to know this is not how I imagined today would pan out. But there is no other place on Earth I would rather be than right here with you, Sara. I'm praying the feeling is mutual."

I still have his dick in my mouth as he says this, which is kinda sweet, but hard to acknowledge in my current predicament. I try to give him a smile with a mouth full of cock, but I can't get more of him in because he's holding me back. I want to tell him to let go of my hair so I can continue sucking him off, but he merely looks at me with my mouth stretched wide, looking slightly confused. Maybe he doesn't like my fellatio skills or maybe I'm supposed to be doing something else? But then he cups my scalp with both hands and starts guiding me further down while pushing himself into me, rewarding me with his sound effects. I thought I was in control of this blowjob business, but I'm mistaken; Liam has full control and I like it.

He has a firm grip on my head as he pumps himself into my mouth. I can see when he starts to lose it. His eyes fight to stay open and he struggles to keep calm. He's acquired that deranged, panicked expression that I had a few minutes ago when I attacked him after he spoke '80s to me.

"There is no way I'm bloody losing it and coming after a one-minute head job. That is not how this will go down in history," he says, which makes me laugh hard. I let go of his dick and continue to laugh with tears running down my face. I've never in my life made a guy come—well, I never in my life made Jeff come from just a blowjob—and if Liam were to come from this simple act alone, my ego and I would be incredibly grateful to him and his impatient dick.

When I stop rolling on the bed laughing, I say to him, "God,

Liam, I wish you would come in my mouth. I've never made Jeff come just from oral before."

His eyebrow turns up at my comment and then he pulls me up on top of him. "What am I going to do with you? I've never come from oral, either, so it could be a first for both of us." He gives me a kiss—it's slow and sweet. He pulls away and adds, "Don't talk about him when we're naked. You can tell me anything and everything about your life, but not yet."

After gazing into his eyes for as long as I have, I could probably describe every magnificent flake and different shade of blue that make up the most beautiful eyes—besides Emily's— I've ever seen. I run my hands through his hair and that, too, is made of different shades of blond. *Fuck*, I hope I don't grow fond of him, because he makes it too easy to like him. We're getting as physically close as two people can and it's perfect. Shouldn't I feel wrong about being with him? *No, it can't be wrong*. With each touch, nothing about us feels wrong. I don't know this feeling of being with someone and not feeling disgraceful about it. I will always look for a reason why I shouldn't be with someone, thanks to my history. Wouldn't it be nice if I could just enjoy a moment like this with a stranger for what it is?

It's peaceful just being by his side in a quiet room, nestled inside a private retreat atop a New York City landmark. My heart beats faster than it has in a very long time and yet it's a calm kind of chaos; I'm at peace. I think of how we pass hundreds of people every day and each one of them has a story. I have a story, Liam has a story, and we know close to nothing about each other, and yet I feel that he gets me better than all my friends and family combined. I haven't told him anything, but he's the only person in the world that I want to.

He looks at me and yet I don't feel ashamed for looking back. I haven't lied to him about my life, and that alone makes me want to live, to keep going, to start again. I haven't wanted that in forever. He doesn't even comprehend what he's doing for me and I'm not sure I will ever be able to repay him for this, but Liam is saving me—one look at a time.

"Thank you, for this," I say, and feel like a moron the second the words are out of my mouth. I blush at my stupidity and can't believe I've said thank you to a dude for agreeing to fuck me. This has to be a new low, even for me. "I'm sorry, I didn't mean to say that out loud. It's like I'm thanking you for being my fuck buddy."

"You don't need to thank me, or apologize, or even say another word. I'm trying to figure out what's happening between us and I'm...I'm...I'm all right with not fully understanding. You're lovely and I'm grateful you're here with me, and it's bloody insane because I didn't even know you existed before yesterday."

I love hearing him talk; his words are just right. If he knew what his words do to me, he would probably run for his life. I want him, and it's surreal being here with him, both of us wanting the same thing—sex! He smiles and I can't help but mirror it with my own lips. Boys could make you smile; boys *should* make you smile! I think I may have found a British boy that can make me smile for a little bit and forget the world.

"Let me see all of you, Sara. Take your shorts and knickers off and sit in my lap," he says very casually, and his naughty request makes my insides twitch and pulse. I don't argue; I mean, come on, even I know that if a gorgeous British boy asks you to sit naked on his cock...you do it!

I remove whatever is left of my clothing and straddle this sexy stranger without needing to be asked twice. He takes one look at my bare pussy and then lifts me up to adjust his erection, placing it up toward his stomach, and lowering me again to sit flush on his massive balls. I love that we're skin-to-skin and his length is right between my folds. His cock is pressed perfectly underneath me, almost reaching his belly button, and the thought of him inside me is euphoric, causing me to full-on leak all over his hard on. He cups both my breasts, giving them a hard squeeze and then circles my nipples with his thumbs. As I look down at his fingers working my nipples, I spot my dark hair cascading down my shoulders, which is probably the longest it's ever been. I almost forgot that my hair is not dirty blond anymore. The color seems even darker against my naked skin. It's weird that this is how he knows me. He's never met the lying, cheating Sara that belonged to Jeffery. He only knows the real me from this point on.

I start to slowly undulate on the length of his pulsating and twitching dick beneath my pussy. I can taste how bad I want him inside me, but I'm enjoying our foreplay. Once you have sex, it's done; you can never have that unknown moment back. I crave the intimacy we're about to experience; however, I do find myself enjoying the anticipation. It's inevitable that we will consummate our "friends with benefits" status shortly, but I need to first commit all the emotions I'm having to memory before we cross all lines. I will revisit and enjoy these memories over and over, and therefore, I must take my time. He likes to watch me, and I love watching how he unconsciously lets his tongue hang out while he plays with my tits. He makes a deep moaning sound every time I slide up and down his hardness. I need to remember these sounds.

"How do you come, Sara?" he asks me breathlessly. "Do you come during or prior to intercourse, or both?" he continues in between our combined groans.

I've never had anyone ask me that before. I don't come during sex since Jeff always makes me come before he's inside of me. I guess I come before sex, then. "I've never come during sex," I decide to say to him, which makes him stop moving for a second before a huge smile spreads over his face.

"Good, you and I are about to have many epic firsts, Sara. It's like you're a virgin."

It's cute that he thinks he can make me orgasm during intercourse. The man I've loved and been sexually active with for over a decade has never been able to make me climax during sex. I smirk, thinking, *I'm not about to argue* as I continue sliding up and down his perfectly hard, lubricated dick.

Liam

"You Spin Me Round³³" by Dead or Alive

My knob is glistening with her juice and I bloody love having sex during the daytime, with the sunlight on her body like a spotlight. I can't take my eyes off our point of contact as she rubs up and down my length. She's beautiful, I don't remember thinking she was this beautiful last night at the pub, but it's undeniable. I've never been with a girl that needed me as much as Sara needs me, not even Emily, and it makes me want her in a strange, wonderful way.

What could she be lying about to Emily? The thought pops in my mind. I don't reckon her lying if she tried. I just hope to God she's not seriously involved with that Rossi fella. The stupid bloke doesn't make her come during sex, he doesn't blow his load while she sucks him off, and I know he leaves her before the sun comes up; what is the matter with him? *I loathe him!* I shouldn't even think about him; I need to just enjoy the way she makes me feel. She looks at me like I'm a rock star, and I love that! *I hope she doesn't look at him like this.* I try and fail not to think about him as I squeeze her petite-sized, perfect tits together. Her nipples are dark and round and practically look painted on against her milk-colored skin. I ought to make her feel special, craved, and instead, I have this egotistical need to make sure she won't fucking look at him ever again without thinking of me. *After we fuck, what if she goes back to him?* This broken ballerina should find a new man, a good man.

I slide my hand down to her smooth cunt and find her clit, giving it a polish with my thumb. My tanned hands accentuate her fair-colored skin. She has zero hair and her softness drives me bonkers. I can smell our arousal and the scent makes my mouth water. As much as my dick tickles to be inside her, I know she needs to come first. A gentleman always lets his lady go first. I don't know her body well enough to make this good for both of us and I'm not sure how many chances I'll have to get it right. We ought to play and get acquainted first prior to fucking. My tongue hasn't even been formerly introduced to her pussy yet.

Her intoxicating scent paralyzes my common sense. I wish to ask her to properly show me how she makes herself come. My mouth salivates at the mere thought of watching her play with herself and then tasting her as she comes. I asked her to bloody sit on me, why can't I ask her to play with herself? I'm being a pussy, afraid to chance pushing her too far by being a bit too kinky for her.

I flip us over gently and kiss her again. I can kiss this bird all day. Every time we kiss, her eyes enlarge and she wears this shocked look on her face. It's quite sweet, almost like she can't believe we're doing this. Well, I, too, can't believe we're doing this. I hope this isn't another big blunder. The thing with Emily and me in St. Lucia is starting to feel like a big muddle and I don't want this to feel wrong, too.

"I know I said no more yapping, but what are you thinking, Sara? You're all right with this, right? I want you to be square and happy about us being like this." I pray she doesn't put the kibosh on this. She gives me a small smile and even that is glorious. Who knew a girl's smile could feel this fucking good? If she laughs, I may die.

"I like this, I haven't felt this good in a very long time. It's nice and I'm glad it's you who's making me feel this way and not him."

Him! Him! Him! There is always a fucking him! Why is there always someone who stands in the way of me having what ought to be mine? I don't know what those two have, so how am I supposed to compete with it?

"Liam, what's wrong?" She cups my face, trying to get me to look at her. I guess I can't fib to her, either, and everything I feel must be written on my traitorous mug. "Look at me, we're having fun, just fucking, right? I'm helping you get Emily out of your head and you're helping me deal with my issues."

I try to shut my brain off and work her out of my system quickly, before she becomes a permanent tenant.

"Yes, yes, we're just fucking, love. My whole life is actually just about *fucking* and this is exactly what I needed. I need to bang a broken ballerina, and you need to fuck a delusional Brit. Clearly, this is what we both need," I say, without chancing a glance at her. The truth in a nutshell: we're two broken people trying to help each other break even more.

I actually don't feel like doing anything with her anymore. These head games that make up my life are starting to make me wish I could be a castaway somewhere far, far away. I wouldn't even bring a wretched ball with me, because I'm sure it would find a way to fuck up my life somehow.

She continues to hold my face as I try to free myself from her grip and get my bum out of here. I've heard enough, I've seen enough, New York hates me and I need to go. If I stay here, yes, my dick will win; I'll get to fuck her...but then what? I don't want to think about her and that fucking Jeffery getting it on once we're done.

"Liam fucking Knight, can you please look at me?" she practically yells at me. I don't want to look at her. I know that if

I look back into her sad eyes, I'll crack…she'll make me lose it and I'll want to make her happy all over again. "Liam, why are you being like this? I want you! Nobody else! But I can't just pretend that I don't have a past with him. We just met. We mean nothing to each other. Let's just finish what we've started. I need to have you inside me." Did she say that? *Wow,* that actually hurt. I suddenly feel like a prostitute. It's odd, I don't remember ever feeling this used before, and yet how could I possibly feel used if I'm using *her* as a cum-catcher just as much as she's using me as a cum-donor? I can't shake this rubbish feeling off. *Bollocks!*

I finally collect my scattered thoughts and answer, "I don't want to look at you. I'm sorry, this was a bad idea." I instantly feel the loss of her hands from my face as she harshly pushes me off her and sprints off the bed. I look at her delicate naked figure as she starts pulling her clothing back on.

Now she's the one who won't look at me and I can't believe I've managed to hurt her. I didn't intend to hurt her, but I just rejected her and she has no idea why. She doesn't look my way or bloody say a word, but the throbbing in my chest tells me she's about to cry. I tried to make her forget that arse Jeffery ever existed and now I'm the arse she ought to forget. I thought she could be mine for a bit and I've managed to make it all go tits up. My feelings and my issues have ruined what could've been perfect—at least momentarily.

"Sara, it came out wrong; let me explain."

She stops fussing with her shorts and turns to look at me, and that look, those eyes, those unshed tears nearly destroy me. I leap off the bed and grab her so hard that she makes a pained noise before her tears pass over her lower eyelids.

"No, love, please. I'm sorry. I want you and me to be together, but I don't want to just be someone you use to fuck him out of your system. I want us to not have to fuck anybody out of our systems. I just want us to be together. I ought to be an option, a choice, not a fucking regret."

Is that really what I want? Her wails echo around me and I think, *I'm a stupid wanker.* How do I fix this?

Sara

"If You Leave[34]" by OMD

Hate and love are different sides of the same coin. I love and hate almost everything and everybody in my life at one point or another. Why this silly, gorgeous man is here and why fate brought us together, I can't pretend to understand. He pushed me away because he thinks I want Jeffery, but all I can think about is him. I'm pretending to use him to get Jeff out of my system, but that's a lie. I want Liam and he needs to understand that. I choose him. I won't allow Jeff to have this kind of hold on me. I refuse to play second fiddle anymore. From this day on, I will not tolerate anybody in my life—even for a day—unless they want me first. I've earned that!

I have once again proven to myself that my dam of tears is bottomless. I understand everything he's said and I feel everything he feels, and yet I can't stop crying. This makes how many times that I've cried today? Why is he still here and not running away? I'm certain that I've provided enough evidence to establish that I'm the biggest mess he's ever going to see. This shit show is slowly starting to get embarrassing. He should go, like now!

"Liam, let go of me. You need to leave." I can't even see

him clearly with the nonstop stream of tears blurring my vision. He holds me ridiculously tight against his chest and his grip hurts, but I can't help but wish I had someone who wanted to hold me this tight forever. "This was a mistake, just go. Don't worry, I'll never speak of this to anyone." My words cause him to clench me even tighter.

"Please, Sara, don't say that. Listen to me; I love being here with you more than anything. I'm just tired of being everybody's second choice. I wanted you to choose me! I didn't mean to push you away or make you bloody cry again. Forgive me. Please tell me you understand that I'm not using you to get anybody out of my system. I'm using you because you feel good in my arms."

He holds my head against his chest as I continue to sob, my tears running down his naked body. This perpetual hell I've made for myself needs to be destroyed. He begs me, *pleads* with me to stop crying but I physically can't. I allow a perfect stranger see the ugliest, scariest side of me—a side I don't even think Jeff has seen. Why have I allowed myself to break down like a weak, worthless fool in front of him?

I feel him lift me up once again and a sense of déjà vu comes over me. "Put me down. I need to go wash my face. Your tea must've been laced with hormones. I never cry this much, especially in front of a stranger," I say between hiccups.

He kisses the top of my head and says, "I stopped being a stranger after I sucked your nipples and played with your cunt, so kindly come up with a new term to describe me because I may be many things, but a stranger isn't one of them."

I'm nestled into his chest as he leads us into yet another room I've never seen before. "Holy shit! How many rooms does this penthouse have? Are we playing musical rooms?"

"I will make sure everything is smashing this time. In the first room you made a bad decision, in the last room I made a bad move. I proper fancy this room for making stellar memories," he says, smiling down at me.

This new room is beautiful. He hasn't released me from his arms and I find it weird how normal this feels. He walks us to one of the two queen-sized beds, closest to the window, and lays me down on the blue and white bedspreads that look almost royal and match the wall coverings. "This will be the last time I'm fetching you a cloth to wipe your eyes...understood?" I nod. "You're beautiful, even when you cry, Sara," he adds before going to get yet another fucking rag to clean my treacherous eyes.

I accept the towel, thanking him. I have experienced too many sensations about Liam to even start to understand what's happening between us. I wipe my eyes as he studies me.

"What are you thinking?" I ask him.

"That I need to know everything. Every last inconspicuous detail about you. New rule—no touching, just talking."

"So, now you make the rules for our fucked-up relationship?" I tease as he breaks his own rule in less than a minute by lifting my legs and placing them on his lap as he sits at the foot of the bed.

"Fine, the no-touching rule blows. I wouldn't be able to stop touching you, anyway. How about no kissing, or sucking any body parts?" he offers as he starts massaging my feet, first gently and then with some much-needed expert strength.

Yeah, that's a good rule, I think, melting into his touch. God, I love having my feet touched; Jeff never has time to massage my feet. I close my eyes and let myself enjoy a few rare minutes of bliss.

"Everything about you shouts ballerina," he says, outlining my high arch.

I smile at his assessment. I hated ballet as a child. I had to pirouette and plié while Emily got to dance hip-hop with all the normal kids. Who needs to stand in a turnout and walk on their toes, wear pink tights and tutus, when you could be learning dance moves that you may actually use one day? Not sure why my mother insisted I practice ballet all those years, when the only person to ever see me dance or come to my performances was Emily. I haven't danced for twelve years and I have no desire to ever put my pointe shoes back on. Perhaps Liam's right—a broken ballerina I am.

"If you get me drunk enough, I may show you the mean split I can do." I smile as my handsome foot masseur continues his job.

"I'm breaking another rule," he says as he brings my foot to his mouth and plants a soft kiss along my arch. "If some dimwit didn't make up some silly rule about no kissing I'd give your feet a proper tongue massage, but it's against the rules." He gives me a mischievous cocky smile.

"I've never had a tongue massage, on my feet, that is." I giggle as everything, including my clit, comes to life and tingles once again as I imagine his tongue doing wicked things to me.

"I'll fix that one day, if you let me." He lifts my feet, slides from under them, and moves up the bed to lie next to me. He drapes an arm over my waist and lays his head on my chest. He's completely naked; his jeans are in the last room. If I didn't know that he owned a hotel in St. Lucia, I'd say judging by his tan lines that he's a surfer. I run my fingers up and down his back and his skin pebbles to my touch but still feels hot. I lower my nose to inhale his hair and it smells of something woodsy and manly. I wrap my arms around him and I kinda sorta feel safe for no good reason. I kiss the top of his head, and it feels strangely natural and calming being entwined with Liam.

"Stop smelling me and start at the beginning, Sara…when did you meet him?" he asks.

"If I rewind and try to tell my story, you must promise me a few things."

He looks up at me and says, "Anything."

"Promise to not react to what Jeffery and I share. When you hear my story, you have to accept that it's not just my story but Jeff's as well. Emily must never know any of this; she won't understand. This will hurt her more than anything, and I can't take that chance. I will lose the only true friend I've ever had. You also need to promise not to feel sorry for me; I don't need pity."

He moves up to my lips and kisses them, breaking yet another rule.

"Enough with the promises, I'm here for you. I can't guarantee that I'll fancy hearing about you and some wanker, but I will endure it for you. Someone other than you needs to have knowledge of your past in order for you to stop hurting and punishing yourself."

I can't believe that Liam Knight is about to hear my tale. He probably assumes that once he knows my truth, he'll just be able to close his eyes and fuck me, as if I'm not the worse person in the world. Once you know the truth you can't un-know it. I've kept secrets and told lies for long enough to recognize that right now is the best opportunity I'm ever going to get to unburden my wounded soul.

I close my eyes and begin telling him the story of Sara and Jeffery Rossi.

Sara

"Don't You Want Me?[35]" by The Human League

I could tell you the exact moment my life changed forever. The exact second, that if given the chance to go back in time and avoid, would positively, unquestionably, without a doubt alter my whole existence as I know it.

I was fifteen years old and I kissed a twenty two-year-old man. It was the first time I saw the inside of a nightclub and it later proved to be a night of many firsts. Eddie, my older brother, and his friends took Emily and me to our first New York City nightclub in the heart of the village. Twenty dollars got two under-age girls inside and my life has never been the same since.

My brother had just graduated from NYU and was celebrating with his friends their acceptances to law school. This was their last celebratory party of the summer before they would all leave the following week for schools across America. Eddie brought Em and me along to have fun… He didn't really want to take us, but we begged and cried until he got sick of saying no and reluctantly agreed.

You should know that I knew all of my brother's friends at that time, to my knowledge, that is. However, that night fifteen years ago, I also met the love of my life. The man who, unbe-

knownst to me then, would shape my existence and mold me into the Sara that the world thinks they see.

Em and I danced inside this human shield Eddie and his friends formed around us. It was amazing how time stood still inside the walls of that club. Deafening music roared in my ears and the vibrations traveled through my body. We danced for hours until we noticed Eddie and his buddies finally loosen their tight shield around us; they even started dancing with some other girls.

You've never met my brother, but you should know that he's extremely handsome: tall, dark, clean cut; you know, that all-American rich preppy boy that girls swoon over. The kind of guy you see in Ralph Lauren ads. I was always secretly afraid Emily and Eddie would hook up, but that never happened. Em was the biggest prude and my brother wasn't into high school girls. He once told me that Emily was pretty but since he remembers her in diapers, he would never think of her as anything other than an extra annoying sister. He wouldn't even look at her gorgeous older sister Jenna. I remember his famous words of wisdom: You shouldn't shit where you eat. The Marcus girls are family. I wouldn't touch them if they begged me. *Well, that was the good news; I wouldn't have to worry about my brother touching my best friend. The bad news was I just saw Eddie talking to the hottest guy I had ever seen. They were now both looking my way. Eddie pointed at Em and me dancing, clearly talking about us. I then saw the tall, dark, sexy stranger walk my way with a big grin.*

"Hi," he yelled over the music.

"Hello," I yelled back, adding a wave as I continued swaying to the beat.

"I was sent to babysit you and your friend while your brother goes to 'talk' to that girl outside." He pointed back toward Eddie who was all over his girl Michelle. They had met a few years back on a family vacation to Europe. Yeah, "talk." I'm

sure that's exactly what they were going to do outside, *I remember thinking to myself.*

"We're good girls. We don't need babysitting," I yelled back as I pulled Emily in for a hug. She'd been dancing with her eyes closed for the past few minutes as if in a trance.

"Sara, you cow, you scared me." Emily giggled as she tightened her hold around my waist. Mystery stranger sent to babysit us spoke again but I couldn't hear him with the new loud beat blasting from the speaker positioned right next to us. I let go of Em to allow her to dance on her own and motioned to my ears that I couldn't hear him.

Sexy stranger with sleek black hair and a Dracula peak on his forehead who hadn't looked away from me smiled and lowered his head to say in my ear, "I promised Eddie I wouldn't let anybody dance with the two of you. He doesn't want some guy thinking he can put his hands on his little sister." As he said this, he put his hand on my back to keep me still while he spoke.

I turned to face him and beckoned him closer so that I could whisper in his ear. "You don't want some guy like you putting his hands on me." I recall being brave and chanced a glance up at his eyes that were overly dilated and glistening with amusement, making it hard for me to see their true color, or in his case, colors.

He smiled before lowering his head to my ear again, this time, cupping the side of my face before saying, "If you were a year older, I'd put my hands on you all night... I'll let you grow up a little before I start touching you." And then he left my side without a second glace as the crowd swallowed him. I spent the rest of that night trying to tell my stupid heart that hadn't stopped beating out of my ribcage to calm the fuck down and pay no attention to the stupid stranger who already touched me with just a few words.

The night ended with Eddie and his mystery friend—whose stupid name I had yet to learn—abandoning their friends at the club to walk Em and me home. Eddie conveniently forgot to inform me that his buddy from school, Jeff, was sleeping over since our parents were away and Jeffery didn't live in the city. My brother left me in front of our house with Jeffery to go walk Emily home. Em lived 557 steps away from me.

I pretended to be calm, but it was hard for me to breathe and continue to be my usual loud, smart-mouthed self, because this guy Jeff wouldn't stop looking at me. He had so much confidence, or maybe it was just liquid courage. I knew for sure he was drunk because he kept swaying a little to the left and I could smell the faint stench of tequila on him. He finally broke our silence and asked me, "How old are you?" as I opened the front door to let us both in.

"None of your business, Jeff," I barked back, not sure what prompted my bitchy response.

"If you want me to touch you, I'll need to know your age, Sara, right? I need to figure out how long you'll need to wait for that to happen." He laughed as if he'd just told the world's funniest joke. What a dick!

I obviously didn't answer the fool and walked upstairs without another word. I think I was upset with myself for actually liking him and letting a drunken idiot see how much he affected me. After his vain remark, I decided I would never say another word to Jeff.

That night, I couldn't sleep. I tossed and turned, trying to get comfortable and calm enough to let my body win the battle with my head and shut down. You see, when I was young, I liked to talk a big game and pretend that I'd "been there, done that." Pretend that at fifteen I'd kissed countless boys and touched their dicks. Pretend that sex was no big deal. I had no choice but to be that kind of girl. Emily was my only best friend and the perfect, prudish one, so I got the role of the cute, sassy, and sexually experienced one. I've watched enough of my brother's stashed-away porn movies to fake it. Thanks to Eddie, I knew exactly

what boys wanted, what they talked about, and how a girl needed to act to attract their attention. *I had no intention of testing
my theories with a boy any time soon; I was just a delusional
hypocrite testing my theories through others. I liked the opinion
my friends had of me. I loved being able to dish out advice and
shock everybody with what came out of my mouth. If you ask
Emily who was the most sexually promiscuous, loose person she
knew growing up, she'd tell you it was me, her best friend, Sara
Klein.*

*So there I was, fifteen years old, trying to sleep in my room,
minding my own business, struggling to forget my first club experience and the way some dumb guy named Jeff put his hand on
me and how good it felt. Trying to ignore the fact that when he
spoke into my ear, every hair on my body—including my pubic
hairs—stood at attention. Pretending that his promise to let me
grow up before he touched me didn't affect every one of my mol-
ecules. At four thirty in the morning, someone opened my door
and stumbled into my bedroom with a loud thump, scaring the
living crap out of me. I remember my heart getting stuck in my
throat as I tried to scream for help.*

*As soon as the shock dissipated and my voice re-emerged, I
began to let out a scream before I felt a hand over my mouth to
silence me. I remember thinking,* it's all over, this is how horror
movies end.

"Shhhhh...sorry-y-y. Sara, don't yell," the owner of the
hand mumbled.

*I knew that voice. How could this be happening? How could
the person that I just had a wet dream about be in my room in
the middle of the goddamn night?* Did I summon him to my
room or was it part of my dream?

*The first song that popped into my head was A-ha's "Take
On Me[36]." I recall thinking that if I lived to tell about this, I'd
call Em first thing in the morning and tell her how Eddie's hot
friend from the club made a pass at me and asked me to make*

out with him by attacking me in my own room. I'd use that song for sure. That song would only make sense to Emily, because there wasn't another fifteen year old on the planet that would know every song from the '80s like she and I did.

We had created our own language of lyrics. The words from the songs would do the talking for us. It was I who came up with that brilliant secret language to help me manage all my lies. I wouldn't have to go into detail, which meant I wouldn't have to remember too many particulars about the fabrications I'd feed Emily in regards to my nonexistent bullshit lifestyle.

"Please, don't yell. I didn't mean to scare you," Jeff whispered to me.

"Jeff, why are you in my room?" I asked as my eyes began to adjust to the darkness and saw him lying halfway on my bed with his arms resting dangerously close to my chest.

"I'm sleeping over, remember? I thought this was my room," he answered, blatantly lying as he then sat on my bed. He really was drunk. The guest room he was supposed to be occupying wasn't even on my floor.

"Okay fine, if that's the story you're going with, let me get dressed and I'll show you your room." I tried to move and put the light on so that I could get dressed and walk that drunken fool back to his room when it happened. I remember him gently grabbing my arm to stop me from turning on the light on my nightstand. When he put his hands on me, it was that same feeling I had at the nightclub—arousal like I've never felt before. I think I even stopped breathing.

He then urged me back down and strangely started tucking me back in. "No, Sara, go back to sleep. I feel stupid for waking you. I can find my room myself. I don't know what I was thinking."

Just as he was about to leave, he lowered his head and kissed my lips. I was shocked—frozen, speechless, definitely not breathing at this point. Thinking back now, I truly believe that since he was drunk and operating at half-speed, he meant it to be an innocent peck, but it wasn't. He was suspended over me, and it looked as though he battled with himself as to why he did it and how he could explain it.

That was the moment I sobered up and chose to be The *Sara that everybody believed I was. That was the moment I chose to help materialize the childish illusion I had over some hot stranger I laid eyes on in a noisy club. I bravely placed my arms around his neck and pulled him down to me, kissing him just like they did in the movies. It was first slow and soft, but as I felt him start to kiss me back, I became braver. He smelled like a man and tasted good. I'm sure he was in shock, but he didn't stop kissing me back, putting his tongue in my mouth and running his fingers through my hair. I remember the deep, throaty sounds he made, clearly enjoying the taste of me.*

"Sara. Jesus. Fuck. Stop!"

He said stop? *When his words and tone sunk in, I stopped and let go of his neck. Why would he tell me to stop? I remember thinking that I must have horrible breath. What was I thinking, kissing him like that? I felt instantly hurt and ashamed, willing my tears to stop from joining the spectacle I'd just orchestrated. I summoned my inner slut Sara, Sara the ball buster, the say-what's-on-your-mind-without-a-filter Sara. I needed her strength to emerge, but she was a coward and I lost it. I started to cry. No! I started to wail. Big, ugly tears. I was embarrassed at what I just did. I forced a drunk guy to kiss me. I'd read his signals all wrong. He evidently wanted nothing to do with me. He was just buzzed and accidently stumbled into my room and I attacked him like a crazy girl who'd never seen a boy in her life. How would I explain to him that I was just kidding? I hoped that maybe he was so drunk he wouldn't remember any of this in the morning. Or maybe I just needed to crawl into a hole and die.*

With tears running down my face, I whimpered, "I'm sorry, I didn't mean to do that. I thought that's what you wanted."

He turned to me, saying, "Please stop crying. The last thing I need is for you to cry. Of course that's what I wanted. I'm piss drunk and things are happening very slow in my head, but I still know I want you." He lowered his head into his hands and started cursing to himself.

I felt the weight of the world lift from me when he said he wanted me. Oh thank God, I repeated in my head. I climbed out of the covers, still sniffling, and sat right next to him on the edge of my bed. I recall wanting to climb into his lap but settled for putting my hand on his upper thigh to assure him that I was on the same page with him.

"Jeff, what's the problem? You want me, I want you," I said between hiccups. I tried to make him understand that this was exactly what I needed or I would die of shame and humiliation. He needed to touch me to validate my feelings. I needed him to make the lies I had told Emily about everything I'd ever done with imaginary boys come true. If he touched me, kissed me, and fucked me that night, then I'd stop lying. I'd have no reason to lie anymore.

"Sara, you're seventeen and you're my best friend's underage sister. I'm going to law school next week; I don't wanna take advantage of you. Especially in the state my head is in."

I was about to tell him that I was actually only fifteen, but before I was able to compose my thoughts, he started talking again. He was so beautiful with his messy, disheveled hair no longer slicked back. The slight curve to his upper lip gave him a constant sexy smirk. The boys I knew didn't have stubble around their jaw, which made me want to pretend I was a real woman and not some stupid, inexperienced fifteen-year-old girl. He smiled at me and it took all my self-restraint not to throw myself at him again.

"Stop smiling at me. You need to be less appealing, Sara! Even your name is perfect. You do know we can't do this, right? Right? Sara, tell me to fucking leave your room and never come

back. Throw me the fuck out, please!" he pleaded, as his face grew serious.

I nodded but couldn't tear my eyes from him. I couldn't utter those words. He probably didn't even know that this was my first kiss. I couldn't believe that a kiss, just a kiss, could feel like that. At that moment, I only wished for Jeffery to stay with me all night and kiss me the way he did a few minutes ago so I wouldn't need to lie about anything ever again.

"Kiss me again," I demanded. I don't know how I had the nerve to ask him that after what he had said to me. "Please, just a kiss goodnight and I'll never mention this again. It will be our secret."

He seemed to contemplate my offer, and I could tell when the devil won. He came at me slow at first, and then the battle was lost and all bets were off. I would've let him do anything to me that night. The way he kissed me, tried to inhale me. His hands were in my hair again. Now, I was the one who started to moan as my heart pounded and my pussy violently tingled from that desperate kiss. When he let go of my lips to kiss down my neck, I remember literally feeling like I'd combust, like his touch had ignited every cell within my body. His hands slowly grazed my erect nipples, which I thought would make me convulse in pleasure, and then boom! He just froze and everything stopped. It was as if my nipples woke him up from a spell.

"I can't do this. I can't tell if I want you because my brain is telling me that I can't have you, or because you're so fucking sexy and innocent and I just wanna ruin you." He started withdrawing from the space that only seconds ago had been completely invaded by him. "Neither of those reasons are good enough to let myself fuck you tonight."

"I'm not some virgin, Jeff!" My first lie to him that night, unless you count the lie of omission—not correcting his assumption of my real age. "I've fucked plenty of guys. I'm sorry to wreck your delusional fantasy about ruining me, but you're too

late." Lie number two. *"I usually prefer having two guys at once."* The lie that probably sealed my coffin. *He silently assessed my divulgence through his drunken, lust-filled haze, trying to decide if those words really came out of my mouth. I knew that* The *infamous Sara Klein would finally make an appearance that night after all.*

"You! You've had sex before?" he asked me with shock and disgust as he continued. "With more than one man, at the same time?" He looked sad and confused, as if I had just told him that Christmas was canceled that year.

"Countless times, Jeffery," I said, almost believing my own words. After all, I was already a skilled liar. "I could blow you." I remember offering, not knowing where my sudden sexual confidence came from. I'd never seen a dick in person besides Eddie's when he was fourteen. If Jeff dropped his pants, I'd have to go into my memory and try to remember what I'd seen porn stars do in the videos I stole from under Eddie's bed while he went off to school.

"Sara, listen, my head is not in the right place for this. I'd love to take you up on your offer and see you take my dick in your mouth, but I'd rather we sleep on this and talk once the tequila exits my veins. Both my heads are about to blow off from all this shit," he said, motioning to the increasing space between us.

"If you don't want to fuck me, then leave. I didn't take you for a pussy," I said, trying to goad him.

"Oh, I'll fuck you, baby, just not tonight. I need to be lucid when my dick enters that wet pussy. Trust me, you won't ever need anybody else once I start fucking you." If I only knew back then how true his prophecy really was.

I have never felt liquid fire until that night. His words enflamed me in ways I never knew words could outside of erotic literature and good old-fashioned porn. When he said "wet pussy," *I could actually feel my pussy raise its hand and say* "present." *I panted while a cold sweat formed around my overheated body.*

"You can play with yourself until I decide what to do with you," he said jokingly. "I'm almost tempted to stay here and watch. But I know if I see you touching those firm breasts and if I hear even a small moan, I'll lose it."

"I want you to play with me. I need to feel you or smell you in order to come." Another line I'd heard in pornos. I had hoped to break him. Push him to the point of no return. He started to remove his T-shirt, giving me my first view of his naked body. At that point I thought this is it, I did it, I won, *but he just took his shirt and threw it at me, adding, "Here, wear this and think of me." And then he left. I'd failed. He was strong-willed even while inebriated.*

His words floated around me hours after he was gone. I removed all my clothes and put his soft T-shirt on and his scent engulfed and suffocated all my senses. I did touch myself that night, and I did have several orgasms thanks to having something of his caressing me. My vivid imagination pressed replay on Jeffery kissing me, touching me, and promising to ruin me.

I'm pretty sure I didn't sleep for one second that night. I couldn't wait to see him in the morning. But morning came and Jeff, the giver of my first kiss, was gone. He never came back to discuss our kiss or when he would have sex with me. He left without even saying goodbye, without even offering me his full name. I was left only with a kiss, a T-shirt, a promise, and all the lies I would fabricate until he came back for me. He didn't come back to see me until a whole year later...

I pause for a moment and look over at Liam to make sure he's still okay with this and ready for everything I'm about to disclose to him.

"Go on, love, you're doing great. I only flinched once when

you mentioned that arse being the 'love of your life.' But since your life is not over yet, I think that was a tad bit presumptuous of you to declare. Do you concur?" he says with his sexy-as-fuck smile.

"No beleaguering the witness, Mr. Knight. Should I be stopping for your smart commentary?" Can this fool be any cuter? I stop to wait for his response.

He shakes his head and adds, "I'll be a good lad and stay quiet as a mouse."

I look over and he makes a pantomime motion of locking his mouth and throwing away the key. I can't resist and I give him a quick peck on his lips. He then fixes my hair again, which I've started to think is just an excuse for him to touch me, which I kinda sorta like.

"Stop trying to be sweet or your rules and my confession will all go to shit," I warn him.

"Sustained, you may proceed," he says, pretending to lock his mouth again.

I've just told Liam about the most important event that shaped my life. He hasn't looked away from me and hardly interrupted, giving me one hundred percent of his attention and it's doing all kinds of things to my insides. I feel like we're in a time capsule, a sort of bubble. It's almost as if nothing and no one can get to us while we're comfortably suspended over 5th Ave.

For the first time in my life, I crave telling the truth, the whole truth, and nothing but the truth so help me God. I've never spoken about the past because I wasn't going that way. But he's right! I need this rewind in order to finally be able to press play. I actually want to tell him everything.

Sara

"Edge Of Seventeen[37]" by Stevie Nicks

I didn't see or hear from Jeffery for a whole year, and yet I slept in his T-shirt and with the image of him every night...

My sweet sixteen wasn't what I'd expected. My parents surprised me and invited all my friends and their friends to the Rainbow Room. They closed down the whole place and tried to throw the party of the year. They spared no expense. Emily's sister Jenna was a party planner and she designed a party like you've never seen before. My parents were both busy with their lives, most of the time dealing with the pressure of being the Jones' that everybody else needed to keep up with. My dad was the philandering lawyer that pretended to have late-night meetings and screwed every secretary, assistant, and intern he ever hired, and my mother feigned that it was all peachy and pretended she didn't drink like a sailor to forget that everything was, in fact, not peachy. I had more freedom and money than most kids my age. I partly attribute my fibbing skills to my lying parents; I'd learned from the best.

If you asked anybody about Robert and Laura Klein, they'd all tell you that they were the perfect Upper East Side family. Emily's mom and my mother were best friends and even Emily's mom, Adele, would tell you that my parents had a flawless marriage. Heck, if you asked my parents, they'd probably believe their own lies and tell you that they were the luckiest two people in the whole wide world and loved each other from here to eternity. I guess it takes liars to raise liars.

I didn't want a party, I wanted to stay home and come up with a cool story to tell Emily about how I snuck out and had sex with some hot guy I met at a club. But thanks to my parents and their brilliant idea, I had to mingle and pretend like I was having fun.

My other surprise that night was that my brother came back from school for the weekend for my big birthday. I was actually happy to see Eddie. I'd missed him a lot while he was away. I came home every day to a quiet house, my mother passed out and my dad coming home late—if he came home at all. The housekeeper would warm my food and say three words to me before going home for the day. The only love I got was from Eddie, who was the only person I had no need to lie to. I could've told Em the truth a million times. I could've stayed at her house and not felt like a lonely, unwanted stray dog, but I didn't want to blow my parents' cover. They had an image to uphold and I was an accomplice.

With my arms still embracing Eddie, I felt eyes burning a hole into me. I turned around to see Jeffery, my Jeffery, watching us. He didn't look pleased; he looked downright pissed.

"Happy sixteenth birthday, Sara!" he said, which almost sounded like a curse coming out of his seething mouth. My heart began beating erratically and the air around me began to thin out as his presence at my sweet sixteen came into focus.

I heard Eddie talk somewhere very far in the background as my heartbeat pounded in my ears. "Jeffery insisted on coming with me when I told him I was going home for the weekend to celebrate your big birthday." As Eddie said those words, fear slowly spread over me like a blanket.

I finally blinked away the fear and summoned the liar to handle that situation. "Thank you, Jeffery. How noble of you, wanting to come to my party." His features softened for a second before he visibly remembered his anger with me and schooled his irate face once again.

"I didn't want to miss your sixteenth *birthday! How exciting that you're closer to becoming a real grown woman, Sara," Jeff, or shall I say Jeffery, said sweetly for my brother's sake, yet I could tell he simmered with anger on the inside.*

"Hey, Sara, let me go say hi to Mom and Dad," Eddie declared while waving to my parents by the bar. I could tell by the sourpuss look on my mother's face that she and Dad just had a fight.

"Okay, I'll be right here, entertaining Jeffery for you until you come back," I politely offered, too scared to even chance a look at Jeff.

As soon as Eddie left and turned his back on us, Jeff took hold of my arm and pulled me with force into a quiet corner, away from the band and anyone overhearing us. I had a silent countdown in my head for the moment when he would unleash his anger and let me have it. Calling me out on my lie.

"You were asking me to fuck you and offering me a blowjob and you were fucking fifteen years old*?" he asked, or probably demanded is a better word. "Answer me, Sara."*

I looked at my heels and refused to meet his knowing eyes. What could I have said to him? I lied and he knew it. He put his index finger under my chin and brought it up to the level of his gaze.

"How could you let me think you were turning eighteen today?" he asked with a mixture of anger and disappointment written all over that beautiful face; the face that I've dreamt about for almost a year. The face that I told my best friend countless lies about. I knew that face so well; even though I'd only seen it once before in my life, it was etched in my memory.

175

"I'm surprised you even remember me or that night. I was going to tell you the truth when you were sober the next morning, but since you decided I wasn't important enough to see in the morning, I really didn't have a chance to tell you my age. I don't even know your full name, so who cares?" I offered as an explanation, trying to pretend I wasn't affected by him and trembling like a leaf.

"Who cares? Who cares? I care, Sara! I thought I was coming back to wish you a happy eighteenth birthday. I was praying you didn't have a boyfriend so I could finally kiss you the way I've been wishing I did that night in your room." He broke our stare and looked down at his feet before pinning me with those unique-colored eyes, which I couldn't look into. *"I have been fantasizing about a fifteen-year-old girl, a fucking child... I'm not some pervert. Look at me when I speak to you!"*

I looked up at him and God, how I wish I never did. God, how perfect my life would be if he never came back and I never saw him again. If he didn't come back that night, I would have eventually forgotten him and his stupid T-shirt. We must've stood there in silence and just stared at each other for ten minutes before he finally let out a breath and said, *"I will continue to fantasize about you and I'll come find you in two years. I will get that kiss and a whole lot more, Sara. You'll pay for this... We're not done!"*

He then turned to walk away. Once my brain registered all the info he'd just unleashed on me, I yelled, *"Jeff!"* I grabbed him by the arm, shouting for him to turn and look at me. *"Jeff, I want that kiss now! I'm not waiting for you for two years. I want that kiss now!"* I remember when he finally turned around to look at me and at my hand holding onto him, he removed it from his arm harshly and I felt like shit—rejected by him yet again. Why couldn't I just let him be?

He must've seen the dejected look in my eyes because he found my hand again. He quickly pulled me toward him before *one of us changed our minds. I can still see the look on his face; it's the look of hating yourself for wanting what isn't yours. He walked us out of that ballroom. He pressed the elevator and practically threw us both in without letting go of me... I know it's hard to understand, but after not seeing him for almost a year, I didn't want him to ever let go of me.*

"I can't leave the party, it's my birthday." I tried to reason with him.

"We're not leaving. I just need to give us both something to help keep this going until I can properly have you." That comment made me weak.

"You mean until you can properly fuck me," I corrected him. He turned to me and looked at me as if he was about to hit me.

"How many men have you had, Sara?"

I had no intention to answer that.

He asked me again, "How. Many. Have. There. Been?"

I looked up at his beautiful face, those sharp, multi-colored eyes assessing me. The lawyer in him questioning me as if I would actually tell him the truth. "Lots and lots of men, Jeffery. Too many to count."

His upper lip lifted and he smiled a painful smile. "That's what I thought," he said, letting go of my hand and turning away from me before pressing the button for the fiftieth floor. His response enraged me.

"What does that mean? You think I'm a slut?"

He laughed without turning my way.

"Tell me!" I demanded.

The elevator finally came to a stop. He walked out and I was tempted to just take it back up and forget about Jeff. He reached out his hand, which my traitorous body accepted without waiting for my brain's approval. He pulled me into him, wrapping his arm around my lower back so we were now flush. I couldn't look up at him. I grew really scared that he would see right through me and my lies.

"Come." And once again, my body responded without thinking. I looked into those eyes, those eyes that would haunt me for years to come. As soon as our gaze locked, at that moment nothing existed but him. He lowered his lips to kiss me gently, raining soft kisses on my lips. It was too much for my sixteen-year-old body back then. He held me close...his scent invaded me, his warm touch encompassed me, and those soft lips destroyed me. I became liquid in his arms. "Was I also your first kiss, Sara Klein?" he asked into my mouth.

When he said those words, tears just rolled down my cheeks, tears that I'd held inside since that morning I found him gone.

"You don't have to answer, I know the truth. I will be your first and last in many things. But you need to wait for me. As much as I think I should tell you to forget about us, I can't and I won't. I'm sure you have the power to do a lot more damage to me than I'll ever do to you. We will have our time, Eddie's little sister. I don't want to make too many promises, but the things I will do to you, Sara, you have no idea how good they're going to feel. In two short years, I will blow your whole world away because you've already fucked up mine. I promise you that I'll continue dreaming about you. But for right now, I think you deserve a proper first kiss on your sixteenth birthday."

He then gave me the kiss that I can still close my eyes and taste. The kiss that eliminated gravity. The kiss that will forever visit me because no other man would ever kiss me the way Jeffery did that night...that was the kiss that sealed my future. He became my religion and I would sign up to endure anything he would have me undergo just to be kissed like that again. I should've known that kiss would be my undoing. It's the kiss that shaped my life. Just one stupid kiss.

I look over at Liam, needing to see how he's coping with the knowledge of the hold Jeff has on me. "Are you okay?" I ask him.

"I'm ace, love. Keep going, you haven't stumped me yet. If you told me he fucked you at fifteen, you know I would go find him and cut his knob off, right?"

I nod. "I know, and I'm starting to like that quality about you. You're like a vicious brother, only you're nothing like my brother and I feel closer to you than any other human on earth right now."

He pulls himself up and gives me a kiss. Not a passionate stop-the-world kiss, but an I'm-right-here kind of kiss, which is exactly what I need to keep going.

Sara

"Love Bites[38]" by Def Leppard

He left me that night with just one deadly kiss. I went back up to my party where nobody even noticed I was gone except, of course, my best friend, or to be more exact, my very livid best friend.

"Sara, what was that? Why was Jeffery so mad at you? Did you guys have a fight?" I recall Emily frantically at my side, questioning me.

Poor Emily, I lied to her so much about Jeff and what we'd done and the number of times we did it that I didn't even know where to begin. I decided more lies were the answer.

"Emily, he was just mad that we can't fuck until later. He said he came over earlier but I wasn't home. He wanted us to have sex before the party. I guess he missed me."

Emily had that face that I can only describe as shocked and embarrassed rolled into one. I was the one saying all that shit and she was the one blushing.

"Sorry, your parents wanted to surprise you so I made you come over to my house to help me get dressed." She looked as if she were the cause of our fight. If she only knew what our fight was really about. If she only knew that I'd just experienced the

second best kiss of my life. That I just signed on the dotted line and sold my heart to a perfect stranger I've only seen twice, all for a kiss. What would she think of me? What would she think of The *Sara Klein if she knew that all I've ever had was a kiss?*

"Don't worry, I'm sure he'll find someone else to screw to-night. He left to go see his girlfriend, I think." *There we go, I loved being able to put that awestruck look on Em's face.*

"You don't mind if he sleeps with other girls?" *she asked in shock.*

Of course I mind, Emily, but nobody needs to know that. *"Of course not, he's had a few girlfriends since we started fucking last year, I think. Em, I have sex with other guys, too, so it's not like we're exclusive or anything." Emily seemed to contemplate my answer in that innocent little brain of hers. The brain that thinks that people only have sex when they get married and that fathers and mothers love each other dearly and would never ever be unfaithful. I hoped for her sake that she'd find a nice guy that would never prove her wrong.*

She did find that with Louis. But I knew the truth about the real world, my world. I knew men needed lots of women to be happy and no man could be with just one girl. How could they love just one woman their whole life? I figured it would be easier going through life with very little expectations from love and from men in general. Love was not beautiful and pure—love was a joke that little girls believed in.

"But you like him, right?" *Emily continued to question me. She still felt the need to make sense of my character.*

I more than like him, Em. I love him, *I wanted to tell her. But I couldn't let him wreck me. I would be in control of my emotions. I would be in control of my reality, thanks to all my lies, and I would have the exact relationship that* The *Sara would be proud of. I would pretend to be the whore that every man wished he had, the kind of whore that men like my father left their families for to have weekend meetings with. If I let the world know what kind of good girl I really was, what would I gain? I'd have no one to appreciate it or pay me any attention, so I got the love and attention I craved by telling lies.*

I remember coming out of my thoughts to answer my confused, beautiful friend. The girl that I'd give anything to change places with. "Yeah, I like him; he's okay. He's great in the sack and he gives me multiple orgasms, so I guess I like him enough." There was that shocked look again. God, I should've taken my fibs down a notch to make sure I didn't give poor Emily Marcus a heart attack.

Liam raises his hand as if asking permission to speak. I smile at him because he's kinda sorta funny. He takes my smile as clearance to talk.

"Emily never questioned you? Or wanted to see any evidence about the fibbing?"

It may be hard to believe, but Em never once called me out on any of my fabricated stories. I think that's the reason we're still friends. I answer Liam's valid question, "Emily only called me out on a lie once, which was followed by us not being on speaking terms for almost two years. It nearly cost us our whole friendship. We only started talking again when Louis couldn't find her and I spent two days this past July visiting every hospital in New York looking for my best friend because she was missing."

I look over at him and notice his eyes are trained out the big window, no doubt thinking of his involvement in Emily's disappearance and what it must've felt like for all of us going crazy not knowing where she was, only to have Louis suffer a heart attack and nearly die.

"I should've brought her back home sooner," he says, still looking away with remorse written all over his features. "I didn't know what was happening on the home front for her. I just knew that Louis Bruel, the person I attribute my sister's death to, was discovered cheating on his wife, the wife that he chose over my sister, and that same wife was delivered to me by fate to do with as I please."

Hearing him talk about Em makes me feel silly for liking him as much as I think I do. He's clearly never going to be over her. Emily is not the type of woman that men forget and move on from. Louis Bruel would start a war for Emily, and this stranger at my side almost gave him reason to. My little epiphany reminds me once again that there is always someone else who gets to have what I want first, someone who stakes a claim before I even get a chance.

"And you had your way with her, enjoying every second. You fell madly in love with her and now here you are in bed with her psychotic best friend, listening to some stupid story no one has ever heard before, wasting your precious time…when all you really want is another chance with Emily." I close my eyes because I don't need to look at him to see how my words affect him. I can't blame him or his heart for wanting what it wants. After all, who but me knows that feeling best?

"The time has come for me to show you who I want another chance with," he says.

Liam

"Doctor! Doctor!³⁹" by Thompson Twins

For the past forty-five days I haven't thought of anything or anybody but Emily, and I refuse to say her surname. The way she looked when she cried, the way her eyes brightened when she smiled, the taste of her body and scent of her skin, the sounds she made, whimpering as I made her come…and every memory is tainted with her whispering and eventually yelling out his bloody name. *What was I thinking?* She wasn't with me that night; she was with her husband. I should've stopped, that's what a gentleman would've done. But I wanted revenge. The joke was on me.

I had no business touching her in the state she was in or wanting her as much as I thought I did. But now, being able to hold this beautiful girl in my arms makes me question every emotion I felt certain of while with Emily. I didn't feel half of what I feel right now being with Sara. The day she appeared in my hotel, I had some warped adrenaline running through my veins I can only justify as a high a robber gets from stealing and capturing something that never belonged to him.

This beautiful, broken ballerina at my side makes me question my whole meaningless existence. Is this my destiny? Did

Isa, Emily, and even Louis bring me to Sara? Did I need to go through hell to find her? She tells me her love story with Jeffery Rossi, the love of her life, and all I can think is...*your life is not over Sara, what if I'm the love of your life, not Jeffery?* Maybe Emily and Jeffery and every other bloody mistake were just an obstacle, a test, a trial, an ordeal we needed to conquer to find one another. Twenty-four hours ago, I thought my mission in life was to break apart a marriage to find happiness, and now my only purpose is to put a broken ballerina back together.

I fancy showing her what she's doing to me. I want her to know that my body is having a primal reaction to every word she gives me and every touch she bestows upon me. My words don't mean anything to her because she's accustomed to fibs and empty promises. I need to make her understand what's been brewing inside me and that she is the cause of it all.

I realize I said no touching or kissing, but my rules are rubbish. I can't *not* touch her; not touching her is not an option.

"I'm not planning to fuck, Sara," I say as I see her roll her eyes and look away from me. She must think this is a rejection again, silly bird. "We won't be fucking because that's what ordinary people do. You and I are not ordinary. You, Sara, are extraordinary, and I'm not certain there is a word to describe our bond."

She finally looks at me. How have I lived almost thirty years without these eyes looking at me?

"Will you allow me to love you? How do I make you believe that I won't go anywhere? I just want to be near you."

She closes her eyes as if in pain, as if what I've just said physically hurts her. "Thank you, Liam, but I won't let you make love to me until you know everything. I don't think you'll look at me and feel the same way after I tell you the whole truth."

"Nothing you can say will make me not want you. We didn't meet by chance, we've been through hell trying to find each other. I wouldn't feel what I'm feeling if this wasn't predestined." I can't help but kiss her and she can't prevent herself from kissing me back. I can be content closing my eyes, knowing I'm slowly drowning and erasing every other kiss I've ever had before. I'm no longer worried about fancying someone other than this perfect, broken ballerina in my arms.

"Liam, don't…you don't know what you're saying! I wouldn't wish someone like me on my worst enemy. Liars like me don't deserve to be happy. Nobody chooses me; I'm not a good choice."

Her words cleave me in two. He did this. He broke this perfect, beautiful creature. She thinks she's not worth choosing! Punishing herself for telling lies to cover the hurt he caused. I can't even make love to her until she comprehends how bloody flawless she is to me and that all her faults are what make her my Sara. How could she reckon being unworthy of love?

"I choose you, Sara Klein. I choose you now, and I know that I will choose you even more after I know everything about you. You're right, you should keep going and let me hear about who you reckon is the love of your life," I say, knowing that nothing she will say to me will make me question wanting to be with her.

Sara

"Tainted Love[40]" by Soft Cell

Liam's words and the way his eyes study me make me question every emotion I have ever experienced in my thirty years on this earth. How can a person I've known for less than a day compete with someone I've known and loved for over a decade?

And yet my heart doesn't care. My heart believes every silly word that comes out of his beautiful mouth. My heart brawls with my head, fighting for my chance at happiness. Could this handsome stranger be my happiness? Have I suffered enough and earned him? Can a worthless human like me get a happily ever after?

Surely not after he learns the truth. Once he knows everything, he will just get up off this bed and this euphoric world of ours and leave me, never looking back.

People like me don't get to live out their fantasies; liars like me get exactly what they deserve. I deserved to get my heart broken and ripped apart, and karma doesn't disappoint, karma always delivers.

In a way, I wish he already knew everything and would just leave. I could stop wasting time and figure out which way to go to start over...or perhaps not choose to go on at all.

I continue with the story of my life, knowing that my time with Liam will end very shortly.

I counted the days until I finally turned eighteen. I may have been the world's biggest pessimist a cynic on the outside, but inside, I was still a hopeful girl. I still wanted hearts and flowers. I still wanted a Julia Roberts, Pretty Woman *moment when Prince Charming came to my rescue. I craved the* Dirty Dancing *scene when Johnny returns for Baby. I may have said something different if asked, but I wanted it all, I wanted the fantasy. I could lie to the world but I couldn't lie to myself.*

It was my junior year of high school. I was almost a whole year older than everybody else in my grade because I started school late, thanks to being sick with the measles at six years old. I had missed a few months of school and then fell behind, so my parents decided that I would start first grade a whole year later. I was beyond happy because that meant I had my friend Emily in the same class with me.

On my eighteenth birthday, I had this romantic idea that Jeff, for whom I'd been waiting the last three years, would finally come and claim me. I had this scenario worked up where he came and swept me off my feet. I'd imagined being with him in so many ways that I actually felt that in some fucked-up way, we were a real couple. I actually thought that he belonged to me because he called me once a month to tell me that on that day he thought about me. I actually believed he'd been patiently and celibately waiting for me, thinking of me, dreaming of me. My infantile imagination was convinced that a grown, gorgeous man that had only called me a handful of times and who hasn't seen me in two whole years somehow wanted me as much as I wanted him. *My stupid self thought that a liar like me could still one day have a happy ending. I prayed that my faithful, imaginary lover would come and make all my lies true. I even promised myself never to make up another story for as long as I lived once we were together.*

If I had actually spoken to my parents, they would've known that I needed therapy. If I had told someone what was going on, maybe they could've explained to me that I was inconsequential to him and we were not meant to be. That it was time to give boys who actually liked me a chance. That it was all just a childish fantasy and it was time to grow up. But I spoke to no one. I was the judge, jury, and prosecutor. I was my own worst enemy.

He didn't come on my eighteen birthday like my head and heart let me believe that he would. He didn't come, he didn't call, he didn't anything. On my birthday, I told Emily that Jeff and I were going to a hotel for the night where it would be okay to stay in bed all day and no one would find us. Well, what I really said was "All Night Long[41]*" by Lionel Richie, which meant we would be fucking all night and that was how I wanted to spend my birthday. Emily didn't question me. Why would she? This was exactly how The Sara would spend her birthday—wrapped up with a hot guy in a hotel on the other side of town.*

I recall not attending school that day, telling my mother I wasn't well. I called my brother because it was almost six in the evening and he still hadn't called to wish me a happy birthday.

"Eddie, hi, it's me, Sara."

"Sara, I know it's you. Is everything okay? You sound upset, is it Mom again?" he asked me, shedding the carefree sound in his voice.

"No, everybody is okay. I just missed you. I haven't heard from you in a while. Wanted to know what you're up to." Truthfully, besides a simple "Happy birthday" from him, I'd hoped to hear something about Jeff. Anything would've been better than nothing.

"Sorry, sis, it's been an insane amount of work for me late-ly. Between studying and writing my paper, I've got no time to call anybody. I haven't even been able to see Michelle. It's just not normal how inundated I am with work right now." He was silent for a bit, waiting for me to say something. I slowly realized that everybody except for Emily had virtually forgotten that it was my eighteenth birthday. Eddie started talking again when I didn't offer any conversation. "How's school? Can you believe you have one more year of high school? Are you looking into colleges? I think Brown would be a great choice for you, too."

"Yeah, Brown would be sweet. I can't wait to leave this house. Well, I just wanted to let ya know I miss you much and can't wait to see you." I tried my best to hold back the tears that came dangerously close to falling and a sob that begged to come out. "Love you, Eddie. Good luck on your exams, and say hi to Michelle."

"I will, sis. And I can't wait to see how tall you've gotten. If law school doesn't work out, you can start modeling at the rate you've been growing." Funny, because I always thought model-ing would be a perfect career choice for me, too. Then my life could really be one big lie. I'd be fake both inside and out.

I remember getting off the phone with Eddie and lying down on my bed. I was eighteen fucking years old and there I was, cry-ing and feeling worthless and unloved. Well, in my defense, not a single member of my family wished me a happy birthday, my fic-tional boyfriend forgot his promise or that I existed, and I lied to my best friend about being with him, so I really was all alone. The sad part was even if I wanted to call Jeffery, I couldn't. I had no idea what his number was. We never got that far, he was the one to always call me from my brother's phone. I just always assumed he would seek me out and find me. Wasn't that what chivalrous men always did in books and movies?

I was delusional in all ways possible. Thinking back now, I don't know why I worked so hard to try and be someone else. I wasn't so bad, was I? I didn't mean to make up stories and hurt people in the process, but the train was already moving at full steam and there was no way for me to jump off. I would no doubt crash and anybody who got too close to me would suffer the consequences.

I fell asleep alone in my room on my eighteenth birthday that night, dreaming up all the wonderful things Jeffery would never do to me. I knew that when I woke up the next day, I needed to find Jeff and have him make good on his promise of ruining me. I had nothing to lose. I would find him and tell him he already ruined me with just a kiss and his empty promises.

The next morning, my phone rang, stirring me from a romantic dream of Jeff nuzzling my neck and repeating how he would fuck me when I was grown up.

"What?" I said irritably into my mobile.

"I'm a shitty older brother. I can't believe I forgot it was your day yesterday. I'm so sorry, Sara, I've been so off and Michelle wants us to see other people, so I've been inside my own head chewing shit up. I'm sorry, sis. Happy birthday! If it wasn't for Jeff asking me what you had planned for your birthday, I probably would've forgotten all about it." Eddie finished his "I'm sorry" speech but all I heard was that Jeff had asked about me. He remembered it was my eighteenth birthday yesterday. My heart pumped so hard it lodged itself in my throat.

"Sara, are you there? Did you hear me?"

"Yes, you're the shittiest brother in the world and your girlfriend wants to find herself a new man," I said, elated with excitement at Eddie's revelation.

"Thank you, Sara. Would you like a knife to finish me off?

For fuck's sake, do you really think Michelle wants to find another guy? I was just thinking that she's trying to get me to commit and see her more often. Shit! What if she already found another guy?" Eddie suddenly sounded frantic. I remember thinking he must really like this Michelle. I'd never heard him panic about anything—especially not a girl.

"Eddie, relax, I was just fucking with you. I'm sure she's just playing games to scare you into marrying her." That seemed to calm him. My poor brother really seemed on edge. But I needed to get the scoop on Jeffery. "So, can I talk to Jeff and you know, thank him for reminding you about your little sister's birthday?" I tried to be sneaky and yet perfectly proper in my request to talk to my brother's roommate, AKA the love of my life.

"He's left for the weekend after our exam yesterday. He said he had a personal matter he needed to take care of. I will thank him on your behalf and give him the message, don't worry."

My heart was now totally outside my body, beating out of control. Was Jeff coming to see me? No, I had to get his number from Eddie if it was the last thing I did.

"No, Eddie, I'd really like to tell him myself. Just let me get a pen so I can write his number and I'll call him later on." I was so nervous Eddie would see right through me that I fell out of my bed in search of a pen. Eddie seemed too busy contemplating his relationship with Michelle to give my request a second thought. He read off Jeff's digits and my hands shook as I copied them down. We said our goodbyes and I was left with my heart thumping, my breath accelerating, and for the first time in twenty-four hours, I felt hopeful.

After a quick shower, I ran downstairs to find a note from my dad saying he had a last minute meeting and not to wait up for him. What else was fucking new? I went in search of my mom, but she was already gone, too. She had a standing break-

fast date with Emily's mom, Adele, and every Saturday, that breakfast usually turned into lunch. The housekeeper had the weekend off, so I was home alone. I had no one to talk to, nobody to see how happy and excited I was.

I was once again reminded of how I'd painted myself into a corner and I had just myself to blame. If I'd never lied to Emily about being with Jeff last night then surely she would've celebrated my birthday with me yesterday. Surely we would've squealed and danced about the chance that he may actually be on his way to see me. But surely didn't change the fact that I stood in an empty house with just myself to celebrate the maybes in my life.

I gathered every shred of confidence I could summon and dialed Jeffery's number. It rang twice before he answered. As soon as I heard his voice, I lost the ability to speak. He said "Hello... Hello" *a few times and hung up.* Fuck! *Why didn't I say something? While staring at my phone and cursing my stupid coward of a brain, it started to ring in my hands. It was him! He was calling me back, and after four rings, I finally said,* "Hello."

"I knew it was you," *he said as chills ran down my spine.* "Have you thought about me as much as I've been thinking about you, Sara?" *Now my sex started clenching, because I've thought of nothing but him.* "Will I get to hear more than 'Hello' from the girl who offered to blow me at the tender age of fifteen?" *He continued making it hard for me to breathe.* "Sara, did I lose you? Say something."

"I'm sorry," *I managed to belt out before sobbing like a baby. I have no idea why I suddenly felt the need to cry. I was usually strong, or at least I pretended to be strong. Emily was the one that always cried, not Sara.*

"No, I'm sorry. I didn't mean to make you cry. I was just joking. You asking to give me a blowjob in your room after I kissed you was wrong on so many levels, but if I'm being honest, it kept me going for all these years. Stop crying, I'll never men-*

tion that again." He sounded like he had a smile on his lips. I could just imagine that face of his with a big smile crinkling the skin around his eyes. "I'm glad you called," he said, which brought me out of my daydream about his smile and back to the fact that Jeff and I were actually speaking on the phone for the first time in months.

"Why haven't you ever called me from your own phone?" I asked him without filtering my feelings. Without trying to sound cool or unaffected by him. "If you thought about me, shouldn't you have called to talk to me more than once a season?" The fact that we hadn't spoken in months started clearing up the fuzzy euphoria I let my mind sink into. I took a deep breath and continued demanding things that I felt I had the right to know. "Is this a joke to you, Jeff?" And the tears started rolling down my face once again. This was all a joke for him. He probably sat around telling his friends how this fifteen-year-old girl once offered him a blowjob. He probably told the girls he dated that he broke this silly little girl's heart and she probably still thinks he's coming back for her. "I just called to say thank you for reminding Eddie it was my birthday yesterday. Have a good life."

I hung up before he had the chance to say anything to me ever again. It was time to forget about Jeffery the asshole and move on. Yes, I lied, but writing him off would be easy. I would tell Emily he had a girlfriend and that we were no longer seeing each other. No, I'd just tell her I didn't feel like fucking him anymore; that's exactly what The Sara would say.

I brushed off the dismal feeling that enveloped me and went back to my room to write down my feelings in my truth book. It was my diary that nobody knew about. After I told stories that didn't exist to my best friend, I would also write down how I felt in my truth book, to stop the overwhelming feelings of guilt. I'm Jewish, so this was my form of confession. It felt good to at least be able to write the truth if I couldn't actually say it out loud.

I spent about two hours that day putting down into words

what Jeff meant to me and how he made me feel. I explained to my notebook that I loved him. That somehow, through all the lies I'd told, I actually fell in love with our bogus relationship. The things that his pretend-self made me feel were very real to me. The words I pretended he would say to me were all I had to keep me hanging on. He was perfect and he was my version of a fictional boyfriend. I guess in some fucked-up way nobody could've taken that away from me.

By the end of my long journal entry, I came to the conclusion that it was time to move on. That I actually needed to give some poor schmucks out there a chance and maybe I'd actually like them. They may not be a certain twenty-four-year-old gorgeous law school student, but I was done with him. I was eighteen, which meant that I could pretty much do whatever I wanted. I had no one to stop me, except myself.

It was Saturday night. I still hadn't officially celebrated my birthday and it was time to start living out some of the lies I'd told everybody, including myself. I found a short black skirt that barely covered my ass. I wore a gold off-the-shoulder sweater and a pair of skyscraper suede heels that probably put me at six feet tall. I applied very little makeup, only lip gloss to help accentuate my lips. In my mind, I looked fuckable as I checked myself out in the mirror. I yelled to my mom that I would be over at Emily's house watching a movie and that I'd call if I decided to sleep over. She yelled, "have fun" and that was it, I was out.

I took a cab downtown and the first lounge I saw, I walked into like a regular. I actually recognized that place because I did tell Emily that I'd gone there often, so once again, it felt as if I really was a regular. I sat at the bar and waited for the bartender to ask for my order. I'd hoped the cute bald guy with a goatee pouring the drink would make his way to me, but instead, I got the woman working the bar serving me.

"What can I get you? And I'll need your ID, sweetheart," *she said between pouring and mixing another drink.*

"I'll have a French martini, and make it strong." I held my tone and eye contact as I pulled out my fake student ID. I remember shaking on the inside.

"Can I see a driver's license? We don't accept student ID's," she barked back, leaning over the bar and trying to be heard over the music that grew louder by the second. I obviously didn't have a driver's license that said I was over twenty-one. But while I pretended to look through my wallet, some dude next to me I hadn't noticed before ordered me the French martini and winked.

I smiled back and at that moment, I knew that this stranger was getting laid that night, and unbeknownst to him, would be taking my virginity. I gave him my version of a sexy look.

"Thank you. I must've left my driver's license at home. I'm usually not such a klutz. Hi, I'm Sara." I gave him a wave.

"I'm Phillip, nice to meet ya, Sara." He lifted his glass with a wink.

"I'll pay you back for the drink. Thanks for ordering it for me."

He gave a cocky one-sided smile, and I realized that it probably wasn't the right thing to say if I wanted someone to take me home and fuck me. *"I think my bank account can handle treating a pretty girl to a drink. Are you at least eighteen? I don't mind buying you a drink but if the cops show up and start carding people, I don't need them shutting down my club for an under-age girl."*

I remember panicking and thinking great, he probably owns this club and will throw me out in two seconds flat. *I didn't want to start freaking out, but my pupils must've given me away.*

"So you're what, sixteen? Seventeen?" He continued fishing for more information.

"No, I'm legal, trust me," I replied defensively with a weak smile.

He grinned back at me, getting up and moving closer as he

lowered his head and whispered in my ear. "*Sara, relax, you can have one drink on me and that's it. I don't want you hammered and getting into trouble tonight. You seem sad so I know you need a drink. Anyway, one drink won't kill ya.*"

He smiled and my stomach churned. I suddenly became very aware of how close he leaned into me. I had this really bad feeling in my gut. I had this two-second premonition that I was about to feel and look even sadder. I started getting up. I didn't need this shit; this guy made me feel uncomfortable and I didn't like it. He suddenly didn't seem hot or sexy; he seemed slimy and wrong. I wanted to leave as quickly as possible. I wanted to be back home safe in my bed, alone. Telling lies was safer than trying to act them out.

"*Where ya going? You didn't even get your drink!*" *Phillip yelled as I started to leave.*

"*Thank you, but I'll pass. I just remembered I need to be somewhere. Ciao.*" *I started to gather my jacket and bag when Phillip, the creepy stranger, grabbed my arm and pulled me toward him.*

"*Did I scare you, Sara? I was hoping to get a drink in you before I take you upstairs to my office. I don't normally like girls as young as you, but you have my attention tonight.*"

A game of tug-of-war went on in my brain. My head tried to convince me that this guy Phillip was a score. He was good looking, tall, well built, obviously older and successful. He smelled good, and his eyes begged me to go upstairs, so why shouldn't I talk to him? Wasn't this exactly what I wanted, to finally get laid? My brain pleaded with my heart. Wasn't this the whole point of the night? Why was I acting like a scared prude? Well, because I was a prude, and I was scared, and I was alone. I'd never had a man besides Jeff talk to me like that. I was never even close enough to a guy to feel what Phillip had made me feel and I was scared. I should've lied to him and told him I had to go. But that was the one time I decided to tell the truth.

"I've never slept with a man so I don't think I'll be much fun for you. Thank you for the drink. I promise not to come back until I'm really twenty-one. We wouldn't want your place getting into trouble because of me." I turned around and headed for the door. I didn't look back to see if Phillip stared after me. I just knew I needed to get my high school, inexperienced ass out of there.

As soon as I made my way outside and tried to hail a taxi, I felt someone standing very close. I turned to see Phillip in a jacket with his hand up trying to hail a taxi right by my side. He smiled sheepishly, and for some reason, it made me smile back.

"What? You didn't think I'd let you go after you just told me you're a virgin? There are like three of you left in New York and I'm not about to let you walk away. I've never been with a virgin, so you're as close to the Holy Grail as I'm ever gonna get." We both cracked up as a yellow cab pulled up to us. "My place or yours?" he asked, which made me laugh even harder at how absurd this whole interaction was.

"Phillip, I'm not sleeping with you. We met like three seconds ago."

He opened the taxi door to let me in and got in right behind me. "I promise, I won't let you sleep. You may eventually pass out, but as God as my fucking witness, you won't be sleeping once I get my hands on you and your untouched pussy." He closed the cab door behind him and called out an address that was also on the Upper East Side a few avenues away from my house.

"Phillip, I'm not going back to your place. I don't know who the fuck you are for fuck's sake. Can you please stop the car? God, is this how it is for you? Do girls just sleep with you after five minutes?" I became mad and somewhat disgusted. This sounded like one of my made-up adventures, but I had no intention of living this out, even if this guy was hot.

"Well, yeah. I usually don't even need to try this hard. I

usually take a few girls at a time, if you really want to know. You should actually feel very lucky that I walked out of the club and I'm in a car driving you to my place. That never fucking happens. You must be a unicorn."

I was shocked and as I stole a glace to the front mirror, I saw the look on the cab driver's face that mirrored my own— shock and disgust.

"Phillip, stop talking, I've had enough. Sir, can you please stop the car?" I politely asked the driver, who immediately began to brake to pull over.

"Keep driving, buddy, we're good," Phillip, the asshole who apparently fucks lots of girls, said back to the driver. "Sara, relax. I know you want this, let me make your first time good. Don't you want to fuck someone who knows what they're doing with their dick?" He continued talking. "Have you ever had an orgasm? If you're a good girl I'll make you come repeatedly and I'll teach you how to squirt. Trust me, baby, you'll be so happy we met. I normally don't do this kind of shit, but I'm really hard for you. I'll teach you everything, let's just have fun. This doesn't have to be more than a good night."

Phillip was the devil, the wolf, and the corrupter that every parent warns their daughters about, and The *Sara would have done everything he'd just proposed. She would already be on her knees sucking him off. She would sit in his lap and dry hump him and let him suck her boobs in the backseat of a dirty taxi. But* The *Sara wasn't really me; I was just Sara and I shook with fear and didn't know how to get home without getting raped. I wanted nothing to do with him. I just wanted Jeff, even if he wasn't real.*

"Phillip, I'm not ready for this. I'm eighteen but I'm still in high school. Can you just let me off? You're making me really scared." I couldn't pretend to be cool anymore and tears had begun to run down my face. I'd hoped he would finally see that he had the wrong girl and let me go. But my reaction had the wrong effect on him, because he got closer to me and pulled me

into him.

"I'm sorry, I didn't mean to scare you or make you cry. I just wanted to make you happy tonight. I don't need to force anybody, I have plenty of girls, you just seemed different. I just wanted to be with you tonight, but if you're not into me, that's cool." He stroked my hair and it felt nice. I closed my eyes and imagined he was Jeff. I was so confused about how I felt. I'd never been this close to a man besides Jeffery before. Just when I worked out that maybe it wouldn't be too bad if I lost my virginity to Phillip, my phone rang. I let it ring, thinking it was Emily, but then it kept ringing. I finally fished it out of my bag and answered.

"Hello," I said a little out of breath and still very emotional.

"Where are you?" It was Jeff.

"Why do you care?" I answered back almost sounding cross with him. Why did it matter to him where I was?

"I've been outside your house for hours. Your mom said you'd be back soon. Aren't you planning to come home tonight?" He sounded pissed.

I looked at my phone and then at Phillip, who was close enough for Jeff to hear him say, "What's wrong, baby? Who's calling you?" And that's all it took for Jeffery to go ape shit and start yelling back.

"Who. The. Fuck. Are. You. With. Sara? Why did he just call you baby? Eddie said you don't have a boyfriend."

I was shocked and couldn't wrap my brain around what was going on. I was in the backseat of a taxi with a guy I met less than an hour ago, driving to his place to lose my virginity. I had the love of my life who hadn't spoken or tried to contact to me in months waiting at my house. And I didn't know what was real anymore. In my world, when it rains...it hails.

"Jeff, calm down, I'm with Phillip. He offered to fuck me at his place and since you haven't made good on your promises, I'm taking him up on his offer," I said before hanging up. I

looked over at Phillip, whose face was split from ear to ear in the most evil of smiles I've ever witnessed in my life.

"Sara, you just made my night. I'm going to be so good to you. My dick just went from hard to bulletproof. If you want a night of firsts, after I pop your cherry, I can call one of my good friends and you can have your first threesome."

He laughed yet had no idea how painful what he'd just said was for me. His disturbing comment didn't help the feeling of worthlessness that had begun to spread across my entire body. My phone rang again and again and again. By the time we arrived at Phillip's apartment, I felt completely numb. I don't remember getting out of the cab, entering his building, what floor we stopped on, or what his apartment number was. I just followed him in. If he wanted to rape me, I wouldn't stop him. I gave him the green light with the stupid response I gave to Jeff in the car.

When we got inside, I do remember him lifting me and placing me on his cold kitchen countertop. He gently took my shoes off then started kissing my neck and squeezing my boobs. Spreading my legs and standing between them, he ran his fingertips up my outer thighs and under my thin sweater. He continued with his hands under my bra, cupping both breasts. He found my nipples and pulled them hard, causing me to wake up from my out-of-body comatose state. Everything he did felt cold and clinical; it felt wrong. There was zero chemistry between us. I wasn't even aroused.

"Sara, how does that feel? Has someone ever touched you like that before?" he asked while licking my neck. "Am I your first everything? You want me to suck your tits, baby?" When he got no response, he abruptly stopped and stepped away saying, "Okay, I'm not doing this shit unless you're into it one hundred percent." I could tell he'd grown annoyed with my aloofness. "I'm fucking Phillip Dashell; I have plenty of willing pussy back at the club. If you're not feeling this you need to go home, sweet-

heart."

He lifted me off the counter and helped fix my sweater, pulling my skirt down. He knelt down, holding my shoes as I stepped into them. He inhaled deeply close to my inner thighs, which once again, should've been sensual and sexy, but just felt creepy and wrong. "Are you sure you don't want this? I'll be gentle with you. I'm having a hard time accepting that I'm about to send one of three New York virgins back home." He was still on the floor on his knees and looking as genuine as a club-owning playboy could.

I probably should've just stayed and let him do whatever he wanted to me that night. The Sara would've been naked and moaning by now. But all I could think about was the boy that I lost my imaginary virginity to. I thought about that night three years ago when he stumbled into my room. I thought about that kiss, that one deadly kiss. When I looked down at Phillip still on the floor, I just shook my head. He got up, grabbed my jacket, and dejectedly walked me downstairs. Before putting me into a cab and sending me back home, he cupped my face and lightly kissed me for the first time that night. Besides Jeff, I'd never been kissed by anyone. I looked up into his dark blue eyes and decided right then and there that I only ever wanted to be kissed by one man, and it wasn't Phillip Dashell.

Liam makes a growling noise at my side and when I turn to look at him, I see him clench his teeth. "What's wrong?" I ask him.

"I want to know when the universe is going to stop fucking me up the arse," he says, shaking his head.

"Liam, calm down. I didn't do anything with that guy from the club."

He turns to me with a death glare. "Were you the one who introduced Emily to Louis?" *Is this boy on crack?* How did he get to that from the story I just told him?

"What gave you that impression from the things I've just told you?"

He starts to giggle like a deranged maniac. "You, Sara! You just bloody told me you almost got raped by Phillip Dashell!"

"And Phillip Dashell is a close acquaintance of yours, I suppose?"

He shakes his head, getting himself up and sitting at the edge of the bed with his back to me. "Nah, Phillip is no friend of mine, but he is your buddy Louis' best mate."

It's my turn to start laughing at his silly comment, because I've known Louis for over twelve years and Phillip Dashell is not in any way, shape, or form any kind of a friend to Louis Bruel.

"You must be mixing him up with somebody else; he is not one of Louis' friends. I should know. Louis or Em would've mentioned him if he were."

He turns and pins me with a look of pity. "If it weren't for Phillip, my sister would've never met Louis fucking Bruel. Phillip, Max, Andrew, and Louis were the biggest pieces of rubbish—or shit—I have ever had the unfortunate pleasure of reading about."

You know that feeling when someone tells you something that they obviously believe, and yet you can bet your life is not true? That's how Liam's statement hits me. Once again, Liam is confused. I need to show him that what he *thinks* he knows and the actual truth are not mutually exclusive.

"I know, let me call Emily and ask her if she's ever heard of Phillip. Surely, if he were one of Louis' acquaintances, she would know his name."

"Yes, that's a brilliant idea, and I'll go fetch you something visual to perhaps shine some light your way."

"Deal."

"Ace."

We both say simultaneously, almost daring each other.

Liam

"Just Died In Your Arms[42]" by Cutting Crew

Phillip Dashell, the devil, the scum, the root of all evil, has had his dirty hands on countless girls including my sister, and now I find out he almost had Sara. My Sara! I'm not sure how these women have managed to turn my whole life upside down, but I literally feel like I'm in space. If I show her my sister's pictures, if I show her what kind of friends Phillip and Louis are, she may stop looking at me like a delusional loon.

I head back downstairs to the kitchen where I left my carry-on. I dig through my things and find Isa's phone, which I charge every bloody day as if she's alive somewhere and might call. I also find and stroke the only copy of my sister's unpublished manuscript that exists in print. I had a paperback copy made to remind me of what she went through and who was the cause of all her pain and suffering. The book has no cliché cover, no catchy title; it's just a piece of her I get to hold on to—her last confession, of sorts. There are parts in it I've only read once, and then there are chapters describing her "what-if" future, which I can read over and over for the rest of my life. What I wouldn't give to trade places with my sister and give her a chance to live again. Even if I were gone, knowing that she could have her life back—that beautiful life she so vividly described—would be worth the sacrifice.

I go back upstairs and I hear Sara talking to someone. She must be talking to Emily already. I stand at the door and catch a bit of their discussion. I hear Sara saying, "I can't tell you where I know that name from, but please trust me, I need to know how Louis knows Phillip Dashell." There is silence and then Sara answers, "Why haven't you ever mentioned any of that to me before?" More silence. "Em, put Louis on the phone now!"

I peek in and see Sara pacing by the window, clearly not pleased with Emily's answers. I'm certain that her reality, which she'd been so sure of before, is slowly about to come crashing down. She has no bloody inkling as to who Louis and "The Boys" really were, are, and always will be.

"Louis, sorry to bother you but I need to know who Phillip Dashell is to you." She nods her head, listening, and then answers, "I can't tell you why I need to know, but I want you to tell me if he's a friend of yours. It's for personal reasons." She shakes her head from side to side, which can only mean Louis has just informed her that Phillip is someone he knows. "Is the name of that club Lunna?" she asks, and I could've answered that question because Isa spent many worthless moments with that group of animals in that dirty club.

She finally turns to see me waiting by the door and her sad eyes are enough for me to know Sara just got a dose of reality. I know that once she sees the rest, she will never look at Louis the same way again. I don't hear her end her conversation with Louis. She just dejectedly hangs up.

"You're right, they were friends. Louis helped him open that club where we met. He said he's not friends with him anymore, but they were good friends, like you said." The words of acceptance seem to fall out of her sad, defeated body.

"They are still friends now. Emily told me that Louis and he were coming out of a hotel room with a young girl on the day she caught him cheating and ended up in St. Lucia."

She shakes her head, not wanting to believe it, but just because you don't want to believe something doesn't mean it's not true. I know that concept all too well. "Show me," she says and I sense she's ready to see the truth.

I take my sister's phone and find the picture that will be enough evidence even for a headstrong solicitor. When she takes the phone and studies the picture, I realize what I've done. I understand in that moment that it's the wrong thing. Sara makes a pained sound before dropping the phone and collapsing. It's the picture of Isa passed out on a couch while at least three naked men, whose faces you can't see, have their dicks inside her. You can, however, see Louis Bruel high-fiving Phillip, who's holding my naked sister's head and kissing her beautiful sleeping face.

Seeing Sara's reaction, I know my fail. In the past twenty-four hours, I've started to abandon all my silly plans, and now I only have one purpose: to mend this broken girl, not break her even more. I lift her off the floor and pray to a God I don't believe in anymore that I didn't go too far.

She comes around a few moments later and I'm not sure where we go from here. I still want to hear about the man she thinks is the love of her life, but at present we need to deal with the big elephant in the bloody room.

"I'm sorry, love, I didn't mean to shock you like that. You didn't need to see that. I know it's hard when someone you know so well lets you down."

"Do you think they raped her?" she asks, which is exactly what I first thought seeing those pictures for the first time, until I read my sister's book and found out it was all planned with her permission. She wanted to do this for Louis so he would find her more desirable, which sounded ludicrous to me, but I didn't have anyone to question…Isa was already gone.

"No, she gave them permission to do all those things."

She nods, closing her eyes before saying, "I'm sorry, Liam.

I wish I could help you change the past. I'm sorry for everything." I feel closer to Sara than any other living person, and I'm quite sure this is what love must feel like.

"Thank you," I answer as I kiss the top of her head. I've never had anyone else understand, commiserate, and comprehend even a small part of the pain I carry.

She finds my tattoo and places her delicate hand over it. She then lowers her head and kisses that same place over my heart, whispering, "Rest in peace, Isabella." And that's when I know there isn't a single bastard on earth who could stand in my way of making this beautiful, broken ballerina mine.

Sara

"I Still Haven't Found What I'm Looking For[43]" by U2

I'm hurting inside and I can't tell good from bad anymore. I always thought that Jeff and I were bad and Louis and Em were good, and now I don't know anything. I only know one thing; I've never felt as safe with anybody as I do in Liam's arms. Every time I get a little glimpse of who he is, I want to hold on to him a little longer. I wish I could help him with the pain, but I can't. I can just listen and hope that when I tell him about my pain, he doesn't start running.

If I knew back then that Louis was involved with Phillip, I would have done everything in my power to stop Emily and Louis from being together. I keep seeing my best friend's husband's face smiling down at Phillip and seemingly encouraging him on. The poor girl, how could she allow those things to happen? Why would she allow Louis and his friends to do that? I suddenly need to know everything. Louis will never answer my questions and there is no way in hell he will give me access to that video Em spoke about. I need my brother's help. It may not be ethical, it may not be legal, but I need to see that video footage if it's the last thing I do. Otherwise, I will never be able to look at Louis Bruel again. There has to be more to that story.

I've been lying in Liam's arms and I don't even know what time it is. Being here with him does feel like our very own world suspended over New York City. His features are becoming as familiar to me as Jeff's. I want him in ways that I can't even articulate, let alone understand.

I reluctantly untangle myself from Liam's warm embrace to look around for my phone to give Eddie a call. I explain to Liam that I need to call my brother and I'll be right back.

Eddie picks up on the first ring, "Where have you been, Sara? Mom was looking for you and said you haven't been answering your phone." Interesting, I wonder what my mom wants from me?

"I'm staying at one of Louis' properties, the one at The Pierre. Not sure if you heard, but Gavin sold the place on Gramercy, so I needed a temporary place to stay until I figure out where I go from here."

"Louis let you stay at the triplex? That's the most expensive piece of real estate in New York City. The Bruels must really love you!" Eddie says with a chuckle. He's also not saying anything about the Gavin news I just revealed, which only means he's already in the know about my stellar pickle with my Ex.

I try to figure out how to approach this without compromising my brother's livelihood and having him feel like he's betraying his best friend. "I need a huge favor. I need you to trust that I would never jeopardize your license to practice law, but you need to do something for me."

"I don't like the sound of this, sis. What kind of crime are you asking me to commit?"

"I need to see the video footage presented at the trial of Isabella Knight. It is very important for my sanity and my future to see it with my own eyes."

Eddie is silent for a few moments. "Sara, the girl is dead. She committed suicide about two years ago. If you or Emily are worried about her book getting published, I assure you that will never happen. The case we built is impenetrable. If anybody ever releases even a line from that book, her billionaire father loses all his loot. Trust me, tell your best friend not to worry, we got this."

"Eddie, it's not about the book, but it is about the role Louis played in that girl's life. I need to know what that footage contains that you guys were able to build a whole case around. Em told me a little about that tape and that it kept Isabella's book from ever being published."

"Sara, I love you, you're my sister, I would do a lot for you, but I can't do this without asking Louis first. If he's okay with you seeing this, then I'll even be able to email you a copy on one of our secure servers. But I need for him to sign off on this. One attorney to another, please tell me you understand where I'm coming from?" I nod because my brother is the kind of guy you want on your team, loyal until the end. He continues, "Let me call Louis."

"Eddie, I'll call Louis myself. Thank you for your help." I wasn't trying to sound fresh or sarcastic, but my reply comes out strained.

"Sara! Don't be pissed. Ask me to help you with something else."

"Eddie, I'm not upset with you. I understand. You could do something for me; I'm leaving New York, I can't stay here anymore. I'm not sure where I'm going but I need you to promise to never tell Jeffery my whereabouts once you find out."

"Are you still involved with him? Didn't he leave you alone after you got married?"

"No, we're not involved anymore, it's been over for years. I just need to make sure he never tries to find me if things don't work out for him and Jacqueline." I'm ready to start my life somewhere else. Once I tell another human my story, once Liam knows my truth, I'll go.

"Of course, sis. I haven't spoken to him in years, and I don't plan to after the things he did to you." Eddie thinks he understands my life, but he knows shit.

"He didn't do anything I didn't allow him to do. It was mutual, Eddie. I take full blame." And I mean every single word I just said.

I hang up and spend the next ten minutes trying to work out what I should say once I call Louis. He's the only person who can make it all better. Only he has the answers.

I dial his number and before I even say a word, the king and ruler of New York starts talking. "Sara, I'm in the lobby. I'll be upstairs in five minutes, get dressed and meet me on the forty-first floor. I'm alone. I want you alone. Tell William I'm just coming to see you." I stare at my phone, speechless. Not only am I about to have words with Louis, he knows Liam is here with me? *What the fuck?*

I walk back to the room to find Liam and give him a heads up about what's about to take place when the phone in my hand beeps with a text from Louis, stating that he's waiting for me. The shit show is about to commence and I must brace myself for a war.

Louis Bruel is a lot of things to many, but perhaps intimidating should be at the top of that list. Still, this shouldn't be hard, right? I want to see that footage and he needs to let me, simple. For both my and Liam's sake we need to see it, and if he's the person that my best friend married, he shouldn't have any qualms about that request. I walk down the stairs to the grand ballroom and there he is, the man with all the answers.

"Eddie said you wanted to see the video," he states with authority.

"Have you been spying on me, Louis?" It's the first thing I need to know.

He smirks. I've never felt intimidated by him before, but I have this unexplained cold chill running up and down my body.

"This is my apartment, Sara. I would never leave my possessions unguarded. Em was adamant about you not wanting any staff here. You're staying in a fourteen thousand square-foot apartment that is valued at over one hundred and fifty million dollars. Don't you think as your friend I should at least do my best to make sure you are safe?"

I wonder briefly if he knew that Liam watched Jeff and I last night. But then the feeling of shame fills me for even questioning him. Of course he has a right to watch over his investment. I now know exactly how Emily feels when she used to tell me that Louis sometimes makes her feel like a spoiled little girl—that's just how I feel. I can't even bring myself to look at him for shame. This man was gracious enough to give me a place to stay and I question him. I literally invited his enemy into his home and I'm the one throwing accusations around like I have a right to.

"Sara, you're a grown woman and who you bring to your bed is none of my or anybody else's business. My only business is your safety, especially while you're my guest. I wasn't concerned and I certainly didn't watch the surveillance footage when the manager informed me of Jeffery Rossi being your guest. However, when I got confirmation of his departure last night and then my security team noticed a man carrying a woman down the hall, I had to make sure you were okay. That's when I recognized your guest, William. And yes, I have been keeping an eye on the both of you since then."

I finally look up to catch Louis studying me, no doubt trying to figure out why and how I got involved with Liam. I should be embarrassed knowing he's been watching us, but I don't care. I only care about one thing as I ask the question I fear the answer to. "Does Emily know?" I ask softly, trying to figure out what will happen once she finds out what I've done.

Louis shakes his head and I'm able to take a deep breath. *Thank God,* thank God she doesn't know, because I have no idea how I'd get myself out of this lie.

"I wanted to understand and hear from you first before I do any damage to your fragile friendship. The two of you have not been on speaking terms for years; I don't need that again. Sara, Em loves you and I'm not going to be the one to ruin your friendship. I'm sure you'll tell her the truth about everything when the time is right," Louis says, pinning me down with his knowing stare, making me feel like the horrible, worthless friend that I am. "I'm really glad you want to see that video. I was under the impression that Liam had a copy; I know his team of lawyers does. That footage played a huge part of the trial. Was he the one to tell you about that video?"

"Why did you just call him Liam?" I ask Louis, confused. I thought I was the only person to call him Liam, since his name is William. I know there are bigger issues as to why Liam said nothing to me about that video when I brought it up, but right now, my heart wants to know why Louis just called William Liam.

"Isabella, his late sister, used to talk about him all the time. She only ever called him Liam. I actually didn't even know his name was William until he introduced himself to me in my office, maybe twelve or thirteen years ago. He came to teach me a lesson and rearrange my ugly face, he told me back then. He blames me for everything that happened to Isa, her life and now her death."

I nod because I can't argue with that. Liam hates Louis, no question about that, and after seeing that photo I can't blame him. "No, he doesn't know anything about the video. I don't think he has much contact with his family, especially after Isa's death," I say, still trying to decipher how he can have no knowledge of a video that apparently was extremely instrumental in his sister's trial.

"Why would his father not show him that footage?" Louis looks confused, which is a rarity. I don't think I've ever actually seen him not be sure of anything. I've only once heard him lose his cool and that was the night Emily left him, right before his heart attack.

"I was just thinking that, too. I would think he'd at least hear about it from his parents or the attorneys on the case." I hope Liam is not fucking around and trying to con me to get to Emily or Louis. It's a dismal thought.

Louis gets up out of the chair he had occupied and comes to sit next to me on my couch. He then asks, "Who told you about that video?"

I'm certain he thinks my brother did. "It wasn't Eddie; it was Em. She told me about Liam and what happened in St. Lucia, and..."

He closes his eyes when I say the last part, undoubtedly not thrilled about his wife talking to me about Liam. "Nothing happened!" he barks out, not giving me a chance to say anything different.

I'm sure even if something did happen, Louis doesn't want to know about it. I nod, knowing that enough happened to make Liam wait for her here for over a month.

"Did he tell you something happened between them? Em told me everything; she told me they only slept in the same bed, but he didn't touch her, right?" Louis demands and questions simultaneously, and we both know he doesn't want to hear the truth so I change the subject.

"How can I see that footage? I'd like Liam to see it, too."

"Are you two ... together?" Louis asks, employing hand gestures.

"I haven't slept with him, if that's what you want to know, but yes, we have been intimate, as you may have seen from the surveillance cameras," I tell Louis, feeling like a slut. I'm sure he already thinks of me as a serial man-eater. He has no idea how many men I've actually been with.

"Are you sure about this? You've already had a run-in with an English playboy, is this wise?" Louis questions me, and I know he has the best intentions, like Em or my brother, but he also doesn't know anything about Liam. Well, I don't know much about him, either, I only know how good I feel in his arms and how my body aches for him. I only know that I hope and pray that he wants to be my friend even after he knows what kind of a person I really am.

"Louis, don't worry. I will tell Emily when it's time. I need to see that video and I need for you to trust me. I just found out that Phillip Dashell is a friend of yours and was involved with Isa. I met Phillip when I was eighteen. I walked into his club and we almost slept together. I would never think that you'd associate with someone like him. But Liam just showed me a disturbing picture and I need to see that video before my head explodes with all the 'what-ifs,'" I say, feeling the pounding of my heart in my throat. I hope Louis understands my concerns and doesn't give me a hard time.

He nods, takes out an envelope from his pocket and hands it to me. "Everything you need to know is on that flash drive, including Isa's book, which Emily read. I don't have secrets from my wife anymore. I had a friendship with Isa and I cared about her deeply. Not the way I care about my wife but I never meant to hurt her. I have an idea of the kind of picture he showed you, Isa had lots of those pictures, and I'm not proud of the things I've done before I met Emily, but I will take the blame for them.

Phillip and I haven't been friends for years; yes, we were very good friends once and yes, I did things with him I would never want my friends and family to know about. I was an idiot on a destructive path together with him and Isa. We were all lost, looking for a quick fix in all the wrong places. I won't ever go back to that horrible version of myself. Phillip almost cost me the love of my life, twice. I'm glad he didn't mar you at eighteen. You should know he loved Isa in his own twisted way and probably resented me for being the man she chose to love over him. He pretended she meant nothing to him but I saw the truth. He did things to her to punish her for how she felt about me. He read and knew about that book before I ever did and that screwed him up even more. Sara, in this life, you can only control your actions and reactions, you can't always help the people around you. You can try, and I did try, but some people can't be saved."

He gets up, kisses the top of my head and starts to leave. As he gets to the doors to leave the grand ballroom of this palatial penthouse, he turns to me and says, "I believe Liam Knight is a good guy, Sara. Isa loved him more than anything in this world. He deserves to find some happiness, just not at my expense." He offers me a pained smile and leaves.

My heart aches at his words. I don't want to think about the person Louis was before he met my beautiful best friend. He's an attractive man with extraordinary means, which makes him susceptible to a wild lifestyle not available to the rest of us. How Emily was able to tame and convert a notorious playboy into an amazing loving husband and father is nothing short of a miracle. Whoever Louis Bruel was before he became Em's husband doesn't matter anymore, he is and always will be a good guy. I look up the staircase and think that the beautiful stranger waiting for me is also a good guy. I know it. I just don't deserve either one of them in my life, not in any capacity.

Liam

"Please Don't Go[44]" by KC & Sunshine Band

I've been listening to Louis and Sara's conversation and I'm having a hard time comprehending why my father never mentioned or let me view this tape they're chatting about. I feel like a loon for never knowing there was a tape involved. It's safe to say that up until today, I felt certain that Louis had somehow paid enough money to make my sister and her book go away. If I weren't a member of a group of strangers that call themselves "my family" I'd call one of my parents and ask them about this. But I haven't spoken to my father in almost two years. My parents always attempted to cover up anything that could possibly tarnish our good name, and my sister's conduct didn't help the façade they struggled to uphold. My mum can't even hear my sister's name without falling apart, and Isa never uttered a goddamn word about that video. *Bullocks!* What can possibly be on that bloody video?

Once Louis leaves, I go back to our room and wait for Sara to get to the bottom of this. Well, it's not *our* room, it's just *a* room. I heard what Louis said about Phillip loving Isa. That's another bit of history I had no knowledge about. I haven't cried in two years but in a span of less than twenty-four hours, I've

218

had to hold back tears a few times. I'm not sure how I was able to keep it together when he mentioned Isa talking about me. When I think of our short time together, I can't recall her once saying she loved me. She only ever talked and cried about loving him. I wonder what she said to him about me? I wish I could talk to someone who actually knew her while she lived in the States.

Sara walks in a few minutes later holding her laptop. I'm seated at an armchair by the window and I'm baffled that the small act of her filling the same space as me calms me. I almost wish we could skip this awkward part and have her be confidant enough to walk over to me and sit in my lap, where I feel she belongs. I know she has the footage and we're about to witness another dimension to my sister's tragic tale, but I'm elated to not be doing this alone.

"Did you know about this video?" she questions me.

"Only after you mentioned it, earlier," I answer truthfully. "Do you not trust me?" I ask, fearing her answer.

"I trust you, you're not a liar," she states, which I'm thankful for.

"Are you ready?" she asks me. I nod but I don't know what I'm ready for. I don't know what missing piece of the distorted puzzle this video will fill. "Liam, I want you to promise me that whatever you and I are about to witness won't change anything between us. We can't go backward, we can't change the things that have been done. The past has been written; it's only the future that remains open, clean, unknown, and untainted. Please promise me you're willing and open to have a conversation with me about whatever this video holds."

I nod again, but how can I promise not to react when I have no idea what kind of evidence is about to punch me in the heart?

She places her laptop on the bed and walks over to me. My heart actually gets lodged in my throat as she approaches. She gives a small smile that may actually make me burst and then she sits in my lap, curling herself into me and nestling every part of her beautiful body as if molding us together. She has no idea what she's doing to me. I wrap my arms around her and bring her as close as I can without crushing her delicate bones. I've never felt this. I don't even know what this feeling is called. I've fancied girls before, I've lusted over them before, I've even thought I found love before, but this is a feeling I can't grasp. I'm not even sure if she's making everything worse or better. Isa brought me to Emily, and Emily brought me to Sara. I just don't reckon letting her go, despite not knowing whom she belongs to. I look down and I'm happy to have this beautiful, broken ballerina trust me and let me be this close. I inhale her scent and it makes me lightheaded. I want to let myself have this moment, to have this small ounce of joy, and then I remember how cruel the world I inhabit is. I recall how everything I've ever loved gets ripped away from me, and suddenly, I want to give her back before she gets taken away, too.

I kiss the top of her head, and whisper to her, "Sara, if I accidentally like you more than I should, will you allow me to keep you?" I feel her kissing up my chest, not answering my plea. "Please don't make me believe I can have you, only to have you go back to him." She still doesn't answer me. My heart literally aches as if she's squeezing it tight by ignoring my request. I shouldn't be scared to make love to her, even if just for one day, even if I'm disposable to her. I will have a part of her to cherish and enjoy even if just during my musings. We ought to have this, even if he comes back to take her away from me, he won't be able to take away what we've shared together... I'll own that.

She finally sits up in my lap and looks at me. I look back into her beautiful eyes. She's not the American girl from the pub, she's not the sad lonely girl I found this morning, she is not even Emily's best mate, she is my Sara. She doesn't have to say another word, her eyes tell me everything.

I get up and lift us both from the chair and lay her on the bed. I don't need to ask her for anything, she already said yes. I remove all her clothes without looking away once. I've shed my clothing, too, and we're both gloriously naked. I look down at her beautiful body and all I want is to be permitted to be the keeper and the owner of every cell, every freckle. I lower my head and kiss those sweet, tender lips. I spread her legs and position myself between her long elegant limbs. What joy would it be to start and end each day with those sexy lips? I don't think I'd be able to sleep at night knowing those lips were sleeping right beside me. I kiss her and can't help but smile, causing those lips I can't seem to get enough of to smile, too. No words, we don't need words. I know I want her. I've earned her. Even if for a moment, I deserve a bit of happiness.

I deepen our kiss, filling her mouth with my tongue. I lower myself on top of her, letting our bodies touch. I may be on top but she's in control; she has me in the palm of her hand and right now, I would do anything she asks of me. I see her start to close her eyes and a slow panic starts spreading down my body. *No! No!* I yell inside, *Open your eyes Sara*, as if I'm about to lose her. As if once those eyes close, our time will be over. I take hold of her face, which startles her and she opens her eyes and looks at me in confusion.

"Don't go," I say to her.

A pained smile forms on her lips and she says, "I have nowhere to go."

Sara

"What's Love Got To Do With It[45]" by Tina Turner

I've always felt that Jeffery loved me, desired me, and wanted us to end up together one day. I am also, however, old enough to know that what we feel and what we want do not always materialize into what we deserve and what we eventually get in the end.

I feel the connection, the pull I have with this beautiful man. I feel how much he wants me, and it feels wonderful. I'm not sure I've ever felt this needed by someone. Liam needs me and that knowledge and these emotions brewing inside of me are gradually paralyzing. I still can't wrap my brain around why someone like him would need someone like me. I find myself doubting everything. Does he need me to help him forget his pain and move on? I am willing and spread out naked before him to do as he pleases. Earlier, I did ask him to do just this—fuck me! But I have this little intuition that I'm more to him than a fuck. He keeps saying sweet things to me I want to believe, but I've heard it all before. He has no idea how much he, and this, and us, means to me. He has given me so much strength with just the way he's looked at me in the last few hours, that if nobody else ever looks at me again for the rest of my life, I'd be okay.

222

I smile to myself, thinking how Liam won't let me close my eyes. That has to be the most beautiful thing I've ever been asked not to do. I know what it means and it makes me want him even more, if that's indeed even possible. I'm turning into the Sara I once was; I don't remember this kind of hope blooming inside me since...since...I did what I did all those years ago. I'm not a bad person. I was young and stupid, but I always feel like a villain.

I'm aware that my pussy actually contracts even though he hasn't touched it. He holds my face as I finish telling him I have nowhere to go. His stare, the way his eyes flash pity and then delight is tremendous; he's sad that I feel I'm a loser nobody wants, but he's happy I'm his loser.

The way his hair falls to one side and almost grazes my chest is picture-perfect. He loosens the harsh hold he has on my chin and moves his finger to caress my neck and lightly graze my breasts. How we react to each other, the things he says to me make what we're about to do not feel as dirty or wrong as it probably is; it makes this feel like love. People who've met only hours ago are not supposed to look at each other this way. He should be crude and blasé with me. Shouldn't he be treating me like a whore? *What's love got to do with it*, I sing in my head. My common sense won't let me enjoy this; it finally wakes the fuck up and starts demanding answers from my useless heart about how I let the situation get this far.

I feel the panic begin in my stomach. If he won't stop look-ing at me the way he is right now, then I'll need to leave. I've been here before; I know what happens when I let someone look at me like this. All I asked is for him to fuck me! Not save me, or pretend to want to keep me! He needs to shove his dick in my mouth and fuck me like someone he will never see again.

I'm a stupid jerk. Why did I climb into his lap earlier? Why am I setting myself up again? We need to stop this pretend bull-shit pretense and watch that tape, now! I need to stop this! But, I can't stop him now. He looks happy and I want him happy. I didn't like the way he appeared scared when he saw me with my laptop. I climbed into his stupid lap as if I belong because I just wanted him to know that I'll be right here for him, no matter what's on that video. Now he's looking at me and his eyes are making promises I know he won't be able to keep once he knows the truth. How do I always manage to fuck up everything I touch?

"I want your dick in my mouth," I say, shocking him to shit with my scummy request.

"Lovely, are we back to that again?" He tilts his head forc-ing a sad smile.

I nod. "Let's just get this shit over with. Let's fuck each other's brains out and get back to business."

He nods his head, agreeing with my statement, or pretend-ing to agree with my statement. I'm too confused to decode.

"What would make you happy, love? Should I climb up your face and gag you with my cock? Will that please you? Or perhaps I should turn you around and fuck you up your arse so your pussy stays untouched for Jeffery, the love of your life? Is that what you fancy? Does that sound nice, Sara?"

I close my eyes because emotionally, I can't do this any-more. My heart and head will never be on the same team. My heart knows what it wants and yet my head does everything to sabotage any chance of happiness I may ever possibly experi-ence.

"I can't play pretend anymore. I can't pretend you actually want me in this hotel and not Emily. I can't pretend that if I keep letting you look at me like that, I won't be even more broken than before we met, once you leave. Where will I go once you finish fucking me? I don't have a home; I just have me and my lies—that's my home. I don't want you to look at me like I mean more to you than just some whore you met in a hotel bar. A whore you've witnessed get fucked and abandoned in the middle of the night. I know who I am, Liam, do you? Just fuck me so we get the tension out of the way and then you won't need to wonder 'what if.' You and I mean nothing to each other, let's not pretend anymore."

There. I've said it all. It hurts and it's raw, but it's true and I'm proud of myself for saying it all out loud.

"Shut up, you stupid girl. I need you to shut your brain for a bit. I'm not a pretender and there is no one I desire to be under me but you. Get that through your head! Just you! You! *You!* Yes, you're right, I don't know everything about you, but you mean something to me…you mean a lot. Stop asking me to fuck you because I won't. I need to love you, and you need to let me love you, and *you* need to start loving you. Your secrets and fibs don't define you. I want *you,* Sara, and you need to stop pretending you don't want me to love you."

All I have to do is let him in. He's already in, but now he needs for me to invite him. I want this, I want him and nothing or no one should stand in my way, not JJ, not Emily, and not some tape. This is different than what happened with Jeff. "Liam, I want you more than anything I've ever wanted in my life, but I'm petrified because I know I don't deserve you. I don't want to cause you more pain, but I do need you, I need you so much. I don't have anybody, I only have you."

I'm on the verge of tears, but he smiles as if I've just given him the best news of his life. Seeing him happy makes me delirious. He has to be the cure to my disease, the cure that I've been praying for. I always believed that JJ would be my cure and make everything right, but even Jeff doesn't make me feel the things I feel when this man looks at me. I feel alive and happy and above all, I feel loved. As fucked up as this is, I think somebody actually loves me.

"No more tears," he sternly warns me. "I just need my ballerina to keep smiling. I think I can handle anything this wretched life hurls at me as long as I have someone by my side. No! Not just someone; as long as you and I are here for one another, I can handle anything. Let me try to make you happy, Sara. You're the first person in a long time I've wanted to make happy for all the right reasons. I don't know what he did to you, but I won't do the same thing. Please trust me," he says, lowering his head to my neck as he begins to softly but thoroughly kiss every inch of me. "When I'm finally inside you in every way possible, you'll know how bloody perfect we are," he adds before taking my whole nipple with his beautiful mouth and sucking diligently.

"If you keep talking and sucking, I may come without you ever touching my clit," I say. I can feel him smiling with his mouth full and I love that little crinkle that forms around his eyes.

"That's the bloody point. Making you come until you can't keep your eyes open."

I like hearing naughty things come out of that mouth of his in his sinfully sexy British accent, but I'm not sure I even could come more than once. I've lied to Em about having multiple orgasms countless times, but is that a normal thing to have? I wish I could just turn my analytical mind off, and enjoy this man and everything he wants to do to me. "Don't beat yourself up if I don't come more than once."

He lets go of my nipple and says with such seriousness that you'd think we're debating world politics and not my potential climaxing tally, "You can and you will come more than one lousy time for the love of God. Got it? I have you under me and I plan to labor very hard and long to make you happy. It took me all bloody morning to convince your Yankee arse to let me do this. Sorry, but once just won't do! I've never given twopence about making any bird come. So please consider how special you are, love. I'm not even thinking about my poor knob. I only care about your cunt and how your eyes will look once you let go and start trembling."

"Then, why are you still talking?" I ask with a wink.

"Cheeky. I like it," he replies continuing with his tongue licking down my stomach.

This boy really makes me giddy. He's beautiful and funny and his sweetness and charm drive me insane. I can probably look at him all day long and not find a single flaw. There is nothing about him I would change except I wish I'd met him fifteen years ago. I wish my heart had only known and loved someone like *him*. I wish I were there for him in his saddest hour like he is for me right now.

"Come back, you need to kiss me." I try to get him to stop tickling my stomach with his hair and tongue and come give me a long kiss.

"Not yet, love, I need to kiss you somewhere else first," he announces, already between my legs.

Oh my God. I look down to see his face positioned at my entrance. He slides his arms under my unsteady legs and brings his hands over the top, holding me open for him and spreading my folds with his fingers. I'm drenched in desire as liquid pours out of me. He adjusts himself and flexes those ridiculous muscular arms of his, getting into the perfect position. He makes a real meal out of this, as if he plans to be down there for hours.

My arousal level is at DEFCON 1. It feels weird to watch, feel, and respond to everything he's doing to me. He uses one hand to spread my folds and the other hand is over my stomach, no doubt trying to calm my shaking body. I shiver as if being cold but I'm overheated and sweating everywhere. He smiles and shows me his tongue right before he slowly and lazily licks into my wetness. *Oh. My. Fucking. God. Oh. My. God.*

Liam

"Nothing Compares 2U[46]" by Sinéad O'Connor

I wasn't nervous until I felt Sara trembling under my touch, and it causes me to lose it and I begin to shake, too. This girl who seems fragile has enough strength to pull every string in my heart and I don't bloody recognize myself. If the Me from yesterday saw the Me today, he wouldn't know who this baffled bloke is. Isa once told me that when she was introduced to Louis at a party, she just knew that he was the one. I remember listening to her and thinking how preposterous that sounded; to see a person and think, *Yeah I'd like to see you for the rest of my life.* Even when I gave Brandy a ring and asked her to be my wife, I still couldn't imagine only being with her for all my days. Then I met Emily, and the things that woman made me feel in a few short days were extraordinary. She woke something up inside of me, making me want to try, and live, and find happiness again. I truly thought I needed her for my happiness, but I stand corrected.

The reactions I have to Sara don't compare to any emotions I've ever felt. I've only known her for a handful of hours and yet I don't recall a time I didn't know her. It feels as if she's been by my side my entire life. I've never met a girl I comprehend as

228

well as I do her and I don't want to know anything else. I don't care about her past and what fibs she told the world, I just care about making whatever's left of our lives beautiful and true... Don't we deserve that? It can't be that everything beautiful I hold in my hands gets ripped away. I didn't think I'd ever find a reason or a will to go on after Isa killed herself. I think this is probably the first time in two miserable years I've even admitted that my sister killed herself.

Her whole body shakes, but I know she's not frightened of me. Her eyes expose just how very much she needs me to love her. It's the excitement of knowing that after this moment, nothing will ever be the same again for us. It seems I've waited my whole life for this hour; the countless girls that have used me for status, the countless girls I've used in vain for pleasure, Brandy making a fool of me, Emily resetting and turning my world upside down, and Sara finally pressing play.

If she never wants to say another word about her dubious past, that will be ace with me. Her choosing me is all the truth I need from her. This beautifully shattered girl, trembling under my touch, is my destiny. Life tried to separate us with geography and circumstances, but fate brought us here. I would endure my journey again to find her and make everything right.

I look up at her spread naked before me. I'm about to French kiss her patiently awaiting pussy, glistening and beckoning me to have my first taste of heaven. I wonder if she knows that everything about her is intoxicating; she's slowly driving me insane. Those eyes are the true cause of my perpetual hard rod. How could those eyes tell a lie? Do her friends and family not look in her eyes when she speaks? We need no words; I already know everything I need to know. I'll be good to her and she'll never look at someone other than me this way. It's funny how I thought meeting and being with Emily ruined me, but surely being with this broken doll will kill me, and I couldn't stop even if I tried.

"Oh, Liam. Oh," she whimpers as I see her cheeks blush crimson.

"You like that? Then I'm sure you'll love this," I say, fully submerged between her long stems, breathing in that sweet cunt. I bring my hands up to squeeze her beautiful breasts, pinching her firm nipples between my fingers. I take my time licking inside her while plotting how I plan to make her come for the first time.

I decide that finger and tongue torture will have to do, for now. I let go of her breasts and bring my one hand down. I slowly insert my middle finger inside her opening, making my cock twitch. The moment my finger is fully immersed, time stops. *Perfection.* I commence the penetration with my finger slowly in and out, and I begin pounding her clit with my tongue. I bring my other hand to start massaging the area right above my tongue and I can bet my left nut she won't last long.

She doesn't make any sounds, just a big, beautiful, inaudible O with her mouth. Her eyes start to close and I've already started the countdown in my head. I can make her detonate and send her flying if I pick up the speed. My fingers continue working her hard as I start sucking all the liquid dripping out of her...and she's gone.

"LLLiammm," she belts out with her eyes half shut, and then repeating my name over and over. Her climax catapults her upper body off the bed. She tries to close her legs around my face, burying me in deeper. Her hands pull at my hair to try and make me halt the sucking and biting, but I know what's good for her—my continuing effort to push her until she comes again, that's what.

I'm euphoric; I don't even fear that her eyes are almost fully closed, since it's my name falling out of her lips.

"Liam...stop...I...can't...please," she begs, still trembling from the first earthquake.

But she needs more! I stop eating her for a bit as I insert another finger. I feel her constrict and squeeze me from inside. *Oh fucking brilliant.* I try to take my time, but I need my dick inside her tight pussy now or I'll bloody croak. I climb up her body to start sucking those tits that require my attention. Does she know how incredible she is? She looks at me with disbelief as if she can't believe we're doing this. I nod my head, *we're bloody doing this, baby,* and she smiles; eye contact is all we require to communicate.

"Are you happy, Sara?" I ask between lapping her tits and harshly finger thrusting her.

"Very," she replies breathlessly with a naughty smile.

"Ace, but I will make you happier," I promise and have every intention of making her smile until she gets taken away from me…like they all do.

Sara

"Love Is A Battlefield[47]" by Pat Benatar

"**I** need to be inside you and...I don't have anything resembling a rubber johnny on me! Please kindly explain to me how I'm going to survive if you tell me you're not on a tablet," he says in all seriousness, letting go of my sore nipple but still pumping his fingers roughly into me.

"I'm not on the pill," I declare, watching the horror spread across his face. "I've only slept with one man in my whole life and he's clean, but—" I state, knowing that Jeffery gets regular checkups and is, in fact, clean. "I'm sure you can't make that same claim and I don't know you enough to let you inside me without a condom."

He abruptly pauses finger fucking me and by the disappointed look in his eyes, I think I've just killed our moment and destroyed him. The truth is, I'm more worried about getting knocked up than anything else. I can't take care of myself, let alone another human. I actually have an emergency condom in my bag but I wanna have some fun with him and let him sweat a little first. Let's see how resourceful Liam Knight is when faced with a naked, willing girl, but no condom in sight.

"That's okay, love, as long as we make you happy I'll explain the situation to Richard and promise him an encore with Kitty some other time," he announces with an eye roll and a smile removing his drenched fingers, he spreads my wetness around my sensitive nipples and immediately sucks them clean.

"I think you're trying to kill me." I say as I feel another spasm sprouting thanks to his expert suckling technique.

"This is nothing compared to what Richard and I plan to do to you and kitty. Everything about you drives me mad. I reckon we may both need a good will because we may just kill each other," he declares with a grin.

"Did you just call your dick Richard and my vagina Kitty, again?" I ask holding back a smile.

"Perhaps," he mumbles, making me want to burst and kiss every inch of his face.

"I have a condom," I declare, giving him a quick peck on his pouty lips. Did he really think I'd let him walk out of this room today without me feeling that magnificent Richard inside of me? "It has your name on it," I add with a wink.

"Sara, you should know that Richard and I are very close to asking for your hand." We both erupt into hysterical laughter. It's been a fucking roller coaster today: laughing, crying, hating, liking, and if I'm honest, slowly but surely falling for this sweet guy.

"I hope I get to pick my ring out. But you should know I'm not the marrying type," I say, still cracking up, only to see he's not laughing anymore.

"Why do you say such rubbish?" Liam asks me. And I honestly don't even know why I just said that. It was a joke. I don't even notice my negative sarcasm; it's just who I am and how I deal with my truths. I shake my head, not knowing how to answer him. "I'd marry you. Please don't say awful rubbish about the woman I and every other bloke in New York would be fortunate to call his wife." He lowers his head to kiss me.

Did he really just say that? I do want him to be mine. I want to stand on top of this building and scream to anyone who hears me that this beautiful man should be mine. I don't want secrets. I don't want lies. I want Liam Knight! What do I need to do to make sure he's mine?

I miss his fingers inside me, as if that's where they belong. I never want him to take them out. If his Richard feels half as good as his fingers did, I'll never let him go.

"Where can I find that Jimmy you spoke of?" he asks, in reference to the promised prized condom.

"It's in my bedroom. I'll go get it." I start to get up.

"Stay; don't move. I'll go fetch it," he says, and then whispers, "Keep pumping for me, and I'll suck your cum off your digits when I come back."

I nod frantically, thinking, *Yes, Sir*. I hope he knows that I'd probably do anything he'd ask of me.

He walks out of the room and I suddenly have a sobering moment of clarity and a cold chill runs up and down my body. *Oh shit!* Louis has surveillance cameras in the halls of this penthouse and Liam just walked out of this room stark naked. *Fuck!* I cringe, thinking of Louis seeing Liam naked. I jump off the bed, stitch-less myself, to go yell after Liam. I don't make it very far before slamming into a solid form as I exit the room; I fall backward from the impact and look up to see Jeffery looking down at me. He looks confused and angry and I think I'm about to faint. *This must be a dream; this can't be happening,* I reason to myself as I hear Jeff and Liam yelling somewhere in the far distance of my mind.

I slowly open my eyes, confused. Was it all a dream? I see a white sheet around my body and I feel somebody holding me tight. I try and lift my face up when I notice his naked body under me. My face is resting on Isabella's name tattooed over his heart and I look up to find him smiling down at me... He's not a dream.

"You blacked out. Are you all right?" I nod my head. *I'll be all right if you hold me like this forever.* "You and I need to leave now; we don't belong here," he states.

"Don't fucking tell her where she belongs," I hear Jeff shout. His voice startles me and I almost spring up from Liam's lap where he has me nestled. I look across the room to see Jeffery pacing, looking disheveled and out of sorts. His hair is a mess, his shirt is untucked, and his tie appears askew. Something happened while I fainted, and when I look back at Liam and see the murderous stare he gives Jeff, I know it wasn't good.

"I'll tell her what I bloody please," Liam replies, sounding nothing like himself.

"Do you even know who I am?" Jeff barks out as he comes our way. I can feel Liam's muscles contract and tense underneath me.

"I know more than you'll ever know. I know you're responsible for all her suffering. I know she's had the misfortune of knowing you for far too long. I know you're a dirty wanker that leaves her in the middle of the night. I know your sort and I know you don't deserve to ever utter her name. Whatever hold you think you have on her is over, because she's not alone anymore. It's best you leave her alone or I'll bury you."

I listen to all the things that this stranger I've only met today, the one I'm certain I've accidentally fallen in love with, says. I hear the things that yesterday I would've given my own life to hear come out of Jeff's mouth. And yet, as Liam speaks them, I am thankful they're coming from him and nobody else. I should look at Jeff, I should plead for him to leave, and yet I can't take my eyes off Liam, nor does he take his off me. It's a spell. It's like all the bullshit has lifted and I see a future covered in truth and happiness and unconditional love. The person I love loves me back enough to choose me and no one else, whatever the consequences. Liam just chose me and I choose him.

I'm brought out of my daze by the sound of Jeff laughing. I tear my gaze from Liam's to see Jeff shaking his head, and I know my bubble is about to burst with his next words. Liam fired the first shot and nothing can stop the war now.

Liam

"I Ran[48]" by A Flock of Seagulls

She finally comes around and I can't tell how long I've held her in my arms like a helpless, sleeping child. I care so much about her and my heart hasn't stopped trying to climb out of my chest since I saw her collapse. I thought he hit her. I was ready to kill him. I was going to kill him if I didn't have the cathartic need to hold on to her and make sure she was all right. My beautiful ballerina lay broken on the floor thanks to him. I don't think it's possible for me to let her go anymore. Even if she begs me, I don't suppose I could leave her.

How can I not have a life with her? I can give Sara a life, a bloody good life, and she can be my reason for getting up every morning. Isn't that what it's all about? Finding someone to love who loves you back? Isn't that what Isa wanted from Louis? Isn't that what Emily feared she'd lost? This despicable excuse for a man thinks he has claim to her. She's mine! I went through hell to find her and I'll go through hell to keep her and make her happy.

This worthless stag has been pacing the room like a caged animal. He won't leave until she tells him to beat it. She needs to be strong enough to tell him to go scratch and leave us. God, I promise I'll be good to her. All she needs to do is choose me, please let her choose anything but him.

He laughs like a deranged clown and I see the fear in his eyes at the realization that he's lost her.

"Oh, that's beautiful, dude. It must be nice living inside your delusional head. Did Sara also tell you that I'm the only one she's ever had inside her? I'm her first and last everything! Did she tell you she and I are indefinitely engaged? Did she tell you about our children?"

My ears ring deafly, the room starts to blur, and my last gulp of air is lodged in my chest. He's still talking but I can't hear a single word that comes out of his mouth. I look down at my broken ballerina, perfectly nestled in my arms, and she's not looking at me anymore. Her eyes are closed and I see the tears running down her cheeks, feeling their warmth as they spill on my chest, and that's enough. We don't need words. I close my eyes and force a bloody smile, imploring my fake grin to make my own tears disappear. It's all I need to know; she's not my broken ballerina, she's his.

I kiss the top of her head and stand up with her in my arms. I make a pledge to never look into those eyes again; they don't belong to me. Jeffery Rossi is now seated on the bed, looking pleased with himself, no doubt recognizing the carnage he just caused and enjoying his victory. I look behind him at the bed he's occupying, the bed that only moments—or maybe it was ages—ago held so much promise. I walk a few painful steps over to him and lay her in his arms where she belongs, handing over to him my little crumb of hope. I won't look at her or him.

I always lose. Why should this be any different? I find my trousers and dress myself as fast as my pride will allow. I won't look at him holding her, I won't. Life is just a handful of moments like this that remind you of how alone you really are.

I walk out of the room as I slowly allow the noise to filter back into my head. Sara cries and calls after me while Jeffery yells at her to calm down. I just need to bloody get myself far away from here and her, before whatever is left of me breaks down. What's left of me is just an empty shell that needs to go home to die in dignity. My body is leaving her but my heart is already long gone.

I walk out of our room, the room that she and I would have made love in, the room that would have given us a future, and I feel numb. I know there is nothing left of my heart anymore. I walk out and head towards the staircase. I take one more look towards the room where I left my pride and see Louis and Emily sitting on the floor by the door watching me run away. I whisper, "I'm sorry" to Emily as she shakes her head with tears rolling down her face. I don't care anymore; both those birds are not mine, and I just keep running.

Sara

"Time After Time[49]" by Cyndi Lauper

Why won't he look at me? He doesn't understand. I haven't told him everything yet. "Liam!" I try to make him look at me. "Liam, please let me explain!" I say over and over as he stands with his back to me and gets dressed. "Liam, please look at me," I beg like a child. But I don't think he can hear me. It's as if he turned some switch off. Jeff holds me in his arms and won't let me move. I try to free myself, I want to run to him, hold on to him. I need to tell him everything. He can't think that I lied to him.

"Baby, please calm down. Let him go. You don't need him, I'm here," Jeffery whispers down at me.

Of course I need him; I don't need anybody but him. I replay the whole scene that just took place. I haven't stopped yelling and crying out for Liam to come back for me, to look at me. He promised to be my friend. He promised to help me get through this and he just fucking left. He walked out the door and didn't even look at me. He didn't say goodbye—he just ran away. My heart aches; my poor, stupid heart breaks into pieces that have left my body and are now halfway down the street running after him. If Jeff would just let go of me, I'd run down the street with all the scattered pieces of my heart to try and explain everything. I'm hysterical as I fight and yell, but nothing's happening. I'm still in Jeffery's arms where I always end up.

In the end, karma always wins, and I always get what I deserve; I get nothing. I'm too weak to keep fighting and yelling. I have no one to be angry with but myself. I did this! I made my bed and I shall die in it. The only reason I haven't run away from all the lies and this place I once believed was home is because of them. I just exist for them! I see them almost every day as they go to school. Jeff sends me pictures and I trick my mind into thinking I'm a part of their world. I haven't missed a single milestone and yet they wouldn't know who I was if they passed me on the street. They don't know I'm their mother, but I know they're mine. My matter and his matter made them and they will always be ours, whether or not they or anybody else knows the truth. In my heart and in my bones, they're mine. Nobody can take that away from me.

"Sara, baby, who was he?" Jeffery finally asks once my fucking tears decide to stop, because they're not stupid like me, they understand it's too late.

"He was nothing," I say, trying to convince myself and Jeff simultaneously of yet another lie. *He really was nothing.* He was probably just using me to get closer to the Bruels. *Right? Right, Sara?* And yet it hurts so much, it hurts like a thousand knives and a thousand bullets. It hurts like everything else that I get only a little taste of before it gets ripped away from me.

"Did you let him fuck you?" Jeff asks, and his question actually makes me laugh. It somehow sounds absurd.

"No, we didn't fuck!" I answer, not sure if that's good or bad. I don't think that having sex with Liam would be classified as "fucking" even if fate did let us have a few more moments together. When we were together, I saw hope, I almost tasted it, and now I'm back to my reality. I should've known no one would ever choose me when given the chance.

"Why did you tell him about the kids? You never call your children *our* kids. Why now?" I ask, as I finally look him in the eye. "We promised never to speak of this. You made me sign papers to make sure I never change my mind or say a word. So why disclose it to a stranger?" I feel a cold chill envelop my body even though I'm fully covered and Jeff still holds me tightly.

"He didn't look like nothing, judging from the way you were looking at him. He and you looked like something. I can't lose you again. When I found out you got married, I couldn't go on with my life. I hated Jacqueline and everything she stood for. I hated not being able to see you every day and love you. I couldn't even look at the twins. Sometimes, they look just like you. If only things were different. I love you, Sara," he says with tears running down his face, a face I know better than my own.

I hold my wrists flush against my heart like I always do. He's the only one who knows that the names of our children are tattooed in white ink on the inside of my wrists. Their beautiful names were the only thing I gave them. I didn't carry them in my empty womb! I didn't give birth to them! I was just the donor, the anonymous facilitator to bring about their existence. I just happen to know and love their father with everything I have and all that I am.

He takes my wrists in his hands and brings them to his lips. He kisses first one and then the other. If their names weren't there, I'd probably have slashed my wrists many moons ago. I stay alive for them, just in case they'll ever need me.

"If only things were different, we would have had such a beautiful life, baby. We would raise our family the way we've always imagined and talked about. I would go to bed and wake up with you every morning. God, I love you," he cries out, kissing the inside of my wrists over and over.

We're both quiet, no doubt wishing our *what ifs* were real, when we hear a loud sound outside the room. At first, I'm startled, but then I let myself believe that it's Liam and hope blooms inside me once again as my heart starts to beat with purpose. *He must've come back for me*, I think foolishly. A minute later, I see Louis Bruel filling the doorway, holding his wife in his arms. My best friend is crying like a baby. He looks at me and in this moment, I know exactly what I've done. I know exactly why she's crying; I did this, too.

Sara

"If I Could Turn Back Time[50]" by Cher

"**E**m, why don't I leave you to talk to Sara while I go have a word with Jeff," Louis says to his beautiful wife, whom I don't deserve to know, let alone call my best friend. She shakes her head, still sobbing and holding on to him for dear life. "Shhh...that's your best friend, little girl. She needs you, she's hurting, too, baby. You know you can't assume anything until she tells you the truth herself," he says, proving that I don't deserve to know him, either.

As I watch and listen to Louis speak to his wife, I think back to Liam and his low opinion of this man. I wish we both got the chance to see what was on that video. I wish he knew Louis like I know him. Isa didn't just fall in love with a handsome guy, she fell in love with Louis Bruel for the beautiful, loving man that he is, was, and always will be. But I don't think Liam will ever accept and understand that. It's ironic that I'm being held tightly in Jeff's arms, the arms I've dreamt about every night for the last fifteen years of my life, and all I can think about is Liam.

I see Louis walk deeper into the room and gently place Emily down on the untouched second bed, lowering his head to kiss her temple as he whispers something inaudible in her ear. She nods in agreement and turns to face the window. He then walks over to Jeffery, who continues to clutch me tightly, and without a single word, takes me from his arms and carries me over placing me next to Em.

"Make it better, we'll be downstairs," he tells me and walks out of the room, motioning for Jeff to follow him.

It's scary when your best friend, who usually can't shut up, is just silent. She stares out the window right past me as if I'm invisible, and in many ways, I wish I were. I wonder what's going through her mind? I don't know how to make it better. What can I possibly say to make her hate me less? I have no excuse for being a lying bitch my whole life. I'd rather have her near and not say a single world than have her torn away from me, too. I decide to just wait and say nothing. If she wants me to explain, I'll tell her everything. Even if it hurts and rips me to shreds, I'll tell her everything... I can't protect her from my ugly truth with my beautiful lies anymore. It's time she knows who I really am, and if she still wants to know me once I say the unsayable, I'll count it as one of my rare blessings.

She finally looks me in the eyes and says softly after a silence that felt like eternity, "'Wind Beneath My Wings[51]' by Bette Midler."

That song is all I'll ever need to know that I'm not alone, that I've never been alone. I don't have words to express my emotions and the love I feel for this loyal woman who tolerates me. She's the only one who ever really loved me. How could I ever question and agonize over her opinion of my choices? Why didn't I trust her enough to know she would never judge or hate me? Wasn't she the little girl sitting with flowers at my ballet recitals when nobody else remembered to come? Wasn't she the first person and sometimes the only person to wish me a happy birthday at midnight? Isn't she the only one who always tried to make me smile?

That song is equivalent to the Holy Grail in our '80s dialect. She couldn't have chosen a more meaningful song if she tried and she knows it. This is the song that started it all; the song that she sang and danced to in our sixth grade talent show. I fell in love with Emily Marcus almost twenty years ago when I heard her sing that song, which I'd felt she sang just for me. I knew at that moment she would be my best friend forever. I created our own secret language just to strengthen our bond more. Our mothers were already good friends and I wanted her to be just mine. My whole life, I tried to impress her, shock her, and I really didn't need to. She would have loved me even if I wasn't *The* Sara; she would be my best friend even if I were just Sara. All I needed was to be honest with her. Everybody makes mistakes and everybody hurts in different ways. I was a lying coward when all she gave me was unconditional love.

"I love you so much. Please forgive me. I'm sorry about everything," I say, squeezing her and melting into her embrace. "I should've told you everything. You wouldn't hate me, you would understand. I'm such a loser; I was ashamed. Please forgive me for all the lies," I cry out into her hair.

"Sara, stop it! There is nothing for me to forgive. The only person that you need to ask for forgiveness is yourself. I've known you my whole life, and I've always known all the stories were a bunch of lies. I never believed for one second you were the slut you pretended to be. I let you be whatever you wanted to be because I love you. How could you be a slut if all you've ever wanted was love? Sluts don't break down love songs and study them like the word of God. I always knew it was Jeffery. I could see him in your eyes and I could see the way he looked at you, I just didn't understand what you two actually shared until now.

I'm upset with myself because I know how much you're hurting and I wish I could make it better, but I don't know how."

Her words are a solace to my aching heart. She could've made hundreds of horrible, painful moments so much better if I had only let her. I always thought the truth would hurt everybody around me, but the truth would've made my life and all my stupid choices bearable.

"I don't know where to start. I have so much that I want to tell you. So much that you need to know about me." I'm scared at the prospect of telling Emily the untellable.

"Start where it doesn't hurt," she tells me, and I instantly think of Liam and his exact words to me only hours ago. Our time together feels like centuries ago.

"'If I Could Turn Back Time[50]' by Cher," I instantly say, which makes us both smile through the tears. When shit gets real, we go '80s. I take her hands in mine and I begin rewinding to that night I first met the man I thought would be my everything.

Sara

"What Kind Of Fool[52]" by Barbra Streisand & Barry Gibb

Emily and I have spent the last hour huddled in bed under the covers, making up for years of me being a stupid cow and keeping shit from her. I've described for her like I did for Liam how I first met Jeffery that night Eddie took us out to that club. I told her how I attacked him when he came to my room that night, and I then confessed to lying about having any interaction with him until he came to my sweet sixteen party a year later. I've told her everything up to my eighteenth birthday.

I then described club Lunna and that night I decided to celebrate alone and make all my lies a reality. I even told her about Phillip Dashell, which made her cringe thinking that I could've been involved with him.

"Such a small world we live in. You encountered one of Louis' then best friend over a year before he and I ever met." She still hasn't asked me anything about Liam and I don't want to go off course and start describing that train wreck, yet. We need to deal with one disaster at a time. Louis has peeked in twice already and sent in sandwiches with full tea service for us, which we devoured. I guess getting all worked up emotionally builds up a good appetite.

I continue telling Em what happened once Phillip put me in a cab to go home, and I remember one of the most important nights of my life.

I finally got home that dreadful, cold night. After the way I'd spoken to Jeff on the phone, I was sure he'd already left and would want nothing to do with me, but I was very wrong. My response must've fueled him; he was a man on a mission.

When the cab pulled up to my house before I could get out, Jeff opened the door and got in. He gave the cab driver an address and off we went. I remember that cab ride like it was yesterday. Even after my traumatizing evening with Phillip, I was still excited to be this close to the boy that I'd lied and fantasied about for years. He looked furious with me, but he was still the most beautiful thing I'd ever seen. He was all mine; he just didn't know it yet. I replayed in my head the things he and I did in the fictional world I'd created for us. This was only the third time I'd seen him in three years, yet I felt like I knew him better than I knew myself.

I remember Jeff finally speaking, and the first thing he said to me was, "Am I too late?"

I looked at him, not understanding his question one bit. What was he too late for my birthday? So I said, "Yes, you're too late."

He closed his eyes as if I had just said the worst thing I could possibly say. I couldn't understand what he was freaking out about, but then it hit me! He was asking if I slept with Phillip. I started panicking and got closer to him to make sure he didn't think that I had just had sex.

"NO! NO! I didn't have sex with him! I pushed him away, I

didn't want him—he wasn't you! I just want you." I remember frantically trying to make him understand.

He looked at me and I looked at him, and I guess you could say that was the beginning of the end for us. From that moment on, I haven't made it through a single day without thinking about him. When we finally came crashing down on each other, we were like two starving animals. That kiss in the back of the cab was beyond intense, it was a hunger three years in the making. I straddled him, letting him know he could have all of me. We weren't thinking, we weren't fighting; our feelings were on auto-pilot. I had no doubt in my mind that Jeffery Rossi was all mine. There wasn't a possibility that we wouldn't end up together after that night.

That was the day I lost everything. Everything I thought was rightfully mine was only an illusion. It's the part of my story where things got interesting and where I should've let my best friend tell me to run and never look back.

"Sara, I waited so long for this. How am supposed to leave you and go back to school?" Jeff asked me after we'd made love for the second time that night. *The first time I was in pain, but the second time was heaven. The way we fit together was perfection.*

We were in an apartment in the village that had a brand new mattress on the floor in the middle of the living room and one lonely chair by the window. The place was tiny; the size of my bedroom, but it was his and I thought it was the most roman- tic thing in the world. Jeff and my brother were still away in law school and he'd rented that apartment so he could stay in the city close to me. Well, that's what I thought, anyway.

"When will I see you again? Will you call me? Can I tell

people we're together?" I rambled off all these questions to him. I'd just had sex with the person I was infatuated with and I was giddy with excitement. I couldn't wait to tell the whole world about it. I came up with songs that would perfectly describe my night. I wouldn't have to lie about sex anymore! I'd actually know what I was talking about from experience.

I remember looking into his eyes, admiring their dual colors and wondering if our kids would have two different eye colors, too. I just wished I could see these beautifully peculiar eyes every day for eternity. His answers to my simple questions should've told me something was off.

"Let me work out a few things before we start telling everybody that we're exclusive and together. I don't want your brother to fuck me up. I'll find the right time and tell him, my way. Meanwhile, we can use this place and I'll try to come every weekend if I can."

And before I could react, he had me moaning again. To an eighteen-year-old girl, his response made sense. I did what he said and didn't tell anybody about us. I would wait to get the green light from him and then shout my love for him from the rooftops.

He came almost every week and I'd never felt more loved and adored in my whole life. He was amazing, sweet, and gentle in bed. He kept promising me the world and describing what our life would be like, endlessly feeding me hope. I could picture my whole life with him. I imagined my future children growing up together with your children. My life would be beautiful and I'd get to share it with the only man I ever loved since I was fifteen.

It was a dream, but it wasn't meant to be my dream.

We had this secret love affair for over a year. He kept saying it wasn't wise to tell Eddie, because he wouldn't understand, since I was still technically in high school. I kinda sorta agreed with him. He was my whole life; I saw him at least three times a month, sometimes for two days at a time. When we'd be together in our apartment nothing and no one seemed to matter but us.

A month before he was supposed to graduate, he stopped calling me. I waited at that apartment for days and he never showed up. I worried something had happened to him so I called Eddie to see if I could get some information; after all, they were roommates. Eddie picked up the phone and told me he was in the middle of a big celebration with Jeff and he couldn't talk, but he'd call me back soon. When he said he and Jeff were celebrating, I was beyond angry—I was enraged. I must've left Jeffery at least three voice messages a day. I would cry myself to sleep every night because I didn't know what I did wrong. I decided not to go to my brother's graduation, I faked a cold; I couldn't deal with seeing Jeff after being ignored for over a month.

But he finally came to see me right after our high school graduation in June. He said we needed to talk. I needed closure after not speaking with him for over a month with no explanation. I wanted to tell him to go fuck himself, I wanted to tell him to forget he ever knew me and never say my name again, but I couldn't; he was my everything. He was my only truth in my world of lies and I couldn't be smart. I was in love.

We drove to his poor excuse for a love pad to talk. After staring at each other for an hour, he finally started talking. "While I was waiting for you to grow up, I was having relations with this girl. She helped me in school and she was there when I couldn't have you. I was going to break up with her once we graduated but something happened."

As he told me this, I could feel vomit rising from my stomach and my legs began to give out from under me. I remember thinking that this is all one big joke. I mean, he couldn't fake what we had, right? I didn't imagine it, right? I didn't make it up. It was all real! He waited for me, I waited for him; he loved me, I loved him. What the fuck was he talking about? We were meant to be. Why was he telling me about some girl? If he had to fuck somebody while he waited for me I didn't need to know about it.

"*Sara, say something. I'm sorry, but I didn't know how to tell you.*" *He then added,* "*Jacqueline knows nothing about you.*"

When he gave the nameless girl a name, it became infinitely more painful. With every word out of his mouth, I died a little more. Once I stopped free falling off a cliff and finally worked through the haze, I started demanding some answers.

"*Jeff, we've been making love for over a year. Why didn't you break up with her? You said you loved me. You said you waited for me.*" *I was still a child asking stupid questions from the person I had entrusted with my heart.*

"*Sara, I don't love her like I love you. You are everything to me, but every time I tried to break up with her, something came up, something that I needed her help with. I was just using her and I didn't think it was anything serious. I was about to finally end it about a month ago when her father came to see me.*"

I remember Jeff's eyes started to twitch as he told me the next part of his sordid tale.

"*He offered me the job of a lifetime once I graduated, and a partnership in his firm. People who graduate law school work years for that kind of opportunity and he was just giving it to me. He started telling me how he knew that his daughter and I were very much in love and he and his wife were very happy Jacqueline and I found each other. I was about to tell him that Jacqueline and I weren't serious, when he told me that his beloved only daughter was very sick. That she was going to break up with me because she was diagnosed with late stage cervical cancer and the doctors didn't think she had long to live. Her father was shaking and crying as he told me this horrible news. He said he knew we'd been seeing each other, and since her future wasn't promised, he wanted me to marry his daughter right away. He and his wife would take care of everything, they just wanted to give their only daughter a few last happy memories.*"

I recall wondering if this was part of some soap opera or a joke. This shit didn't really happen.

"So what did you tell him?" I probed, as if I didn't already know the answer. "Jeff, are you telling me you're engaged?" I was on the verge of having a mental breakdown if he told me that he put a ring on her finger instead of mine.

He nodded. "What was I supposed to do? Break up with her and let her die alone? If I told her about us, it would kill her, and then what? I would be an asshole and lose the job of a lifetime. You're too young to even think about marriage, so I did the right thing. I will give this poor girl a few happy memories for a few months, or as long as she has left to live, and then you and I will have a lifetime to be together."

He held my face in his hands and kissed my lips, telling me how this was the right thing to do. Why hurt a dying girl if he could just make the last month or year of her life beautiful, and then we would benefit our whole lives from this one right thing. "Sara, I love you," he said. "I will always choose you, but this is different. This isn't about making a choice, it's about doing the right thing."

He made love to me that day for hours, promising me paradise with every kiss, every trusting word. It all made perfect sense when he explained it. He would marry Jacqueline, take care of her, and give her a few beautiful memories while I went to school. Once I finished, we would pick up where we left off. It was a brilliant plan. He just didn't take into account that I was the girl dying inside, not Jacqueline.

Sara

"Live To Tell[53]" by Madonna

"You think I'm an idiot, right?" I ask Emily, fully aware of how stupid and juvenile everything I just told her must sound. "You think I'm a dumb cow, don't you? It's okay; just say it! I think I'm a dumb cow at least twice a day." The truth is I think I'm a dumb cow at least once an hour.

"Shut up, you're a dumb cow for thinking that I think you're a dumb cow. I totally get it! When you're in love shit that sounds crazy to someone else seems perfectly normal to you because you're in a red fog. Do you remember when Louis and I first met? We used zero common sense. We just jumped and I agreed to marry him after knowing him for only a handful of weeks. It wasn't logical; it was love! I don't think you're an idiot, but in hindsight, you ended up with nothing but promises.

"Sara, you need to tell me more. I need to know what happened once you graduated. I understand that you and he were always together, but tell me what transpired once you figured out that his wife wouldn't be dying?" Em closes her eyes as she says it and quickly corrects herself. "I meant to say, what would happen to your plans if she got better and lived?"

"It sounds awful, I know, and I've hated myself for years

255

every time he'd tell me that she was doing better and that the doctors gave her a good prognosis. I would pretend that it was great news but I was fading; her living meant us dying. I'm not a monster, I didn't want the poor girl to die; she went through so much! But her getting better directly translated into Jeff and I never being together like we've always imagined.

"Remember that apartment I told you he had in the village? He ended up buying three more apartments in that building and combining them and that was 'our' place. I would go there every night and wait for him until he'd come see me. For years, her health was always in limbo. She would get better and then something would set her back. It wasn't like her doctors said she'd live to be a hundred. If either one of us believed she would recover and go on to have a normal life, we wouldn't have continued our affair. We didn't think it was an affair until it was. We became liars and cheaters.

"She also really wanted to give him kids. Jeff used to ask me if he and Jacqueline had children, and if and when she passed away, would I love those kids as if they were my own. I would always answer 'no.' I mean, obviously I would still love them, but I wanted us to have our own kids. They tried for years and couldn't have kids; even though she didn't have a hysterectomy, she still wasn't fertile. They were going to use a surrogate and Jeff's sperm so at least he would be the biological father. It was my idea to be the egg donor. Why should they use someone else's eggs when I had perfectly healthy unused eggs waiting for him anyway? My logic was once Jacqueline was gone, those kids would be ours in every sense of the word.

"We had twins, Em! Can you imagine...I'm biologically someone's mother? Well, not emotionally or socially, but physically they're made from my DNA. Two fools who loved each other too much to stop and think about the consequences made those two beautiful kids. Jeff promised me I could name them Juliet and Jacob. I call them 'JJ.' It gives me a chance to say their names all the time and nobody knows that I'm talking about my family—Jeff, Julie, and Jacob! Only you, me, and Jeff know about this."

I look up at Emily, wondering how psychotic she now thinks my life is.

"Wow!" she exclaims.

"Yeah, wow is right. Welcome to the fucked-up world I created for myself. Would you like to see pictures?" I ask her, excited for the first time in my life about having someone other than myself to share my kids with. I've never shown their pictures to anyone. My parents don't know they're grandparents; my brother doesn't know he's an uncle. But finally, my best friend knows.

"Yes, of course! What kind of question is that?" Emily answers and I leap off the bed to find my phone. I get back and start showing my best friend what my babies look like. Juliet looks just like Jeff, with blue eyes and dark almost black hair. Jacob is all me. His hair is dirty blond and he has a lighter version of my eye color but his features and his lips and chin are all me. They don't look like twins at all. Jacob looks much older than Juliet. Emily cries as she goes through my pictures. I probably have thousands of photos of my beautiful little babies.

"Sara, there are so many pictures here," she says in shock, as though she thought I would show her just one lonely picture. I have five years' worth of priceless memories captured in pictures and video—my reasons to live.

"He sends me a few every day and I see them every morning when they go to work and school. I love them; they're perfect. They're my life and they're amazing! I've never held them or met them in person, but every minute I wish to one day be able to hug them. What would it feel like to touch them?" I cry as I always do when I think about JJ, and how I'll never be a part of their lives while she's alive. "I'm only crying because I feel sorry for myself, but I know they have a great life; I see it every day."

Emily wails, probably imagining what it would be like watching her children grow and be raised by someone else. "Why hasn't Jeff let you meet them?" she questions between sobs.

"We both decided it would be too painful." Which is the ugly truth. "I think if I ever had the chance to hold them, I would never be able to let them go."

"Why did you marry Gavin?" she finally asks me, changing the subject so we can catch our breath. Em hated Gavin, so I knew she would need to address that disastrous portion of my life.

"He needed to be married to get his parents off his back and release some of his frozen funds. They thought he was spending all his loot on whores and parties, and he was! He's a good guy to know but not to marry. Believe me, no normal woman would agree to marry him. We had an agreement to stay married for five years, but once we got hitched, his parents released his trust funds and his lifestyle choices made me look like a total idiot. I couldn't even pretend we were married. He said that I was ruining his vibe because I scared his girlfriends off. Relax, don't give me that look, I've never even slept with him. All we did was kiss in front of people and even that was faked most of the time. We were just helping each other out. I helped get his uptight parents off his back and he helped me momentarily make Jeff believe that it was over between us. I wanted Jeff to see that I'd moved on and that I wasn't that stupid twat who'd wait for him forever.

"I know what you think," I say, looking at Emily. "You think that Jeff is horrible. You think he tricked me into being the other woman. Well, he didn't! I really believe our reality is a product of stupid choices made with the best intentions. Em, I promise you I always felt loved and adored by him...it's only when he went back home to his family that I felt alone and unwanted. He thought he was doing the right thing by accepting a job and standing by a sick girl. He didn't fathom that his chivalrous choice would jeopardize our future. The problem was, as he was trying to do the right thing and be a good guy, I believe he fell in love with her, too. She's a good girl and God knows she's been through hell. I know when we're together, he feels guilty for loving her enough not to leave her and cause her more pain."

"But what about you?" Emily says in a small voice. "Doesn't he love you enough to stop hurting you? He has his family—with your help—and now he needs to love you enough to let you start your own family. He needs to love you enough to let you go! I want you to know what it's like to hold your own children in your arms. I don't want you living your life by watching a home from the outside. You are kind, beautiful and smart and any child would be lucky to have you as their mother. You need to start again. A blank page with no secrets, no lies, no Jeffery, just Sara!"

Sara

"We Belong[54]" by Pat Benatar

Unburdening my conscience and telling Emily everything feels fucking exhilarating! The last twenty-four hours have turned my whole life upside down and yet it's the most right my life has ever been. I thought she would hate me, I was sure she would spit in my face and cuss me out and tell me that she's embarrassed to even know me. But Emily is right here, holding my hand and supporting me, loving me, after I've done nothing but lie to her. The images of my kids dance around in my head and it doesn't hurt so much now, knowing I can talk about them and share them with Em without her judging me. I should probably go and offer a sacrifice somewhere to thank whoever or whatever decided that I deserve to have her in my life. Having her near is everything.

Liam's eyes and beautiful smile keep coming into view and I physically miss his presence, as ridiculous as that may sound. I wish he were still here. I am beyond thankful I got the chance to disclose the truth to Emily first, but I wish he'd given me the opportunity to tell him everything as well. He's the only man besides Jeffery I've ever had this unexplainable bond with. But he left me, ran away like I knew he would. I don't even blame him. I wouldn't wish me and my problems on anybody, let alone a nice guy like him. He has enough of his own issues to work through, he doesn't need to try and understand mine.

Emily is still looking through my phone at all the pictures I've collected over the years of Juliet and Jacob. She finally tears her eyes away from the screen and pins me down with her baby blues, saying, "William Knight... Start talking."

I'm scared because I can't tell if she's mad or curious or both. "I'll tell you whatever you want to know! But, promise to not go ape shit or try to murder me until I finish telling you everything."

She begrudgingly nods. The poor girl knew she signed up for crazy the day she agreed to be my best friend. That's it, I promise from now on to always tell her everything, good or bad, she can handle it.

"The truth is, I can't stop thinking about that damn British fool, Em. It all started by me trying to do the right thing, as usual, and get rid of him for you. At first, it was all about you and him and his feelings for you, and I don't know how and when, but something just shifted and started happening between us. You must believe that my only agenda was to get him out of your lives. I didn't want him to try and come between you and Louis, not that he could. You see, I had a whole plan worked out to get him to talk to me about what happened that night with you. And once he revealed what you and I wanted to know, I was hoping to convince him to go back to wherever he came from.

"The good news is I got him to talk, but the bad news is, you're not going to like what he told me. You should know that something did happen in St. Lucia, whether you remember it or not. The two of you didn't just fall asleep in the same bed, you were intimate that night you got trashed. I'm almost a hundred percent sure you didn't fuck each other, but he did touch you and I'm pretty sure some kind of orgasm inducing activity was involved."

I wait for Emily to freak out, but she's calm and poised and strangely, doesn't react at all so I keep going.

"I can also promise you that he has no intention of ever publishing his sister's book. He just wanted to be your hero, and it was kinda sorta sweet the way he wanted to protect you from Louis. He's a bit confused about who the real villain is, but in his defense, he only has his sister's accounts and narrations and her horrible death to go by. He wanted to believe that Louis was this horrible guy that cheated and sexually abused her and you. He wanted someone other than himself to hate for failing to save Isabella. I tried to explain to him how great my friend-in-law actually is without hurting him too much. I did my best to enlighten him as to how much Louis loves you and the kids, and the kind of love you guys share. I think he was starting to understand."

I hope she knows I had really done it for her. My intentions were honorable; I wanted to help them.

"Then Louis came and brought that video you told me about. We were going to watch it together, and everything would make sense and be okay. I was hoping that footage would make him understand that Louis isn't a monster and that Isabella died because she was mentally unwell, and no one is to blame. However, before we got a chance to watch it and allay his worries, things started escalating fast between us. He was making me feel things that I had no right feeling and I think he felt them, too."

I tell Emily how Liam and I came close to having sex and how Jeffery appeared and the shit show that ensued. I know I left out just how intimate Liam and I really got but she doesn't need a detailed account of that. I'm sure I gave her enough information to make her poor head spin. We're both quiet and I think I'm just waiting for her to finally run away, too. I've said it all. Emily needs to say something and give me a freaking clue as to how she feels about me being with Liam.

"Okay, now *you* need to promise to not be mad at *me*," she says, and I nod. "I heard almost everything. Well, Louis heard everything first. This whole place is under video and audio surveillance on all three floors. He wasn't trying to snoop or spy or intrude in any creepy way, but Louis was worried and when he told me about you being here alone with Will, and Jeffery coming back to see you, I was too! Don't worry, he didn't watch any footage, but he heard everything. He told me about all the conversations you and Will—or Liam—had since this morning.

"After Louis came to give you the video, Miguel, the manager, informed him that Jeffery was coming up to see you. He knew you were with Will, so he decided to tell me what was going on and intervene to make sure nobody got hurt. I was going to let you know we were here but then Louis talked me into letting you guys work things out for yourselves first, knowing we'd be outside in case you needed our help. I'm sorry," she says and as mad as I probably should be, knowing that she and her husband have been eavesdropping on Liam and me, I'm not! Those two love me enough to worry about my wellbeing. Louis and Emily Bruel stopped their lives to make sure I was okay. If that's not love, I don't know what is.

I hug her and say, "'Endless Love[55]' by Diana Ross and Lionel Richie."

"Ditto and 'Always On My Mind[56]' by Willie Nelson."

"Emily Marcus Bruel, you are and will always be my first love. 'We Belong[54]' by Pat Benatar."

Liam

"Sara[57]" by Jefferson Starship

"**M**r. Knight, this is the second ticket this lovely police officer has written us. Shall I move the car or continue to stand here and smile?" the driver questions me for the second time.

"Don't you dare move this car! I'm not going anywhere until I see her leave that bloody building," I bark, not sure why I'm taking my anger out on my poor driver. He's had to put up with my cross mood for weeks, ever since I came back to this dreadful city. New York hates me and has always triggered nothing but pain for my family. He nods and accepts another citation from the livid old bill who very colorfully threatened to have our Benz towed. I don't care! I only care about seeing who leaves this wretched hotel. The way our car is positioned, I have both hotel exits in perfect view and I won't miss a thing.

I've gone through at least twenty different emotions over the past two hours I've been sitting here physically trying to contain myself from running back up to fetch her. When I first heard Jeff, or the love of her life as she refers to him as, mention that they have children together, I was certain it was a hallucination. I mean, bloody come on, if they had children, she'd have told me, wouldn't she? Does she think me that thick? Once his words penetrated the proper side of my brain, I began to operate on autopilot. All I wanted to do was run away and never look back, pretend the last twenty-four hours were all a bad dream.

Then, to make sure I lose the plot, after weeks of waiting, I finally see Emily. But since fate is a blind whore with mental disease, she had to make sure I saw her with Louis, crying. I didn't feel the way I'd imagined I'd feel seeing them together. All I could think when I saw Emily upset and in tears was, *Please take care of Sara... Please don't be hard on Sara... Please don't hurt my Sara more than I just did.* Which only confirms that I must be delusional to be infatuated with yet another unattainable woman: Sara, a girl I clearly know close to nothing about, who's told me about a whoreson she loves, a dickhead that abandons her in the middle of the night, with whom she happens to also have children. It's safe to say I'm well past livid. I'm not even sure my body has gotten enough oxygen since I haven't been able to breathe properly; I'm just numb. Words mean nothing, they're just an arrangement of letters, and yet I'm certain they just did more damage than any bullet ever could.

I'm still here at the corner of 5th Avenue and 61st Street waiting for her like a lifeless loon. She pulls every string in my heart and by walking away, I just stretched those strings even tighter. The poor girl had begged me to stay. I can hear her tormented voice echoing in my head as she yelled after me. She was crying. I'm no different than him; I also made her cry. But she must understand I couldn't just bloody stand there and hash things out in front of that bastard. I couldn't have her announce that she chooses him right to my face; I wouldn't survive it. Not her, I couldn't let her do that to me. How can I expect her to choose me if they have children together and they have a history? What if he was her husband? *Fuck!*

Now that I've had a few hours to be away from Sara and simmer, I'm rather upset with myself. I acted cowardly—not like a Knight, not even like a man. Jeffery Rossi may be a monumental arsehole, but he continued to fight for her, he was ready to do or say anything to intimidate me and break the bond he felt we shared, and he did. If he was our first test, then I failed miserably; crash and burn fail. She begged me to stay, why didn't I listen? Why did I leave her? She deserves a man who will fight for her. I reckon she needs a real man and not a wally like me. I only wanted to make those beautiful, sad eyes happy, and yet I made everything infinitely worse. I fucking ran the first chance I got.

I'm buggered and famished and logic tells me to leave. I had my chance with her and I handed her back to him. I don't deserve Sara, and she certainly deserves much more than me. Why am I still sitting here, holding on to hope? Hope is gone. Is this my family's curse—to love and never be loved back? I only need to see my broken ballerina one last time to say goodbye. She won't know I said goodbye and she will always think me a coward, but I'll see her and know I did the right thing by handing her back to him.

At first, I felt lied to and outplayed by her. She should've been the one to tell me that she shared children with him. I never asked her if she was a mother or someone's wife, I just assumed she was mine for the taking. I just assumed it would be okay to love her. I don't fancy being like everyone else she fibbed to her whole life. *She lied!* Even if this was a lie of omission, I still feel lied to and it hurts terribly. But I know that it's me who made everything much worse for her, like I always do. I'm certain she felt what I felt because her words, or lack of words, may have been a fib but her eyes bared the truth. I should face it that I'm as much of a liar as she is, promising a safe haven and at first sign of difficulty, scurrying away. I did the square thing; she belongs with the father of her children, the one who stayed to fight for her. I'm no good for her. I just pray he looks after her the way a beautiful fragile ballerina ought to be handled…with loving care.

Once I see them walk out together, back to their children, I will allow myself to finally close my eyes on Sara and the delusional fantasy I concocted with her. I am, after all, William Spencer Knight! No, I'm *The* William Spencer Knight! I am the last fucking Knight left. I don't need her or anybody else's love; I have responsibilities and obligations that I should be attending to, for Christ's sake. It's time I forget that only hours ago I was a normal bloke named Liam who promised a beautiful girl named Sara a fresh start and a real place to call home. She doesn't need me; she already has a home.

As the hours melt so does my resolve and I decide that nobody is going to save me, she won't come running out looking for me. This is life, not Hollywood. I must cease looking for love when it's all a bloody illusion.

"Mark! Go! I'm ready to leave," I say to my driver and he drives us into New York City traffic. He takes me farther and farther away from her and it stings like hundreds of knives piercing through me. It becomes tougher to take a full breath in as the distance between us grows. I can't deny that I'm in pain knowing I have to leave her behind. The urge to cry slowly chokes me. It's the kind of pain you feel when you've done your best and still failed the most important test of your life. I get enough air to say, *"Goodbye Sara"* out loud to no one in particular but myself. I've been thinking it over and over, but saying it to the universe makes it real. I'm doing the right thing; she deserves someone who can say goodbye to her beautiful eyes like a man, not in the backseat of a car to the ghost of her. I am beneath her, just a delusional coward.

"We're here, Mr. Knight. Your jet should be all ready to go when you are. Have a safe trip home."

One Month Later

Sara

"Here I Go Again[58]" by Whitesnake

"Sara Klein, please initial and sign right here." My brother points to an empty line at the end of a long contract he's just spent the last twenty minutes reading and explaining to a room full of attorneys. I sign my name with a shaky hand and look up to see Jeffery studying me before meeting my gaze and looking away. Emily is at my side, squeezing my left hand, which she hasn't let go of since the moment we arrived. *I can do this... I'm not alone.*

This has been a difficult and tumultuous month in my life. Not that my whole life has been peaches and cream, but the last four weeks have brought a different kind of pain that I had to learn to endure—finally speaking the truth out loud and dealing with the consequences. *There will be no more lies,* I chant to myself. The biggest lie and truth of my life sits across a long table in a cold, opulent boardroom with his loving wife by his side. I finally understand that there isn't always a clear winner or loser when it comes to matters of the heart. Love sometimes annihilates all involved and everybody loses. Our vicious, obsessive affair is finally over and brought to light. We've sold, or to be more exact, I've sold *our* apartment, which had legally been mine, thereby dissolving any remnant of our lies. Jeffery won't have me as a crutch anymore, but he does get to keep his understanding saint of a wife, who, like me, has endured a hard road loving him. And he has our children to come home to.

I sit ten feet away and watch them together, and strangely, I still don't feel like a loser in this game. I look down at the document I've just signed and smile at having this small victory for myself: a gift, a sliver of hope, and acknowledgment at being named one of three legal guardians for my biological children. I've relinquished the opportunity to go meet my beautiful Jacob and Juliet because I want them to continue living a normal life. A life in which they come home to the loving mother and father they've known their whole lives. They will have the truth presented to them once they reach the age of eighteen; that Sara Klein and their father Jeffery Rossi are their biological parents. It may not seem like much, but it's the truth and that's everything to me.

I get to start over, but I get to do it honestly. I've spent the last four weeks cleaning up the dusty shelves in my heart and making room for me. I choose me. I choose to love me and make sure that I will be good to me. I have everything I need, and most importantly, I have my friends and family to support me every step of the way. I look up and see my brother wink and smile my way.

I have decided to return to London. I love it and feel most at home there, even more so than in New York. I will miss living close to my children and seeing my best friend, but ultimately, it's the right choice for my future and my sanity. I am still a partner at my ex-husband's law firm, and I will continue to practice law from our London headquarters, which are far superior to our New York offices. I've finally used my negotiation skills to reach a deal with Gavin for the transfer and ownership of the apartment in London, since he sold our New York digs right from under my nose. I have enough dirt on him that he agreed to almost everything. I will not be a victim any longer, I know what's lawfully mine and I will from this day on, demand what's best for me.

My parents have announced their separation, which is also a kind of end to a lie I've kept all my life. If it weren't for our babies, I'd be able to cut all ties with Jeff; well, almost all ties. I still can't let go of his old grey T-shirt; I can't fall asleep without it. But I'm proud of myself for the choice I made when Jeff was prepared to leave his wife and his home to start a new life with me, but I refused. I did enough damage and I own the role I've played in his bad decisions and I don't want to hurt anybody else anymore, myself included. He finally chose me, but I chose myself. I've made amends with karma, because looking at my children, I understand they're the reason Jeffery and I met and I wouldn't change a thing, I love and will continue to love their father, but I love them and me more. I can leave JJ knowing that they have a beautiful, loving family, and I've made peace with the fact that at this point, their lives don't include me. I will always be their mother and I will forever be here for them, and finally the world knows that I had a hand in creating them.

Liam still frequents my thoughts and dreams. I try not to dwell on him if I can help it, but my mind always wonders back to our short encounter. As much as my body longs for him, I'm glad he never came back for me. I'm sure someone more worthy than me is out there for him. I hope he finds the peace and the love he so desperately craves from a nice girl with a clean past. I pray that the universe has a good life in store for him after all the tragedies he and his family had to endure.

I've watched the video of Louis and Isabella. I've watched it countless times, always learning something new. I wish for Liam to one day see this footage for himself; it would help him let go of some of his misplaced hurt and pain. Seeing Liam's beautiful sister for the first time, knowing her tragic end, was an incredibly painful experience, but it brought closure to her story for me. Isabella Knight was, in fact, a stunning woman and in many ways reminds me of her beautiful brother. The footage clearly shows Louis having a fight with her in his apartment, telling Isa that he would not take part in any crazy orgy she'd orchestrated on his behalf. He pleaded with her, cautioning her to stop trying to get attention from the wrong people and start respecting herself more. He even threatened to call her father if she didn't start taking better care of herself. He was worried about her drug use and the company she kept. He practically begged her not to get involved with men that proposed short-term affection and lived a despicable kind of life that involved drugs and unsafe, dangerous sex.

The tape also shows Isabella's plea-bargain with Louis, which was that if he declared to all his friends that he loved her, only then would she call everything off. It's clear that Isabella Knight had tried to manipulate Louis Bruel to commit and become involved with her as more than just a friend. Louis apologized over and over and tried, but failed, to explain to Isa that he cared for her as a friend and not as a lover. He informed her that Phillip had real feelings for her and that she should stop taunting him and give him a chance. The footage clearly shows she had real psychological problems when she began threatening to destroy Louis' career and kill herself and him if he didn't continue to have sex with her and tell her that he loved her. I believe that Louis was present at that private, debauched party that Liam had pictures of to make sure that nothing bad happened to Isabella, because he knew she wasn't well. She definitely wasn't his girlfriend, but he still felt responsible for her because she cared about him. Louis Bruel may be many things, but he's still a good guy.

I no longer speak '80s with Em since our language's inception was the result of an alibi needed for my web of lies. We speak the truth now and I don't need to hide behind lyrics anymore. We sometimes slip and digress back to our beloved lyrical dialect, but most of the time, we're good. I'm excited for this new chapter in my life and I can't wait to see what the future holds for me.

One Month Later

Liam

"Still Loving You[59]" by The Scorpions

I left London almost two years ago—a place I once called home. It won't ever feel like home again, but at least I can go see my sister's resting place whenever I please. I've had several meetings with my father now that we're in the same country. He acts as if nothing has happened to our broken family, as if it's no big deal that we haven't spoken to one another since my sister was laid to rest. I can't say that he treats me poorly; he just treats me like one of his employees and not like his only son. Not once has he gone off course to ask if I'm all right, or how I'm doing and what's new in my life. My mum is always too busy for us to meet; she has too many obligations to try and fit her only child in for a visit. I'm not cross with her, and I love her enough to comprehend that she just can't stand to look at me and see my sister's blue eyes gazing back at her. I've been to Isa's grave five times in the last two weeks because although she doesn't ask after my wellbeing, she does listen, and I feel most loved being at her side.

Two months ago, when I left New York, I immediately decided to head back to St. Lucia. It may seem juvenile and cowardly, but that's the place I run away to when my life starts spinning out of control. I think about Sara every minute of every hour of every day. I allowed the most beautifully imperfect creature I've ever met to slip away. I was a fool and I don't deserve her. I would've stayed in St. Lucia forever if I wasn't the majority shareholder in my family's empire.

It's a bit odd that there are over eight million people in London but I have a reoccurring hallucination of seeing her pass me on the street, which I realize is preposterous since I'm in London while she's in bloody New York City, but my mind sees her everywhere. For instance, just this morning as I left my flat on One Hyde Park, I could bet my left nut I saw Sara cross the road. I am fully aware that I may require treatment for my overactive imagination, but I can't fucking help it. I walk along shops on Knightsbridge and imagine Sara wearing dresses I spy in the Harvey Nichols store windows. I even took a liking to drinking tea with milk and two sugars, and my new dietary intake includes a chocolate croissant for breakfast. I regret not asking her more questions; I wish I knew more about her like what types of food she fancies, whether she drinks red or white wine, if she likes dogs. I try to keep her memory alive along with all her little idiosyncrasies; the small little nuances that help me keep her close. I don't reckon I'll ever find another person that will compel me to feel what Sara made me feel in a handful of hours. Allowing myself to think about her gives me a reason to go on, knowing she's out there, hopefully happy. I found her Instagram account and I frequent it every chance I get like the proper stalker that I am, hoping I may catch a small glimpse into a life I yearn to be a part of.

I haven't called a soul to announce my return to London; I don't fancy being social and when I catch my reflection in the mirror, I don't quite recognize myself. I'm not myself. I left my heart in New York, specifically in Louis Bruel's penthouse, and I doubt I'll ever get it back. I did my due diligence and tried to work her out of my system. I got pissed and high, tried banging a pretty girl as soon as I got back to La Spa, and still bloody dreamt of nothing but Sara and those fucking eyes. I know that she and Jeffery Rossi are not and have never been married. Jeff is married to some woman named Jacqueline and they have two offspring.

There is no record of Sara and Jeffery being involved any-where except in my mind as I reminisce about the night I watched him bang her. I replay that scene over and over in my head to punish myself for my careless callousness with her. She must surely be his longtime mistress and that would absolutely make sense with the few things she did reference about how the truth getting leaked would potentially harm him. I found out she was, in fact, married, here in London, but to some bastard named Gavin Masters. I battle with myself every morning and every night to stay put and not try to ring her, or go find her to try and save her again, but then I recall the stellar job I did the first time around. She doesn't need a hero like me; she needed a man, not a coward. A real man would've waited to hear his lover give rea-son and not run like a child at the first sign of trouble. I'm left to drown in a sea of queries, but no one to offer any explanations to save me.

It's lunchtime and I've decided to take my second cup of tea with milk and two sugars and get some highly polluted air on Piccadilly Circus, right outside my office, which actually seems on the tame side today. I fancy coming here, especially early in the morning, and I take a seat by the statue of Eros. Eros, or as the Yanks call him, Cupid, is the Greek God of love and I'm the

British fool of love; therefore, I feel we're old mates and he must understand me above all other inanimate objects. I laugh to myself as I hear my name being called; my name is rather common so it's usually someone other than me being beckoned.

"Will!"

I look around to see who has called my name and I see Emily, no longer *my* Emily, but Emily nevertheless.

"Hey, mate," I answer, getting up to go greet her and feel slightly at a loss for words. "Fancy seeing you here," I offer. I feel silly giving her a peck on the cheek so I decide on a friendly hug, which feels a bit less awkward. It's odd seeing Emily in London on fucking Piccadilly at the feet of Eros, no less. The last time I saw her, she was with her husband, crying while I ran away from my crumbling world. I wonder how her nutty prison ward let her out of his sight to come this far?

"It's nice to see you, William." She smiles and I instantly want to ask her about Sara, my Sara, but I can't and I won't.

"It's lovely seeing you, too. What brings you to West End, or London, I should say?" I hope and pray she came to find me and bring me news of Sara. I hope Sara's all right, I hope nothing bad happened to her. That stupid thought enters my mind and I unconsciously hold my breath.

"Louis had some business here and I came along to see how Sara was doing back at her old position. I'm sure you know she lives in London full time now. She also got her place in Mayfair back and she's working at the firm she owns with her ex. It's on Fleet Street. I'm actually headed to her office to have lunch with her."

I listen to Emily and study her face as she smiles with a knowing, conspiring smirk. I'm still not able to breathe; my heart beats funny and I don't reckon what this means. Should I ask Emily if she's here with Jeffery? *No, I can't ask that.* Should I ask Emily about their children? *No!* Truth is, I don't bloody care if she has children or not, if she'd have me, I'd take her with ten kids and all her baggage as long as there's a chance for us to get another try. I've thought of nothing but her. I close my eyes and picture her smile and I can't help but be giddy.

"You didn't know she was here?" she asks while I shake my head repeatedly.

I look over at the angel by my side, who yet again has brought me back to life. "What do I owe you?" I ask Emily, grateful for her existence.

"You brought me home to my family and I brought Sara home to you, I say we're even." She comes closer, handing me an envelope, then she takes a few steps up on the statue to reach my height and plants a kiss on my cheek, whispering, "'Broken Wings[60]' by Mr. Mister."

I look at her and answer back in her own tongue, clearly in reference to Sara and I, "Thank you for finding me, I can't stop thinking about her. 'Still Loving You[59]' by The Scorpions." I've actually been studying and I think I got it right when I'm rewarded with an even bigger smile and nod as she proceeds to walk away chanting, "*Yes, yes,*" over and over to herself.

"Will!" she yells, right before reaching her chauffeured Phantom waiting by the curb. "'Every Breath You Take[5]' by The Police, remember that." She makes the universal signal for "I'm watching you" right before entering her ride with none other than her husband, Louis Bruel, waiting, watching, and smiling from the backseat. *He loves her, how could he not?*

I look down at the envelope Emily entrusted in my possession, imagining millions of options as to its contents. I don't quite know what to do with my newfound knowledge of Sara being within my reach. I suddenly feel restless and my mind is already racing to see her. I smile because today is a good day. Today I was gifted with hope.

Ten Months Later

Sara

"The Winner Takes It All[61]" by Abba

Emily and Louis are coming into town this weekend and I can't wait for us to go out and catch up. I'm excited to finally start dating one of my former clients, Danny, a super sweet guy with whom I've been texting back and forth for over a month. Today is the one-year anniversary of my eviction from Gavin's place and thus a turning point in my life. I'm at a beautiful place right now and in a weird way, I have him to thank for kick starting me into a different lifestyle. I've finally stopped looking for someone to love me in order to validate my existence and I enjoy being on my own.

I talk to Jeffery once a week to find out how JJ are doing. He is where he belongs, with the woman and family he loves, and I will be okay one day. I don't resent Jacqueline anymore, I respect her and thank her for being nurturing to the many people we love in common. I think she's grateful to me in a fucked-up way for walking away and letting her keep her husband and children, and for not making a bad situation infinitely worse. I also, for the first time in my life, love my job and enjoy the people I work with. Eddie and Michelle promised to come spend New Year's Eve with me and I may go back to visit my folks for Thanksgiving if my work schedule allows it.

I honestly can't complain about a thing. Well, that's a lie. I can complain about being possessed by a person I met for five minutes and know nothing about, but it wouldn't do me any good. Time will heal everything, even my hopes to one day belong to Liam Knight. Emily brings him up all the time and I know they speak, which makes me extremely jealous, but this too shall pass. I know I shouldn't care, but I'm proud of Liam for making amends with Louis. I wish him well; however, I try to ensure I never hear about who he's with from Emily. I don't need a reminder of what's not mine. I told Em that I would prefer she not speak about him unless absolutely necessary because it hurts too much to pretend that I don't care, and she understands. I did enough research about him and Isabella to know exactly which hotels his family owns in London and around the world, and I will do my darnedest to never step foot in any of them.

I have this recurring dream that he and I bump into each other on the street and when our eyes meet, I always wake up. I wonder if I enter his thoughts as much as he invades mine? I wonder who gets to call him Liam and if he fixes her hair constantly? When I'm weak and lonely, I let myself enjoy his memory for a few moments of bliss before I talk myself back to reality. I still can't decide if it would've been better or worse if we'd actually had sex almost a year ago.

I've decided to treat myself to a special gift today. No one, not even Jeffery, has ever bought me a piece of jewelry, so I've elected to splurge and buy myself something ridiculously expensive and beautifully special to celebrate my emotional independence and for not telling a lie for a whole year. I'm proud of how far I've come and I'm okay with sharing these achievements with myself by myself. I decide to take the day off after lunch to find the perfect gift.

My career has completely and utterly monopolized all my free time this past year, which I'm thankful for, and this sporadic treat of walking the posh area of New Bond Street to find the perfect trinket for myself is a rarity. I wind up window-shopping in the most beautiful high-end jewelry stores in the world, trying to conceptualize what object would be the perfect symbol of my self-love and emotional emancipation. I pass Chopard and spy stunning watches and then I move over to Van Cleef & Arpels, with their beautiful Alhambra iconic flower pieces beckoning me. I decide to cross the street to window drool at the one and only Harry Winston, which is hands down every girl's fantasy shop. I'm sure most women dream of getting a diamond rock presented in a Harry Winston box, and although I can finally say out loud what I've held inside for years, acknowledging that I want a happily ever after and for someone to put a ring on it is still too painful. I'm aware that marriage may not be in the cards for me.

I stand at the window and study the exquisite fine jewelry gracing the small-framed vitrines as a guard at the door smiles when our eyes meet. I catch a glimpse of a man and a woman seated at a table inside the store inspecting jewels. I imagine how excited and happy the couple must be, probably choosing the perfect engagement ring to declare their love and commitment. I'm about to leave when the man turns slightly to look at the girl by his side and my heart withers when I see him. My heart. My poor heart, my poor stupid heart, my poor stupid worthless heart will never know love.

I've walked the streets of London for the last nine hours. I feel lost and numb. I don't need food or water or rest or a bathroom; I just need to disappear. Why am I surprised? Did I think I meant something to him? Did I think I was destined for something other than pain and disappointment? I've been put on this earth as a spectator. I see others being loved and cherished, building families, and raising their kids while I just watch and admire from afar. I've been barefoot for the last few hours, heels in hand, and I can't bring myself to go home because nothing feels like home.

It's almost midnight when my aching feet finally near my building. My phone has been vibrating in my attaché case for hours; it's Emily, no doubt, wondering why I haven't answered her texts, which have been coming in non-stop.

I answer, "Hello," and I know I sound exhausted.

"Hello, hello, you stupid cow, where have you been?" It's Emily, sounding wild and frantic, and well…like Emily.

"Sorry, long day. I'm a bit blue today. I've been aimlessly walking around trying to clear my head. What time are you and Louis arriving tomorrow?"

I hear her make some animal growling sound. "Fucking say it!" she barks.

"No, I won't. We swore we'd stop. I promise I'll be pink tomorrow, and by then, you'll be here and we can discuss this over drinks and sushi."

Emily is back to making possessed sounds on the other end of the line. "Sara, if you don't give me a song right now I will kill you and you won't see tomorrow, and that's a promise."

I'm too weak to argue or fight with angry Barbie so I just say, "'The Winner Takes It All[61]' by Abba."

"But you're the winner, right? You won! You get to take it all, right?" She sounds frantic and it's kinda sorta comical how she gets worked up over nothing.

"No, Em, I'm pretty sure I lost."

"You don't need Jeff. Listen to me, something a million times better than Jeffery is waiting for you. Please tell me you believe me," she says with such passion and conviction that it makes me smile and love her even more than I thought possible.

"Not Jeff, this isn't about him. I accidently talked myself into loving someone just as unattainable as Jeffery, and I know that it sounds ridiculous because of how he left me and never looked back, but I thought what we had was different and perhaps special and that he felt it, too...and maybe, just maybe he'd wake up one morning and come find me. But that will never happen." My voice cracks as a tear leaves my eyes and I start laughing at how stupid I'm being.

"Are you crying?" she asks and I shake my head, because I'm really not crying. I'm laughing and crying simultaneously, which is something totally different. "Go home, please. I don't understand why shit can't just go smoothly. But just get yourself home safely," Em mumbles and I'm thankful she's not pushing me to talk more because I'm wrecked.

"See you tomorrow. Have a safe flight and if you get a chance, grab me a couple cans of Bumble Bee tuna in spring water...I need to make myself a real tuna fish sandwich and I can't deal with the tuna here. Love ya, kiss the kids for me," I say and hang up just as I reach my building.

Tomorrow will be a better day, today just needs to end.

Liam

"Every Breath You Take[5]" by The Police

I'm at my usual table eating my usual chocolate croissant and sipping black tea with milk and two sugars. I wait almost every single morning at eight sharp at this tiny corner café across the street from her flat as I watch my beautiful ballerina head out to work. I've watched Sara transform before my eyes and become more beautiful than any woman I've ever known. Her hair is slowly becoming lighter and she always has a smile on her lips as she leaves for work. She doesn't seem like the sad girl I left with my heart back in New York almost a year ago. My day ends when I see the lights go off in her flat; only then can I rest, knowing she's in bed safe and sound and that I'll see her first thing in the morning.

She's been on several dates with various wankers in the past year. I've considered very hard accidentally plowing the bastards over with my car, but fortunately for me—and them—none of her dates ended with more than a friendly peck on the cheek. I've been testing myself. The easiest thing for me would've been to run to her and ask her for another chance, but the correct thing is to earn another chance with her. What I did to her and the way I abandoned her is unforgivable. She trusted me above her best mate and I demonstrated my disloyalty almost instantly.

She may not know it, but I'm courting her. We have been dating from the moment Emily informed me she was within reach. I know everything there is to know about her, from what and where she eats to what she drinks. I know which underground tube she rides to get to her firm and which co-workers she frequents the pub with after work. Her favorite store is Selfridge & Co. and I even know where she buys her knickers. She treats herself to flowers every Friday and walks into Hamley's toy shop at least once a week. She goes out to dinner on her own frequently and stares at her phone screen entranced for hours. I long to sit next to her, just be by her side and fix that hair that always falls into her eyes, but I haven't earned it yet. The bottom line is I'm in love with Sara Klein; she just doesn't know it.

I have been in contact with both Emily and Louis since watching and learning of the video footage of Isabella and Louis all those years ago. I forgave him and myself for failing to save my beautiful Isa. She had drug addiction issues that caused many of her heartaches and eventually took her life. I respect him for trying to help her and I've apologized to him on behalf of my sister for the turmoil she and I caused. About three months back, Louis paid me another visit that ended differently than our previous encounters. It actually ended with us visiting my sister's grave. I've told Emily of my feelings toward her best mate, which she urges I make known.

I've been studying and with Emily's help, I now speak fluent '80s. I know almost every song—well, every *important* song from that era, and I can recite the lyrics, and in most cases, I can even sing it. I long to be Sara's everything, not just her lover and partner. I must be her best mate and whatever language she speaks, I ought to speak as well. Tomorrow will be the one-year anniversary of our lives colliding at that restaurant within The Pierre hotel in New York City. I have a bloody plan that I can't wait to finally reveal to her. Tomorrow will be brilliant.

Liam

"Take On Me[36]" by A-Ha

You know you love someone when the thought of something bad happening to them paralyzes and hurts you more than the thought of anything bad happening to you. I had it all fucking figured out. Got dolled-up like a loon with my gift and speech and all systems were set to go, and yet I never once stopped to ponder that something could happen to her. That perhaps there were circumstances beyond my reach.

I don't bloody know where she is; it's not like her to not come home this late. She left work at noon and nobody—I mean, not one goddamn human—knows where Sara is. Emily and Louis are running around London trying to find her and I've been here, pacing aimlessly by her door for the past seven hours, scared to hell with my mind racing a million miles away. I've already called the police, they're on alert, but they can't claim her officially missing until twenty-four hours from the last time someone saw her. In an hour, I plan to break down this door and go inside to see if the doorman perhaps didn't notice Sara return. Maybe she's inside her flat and just fell asleep, or maybe something happened. I know I shouldn't go there, but this reminds me of how I waited for my sister and then gave up and didn't go looking for her and possibly saving her like I was supposed to. I won't do that again. I won't give up.

Why did I wait this long to tell her? Watching and following her for almost a year like a stupid spy—why didn't I try to see her sooner? If I didn't make believe that we were together, and instead actually tried to be with her like a man not like a child, then maybe she wouldn't be somewhere, God knows where, on her own right now. *I'm a joke.* Everything I've planned seems silly and meaningless if something—God bloody forbid—were to happen to her.

My feet throb from the back and forth pacing. My cell is completely lifeless, but Emily and Louis know I'm here and if they have any news, they'll come find me. I slide down and sit by her door, no longer able to stand. I close my eyes and start to pray again. I pray to anybody who will listen to please help safeguard my Sara from any harm. What if she's in trouble? What if she's hurt?

"What the fuck are you doing here?" I hear her voice and almost faint with relief at hearing the best sound in the whole bloody world.

I open my eyes and look up to see my broken ballerina standing close enough for me to finally touch her. I don't know who heard my prayers, but I am indebted to them for life. I grab hold of her legs like a child and clasp her close to me, kissing her thighs, not caring one bit that I must look like a deranged freak. I will never let go of her; they'll have to extricate me by force. Thank you, Lord! Thank you for making sure she's alive and safe and yelling at me.

"Liam! Are you crazy? What are you doing here? Let go of me!"

I don't bloody care what she says, I love her and she may not know it yet, but she loves me, too. "Say my name again. Fucking Lord, I missed hearing my name come out of your mouth. Say it again!" I demand, because my name sounds like a gift as it comes out of her mouth.

"Why are you here? Please let go of me and tell me what's going on," she pleads.

I loosen my hold to look at her, noticing she's barefoot and looking like she's been crying. "Where have you been? Are you all right? Did anybody hurt you? Why do you look as if you've been crying?"

She shakes her head and tries to create distance between us, which I won't allow after not touching her for a whole year. "I'm not sure why you're here, but you should go. I'd like to go in and take a shower; my feet are filthy and I stink. Did you come in person to tell me your good news?" she questions, sounding as cheeky as ever.

"Yes, I have lots of things to tell you," I say, failing to contain my excitement at finally being close enough to tell Sara, my Sara, all that she means to me.

"That's very magnanimous of you, but I already know your wonderful news. Congratulations, I wish you both only happiness," she says without looking at me, and it sounds a bit odd.

"Thank you, I think. And by 'both' you mean you wish you and me happiness?" I ask because I'm confused. How can she congratulate us if I haven't told her my plan or asked for her hand yet? Did Emily spoil my surprise?

"Yes, I wish you happiness and I hope to one day find my happiness as well. Thank you again for coming to tell me in person. Goodnight. See you around," she says, not at all as excited as I've let myself imagine she'd be. "Excuse me," she adds as she moves past me, still on floor, to open her front door.

She's about to close the door on me as I jump up and hold it open. "Sara, are we not going to talk about this?" I'm very confused; I don't understand what's happening. Why do I feel like she's about to slip through my hands again? "I've been waiting for you for..." I look at my watch. "...nine hours."

"I'm sorry, I'm not sure why you couldn't just call or text

me your announcement. I don't know why you'd wait for nine hours at my door to tell me you're engaged."

"Well, I had to ask you first! I thought you'd want to know, it's a big deal. I've waited almost a year to be able to tell you how I feel."

She bloody laughs at me. "You waited almost a year to tell me that you're getting married? Were you engaged when we met in New York?" she asks me, looking as confused as I feel.

"Of course not! It was only after I left New York that I realized who I want. I don't reckon being without you anymore. I made so many mistakes, but I'm ready to make it up to you. I almost didn't survive waiting here for you all day. If something were to happen to you, I wouldn't forgive myself. Where have you bloody been? It's not like you to come home this late." I speak to her in English, but it might as well be Cantonese. We're having a failure in communication and I'm not sure who needs to explain what. However, I am sure that I won't surrender or fucking relinquish her to anyone ever again!

"Are you stupid? Or do you think I'm stupid? I saw you picking out a fucking ring for your girlfriend at Harry Winston this afternoon. And now you're here at my door telling me you want me and that I came home too late! Is this some kind of joke?"

I start to slowly piece together the scene she just described and I can't help but laugh. I mean, I should probably start crying because this bloody proves that a higher power is absolutely trying to fuck me in the arse. I laugh hard enough to know that I may piss myself if she doesn't let me in to use the loo.

"Did I say something funny? Are you unbalanced? Should I be calling for help?" She continues with that sweet, awestruck look on her lovely perfect face, but everything she says makes me laugh even harder. She hasn't once seen me follow her for almost a year and yet today, of all bloody days, she spies me.

"Sara Klein, please stop and listen for once in your life. I am an idiot. You deserve far better than me. But I am not letting you go ever again because I am madly in love with you. I have been watching over you for almost a year. I couldn't come see you until I knew for sure that I wouldn't hurt you like I did in New York. I had to ensure that I was the kind of man you needed and not the coward who handed you over to someone else. I've been watching every morning and every night, and I have been falling in love with you every single minute.

"I think of nothing but you and all I want is to make you happy and smile. I want to make up for all the tears you've ever cried. I feel personally responsible for every tear because I should've found you sooner. I promise I will take care of you and your children and anybody else I need to take care of just to be with you. You must know I've never felt this way and I won't feel this for anyone but you. I was an arse and let you down, and I'm prepared to do anything to prove my devotion. I shouldn't have left you in New York. I was afraid you'd leave me first and I was a bloody coward. And it's okay if you don't feel what I feel, I'm willing to do everything to earn your trust, but I won't let you go, I won't let you turn me away. I want you, I choose you, only you. You will never be alone; I will always protect you."

I will say and do anything for this woman, and all she needs to do is trust me. I know I haven't done a thing to receive her trust, but I pray she takes a leap of faith and lets me love her. "I was in Harry Winston today, not with my girlfriend, but with your best mate, Emily. We were picking out a gift for you. When she told me that she wanted to buy you something special to celebrate your friendship and then mentioned that you haven't been showered with gifts, I promised her that I would be buying you enough gifts to make up for everything you've been lacking. Anyway, it's our one-year anniversary today, and I fancied surprising you. I shaved and got all dapper for you—I even got a hair snip. I had this whole speech worked out and I was going to beg you to be mine indefinitely, and then it all went tits up."

Why is she silent? I just told her I love her! She must say something or I'll die. She must!

"Let's hear your speech. It better be good, Liam." She sounds harsh, but I can sense the beginning of what may possibly be a smile, and she just said my name again.

I find her gift on the floor and pick it up. I ask her to hold it and she takes it, rolling her eyes. *God I love this bird.*

I position myself perfectly in front of her, stretch my neck and begin the most important speech of my life. "I was going to come and tell you that I, Liam Spencer Knight, have been 'Free Falling[62]' by Tom Petty ever since you brought me 'Back To Life[63]' by Soul II Soul. I have been 'Waiting For A Girl Like You[64]' by Foreigner my whole life, and you 'Sara[57]' by Starship 'Take My Breath Away[65]' by Berlin. 'When I See You Smile[30]' by Bad English, I understand 'The Power Of Love[66]' by Celine Dion because "Nothing Compares 2U[46]" by Sinéad O'Connor. I've been 'Alone[67]' by Heart and 'Living On A Prayer[68]' by Bon Jovi trying to not 'Run To You[69]' by Bryan Adams every day because 'How Am I Supposed To Live Without You[70]' by Laura Branigan when all I want is for you to 'Hold Me Now[71]' by Thompson Twins.

"I have 'Sweet Dreams[72]' by The Eurythmics about your beautiful 'Hungry Eyes[32]' by Eric Carmen and remember 'Time After Time[49]' by Cyndi Lauper how your 'Lips Like Sugar[73]' by Echo & The Bunnymen taste 'Just Like Heaven[74]' by The Cure. 'I'm Crazy for You[75]' by Madonna and I don't care about your 'Little Lies[9]' by Fleetwood Mac or your 'Tainted Love[40]' by Soft Cell. I've been 'Working My Way Back To You[76]' by The Spinners, chanting each day I see you; 'Don't You Forget About Me[77]' by Simple Minds.

"Baby, 'Don't Stop Believin'[3]' by Journey because I know that 'Love Is A Battlefield[47]' by Pat Benatar, and we will make it 'Against All Odds[78]' by Phil Collins. I will go 'Through The

Fire[79]' by Chaka Khan to prove to you my 'Endless Love[55]' by Lionel Richie and Diana Ross because I'm 'Still Loving You[59]' by The Scorpions. And I promise you they will 'Never Tear Us Apart[80]' by INXS! Sara, 'You and I[81]' by Eddie Rabbitt and Crystal Gayle, 'We Belong[54]' and we'll be 'Invincible[82]' by Pat Benetar since I'm 'Never Gonna Give You Up[83]' by Rick Astley and 'I'll Always Love You[84]' by Taylor Dayne. Now all you have to do is 'Take On Me[36]' by A-Ha."

I finish my speech without having to check my cheat sheet because I've read it hundreds of times in front of the mirror and in my car every morning waiting for her. She stares at her feet and if she laughs at me or sends me away, I'll collapse.

She finally looks up at me with the most beautiful eyes in the world, then stretches out her hand and says, "Hi, I'm Sara Klein, it's nice to finally meet you Liam Spencer Knight. It means everything to me 'When You Tell Me That You Love Me[85]' by Diana Ross. Would you like to come in?"

"Wait! You speak '90s? I only studied '80s, but I can learn '90s, too…"

Not the end, just the beginning…

St. Lucia

One Year Later

Sara

This view has to be the best view in the whole world. All I see is a green paradise engulfing calm blue waters and Emily & Louis' yacht docked in the distance. The sun rises above the horizon as Liam sleeps, and I'm itching to wake him up in his favorite way.

I move away from the balcony and inch closer to my beautiful, naked Adonis sprawled in bed like a king on top of rumpled sheets that smell of him and me and us. His blond hair covers half his face. He must get a haircut before we get married next week, he looks like a hobo—a sexy, loaded hobo, but still a hobo. I spy his dick, or for all intents and purposes, it's safe to call it *my* dick, just patiently resting, waiting for me to play with it and bring it back to life. *Perhaps it needs CPR*, I think and giggle as I touch my aching, overused jaw. No, definitely no more CPR.

I make my way up the bed, quietly attempting to ambush him in his sleep, when he grabs hold of me and pins me under him in the blink of an eye.

"Are you trying to attack us, comrade? Richard and I can always sense you coming," he says, already sucking down my neck and heading lower toward his favorite left nipple.

"If you don't harm the nipple I'll surrender and tell you everything, Agent Knight," I say, cracking up and trying to wiggle out from under him.

"Tell you what, Special Agent Sara—soon to be Mrs. Knight—if you reveal who the love of your life is, I'll let you keep your nipple and I'll throw in a wicked tongue massage on an area of your choosing for good measure."

I laugh at our silliness and cup his face for a kiss. This man tastes perfect at any hour of the day and I could kiss him like this for the rest of my life.

"The love of my life is the one and only Liam Spencer Knight. I love you with all that I am and everything that I have and I thank God for you every day." As I say those words, tears form in my eyes because I honestly can't imagine my life without him. Liam has brought so much joy into my world by merely existing. He makes my life brighter, louder, truer, happier; he just makes everything better.

"You, baby, are my life, and this little baby growing inside of you is going to fuse us forever." He lowers his head to kiss my stomach. You can't even tell I'm pregnant, it's that early, but the pregnancy test and my missed period definitely confirm that I'm gloriously knocked up. We've decided to wait and announce the pregnancy after we return from our honeymoon.

Liam is already kissing and flicking his tongue near my soaked pussy. I don't even know how his dick still functions after last night's performance, because I'm ridiculously sore. I shouldn't be complaining since he did shave for me; I could've been sore and chafed. He's already working me to my first orgasm, pumping two fingers and sucking my clit like a hungry beast.

He has a very peculiar relationship with my vagina. He's being nice and gentle now, tenderly kissing and licking it clean, but once he comes up for air, I know his greedy cock will be punishing that same vagina as if he didn't just make out with it. Once Liam crams himself fully inside me and finds his rhythm, he can't seem to pace himself or stop from harshly pounding me until he violently detonates and collapses, crushing me. But I love it and crave the feeling of his weight on top of me. Knowing that he's satiated and out for the count because of me is intoxicating.

"Oh...oh, yeah... oh, fuck... I'm coming...I'm coming, baby!" I yell as he ruthlessly pounds me with his tongue. I try to keep my eyes open because I love to see him smile as he feels my climax coming in waves from inside me.

I continue to spasm around his submerged fingers as he mumbles from between my legs, "Name...you didn't bloody say it."

"Liam! Liam! Liam... Only you, Liam!" I say as we both laugh at how stupid we are together. But it's perfect, he's perfect, and there isn't anyone else that I would want to be stupid with but this beautiful, crazy man that spends way too much time between my legs.

He starts to move up, stopping at my belly to whisper, "'She Drives Me Crazy[86]' by Fine Young Cannibals. Your mum, not you, little one." I can't possibly love this man more.

He moves to lie down at my side and asks me, "Are you game for French kissing Richard? He's been laboring hard, you know." He raises his eyebrows suggestively, stroking his hard working Richard.

I physically can't even open my mouth. "My jaw still hurts

from last night. Richard is too big to frequent my mouth as often as he does. Tell Richard he can play with Kitty while my jaw recovers."

"Richard loves playing with your cunt and he's counting the days until you let him inside your sweet arse again." I blush any time he brings up anal, and I'm convinced that my blushing turns my kinky fiancé on even more. I turn to lie on my stomach, presenting my ass to Liam for the taking. I can feel him already climbing up my body. I can't see him but I can hear the guttural sounds he makes and I can only imagine the ridiculous smile he must be sporting. He's fondling my ass cheeks with both hands before starting to rub his dick along my crack. I wait for him to begin probing my hole when he suddenly bypasses my ass and goes straight into my drenched pussy; with one hard thrust, he shoves himself fully inside of me.

"I'm too horny to try and cram into your arse right now, I need that cunt to squeeze me tight, love," he exclaims, panting while working his cock in and out of me. "I'll try to last a bit longer; I wanna see you come in this position."

I imagine how fucking sexy he must look straddling and working me from behind. I don't think he can last long with me in this position, and I love that I can make him lose control. He moves slowly in and fully out of me with a pop, slapping my ass every few minutes, and getting himself and me going from the sound his dick makes every time he reenters my pussy.

"I bloody love watching my cock disappear into your cunt," he informs me. He lets go of my ass cheeks and lowers his body to find my sensitive, overfilled breasts. "This baby is gonna make your tits huge. I'll be fucking you all day," he adds breathlessly, already picking up the speed. He holds himself up with one arm, and without changing his glorious rhythm, he starts massaging my clit with his other hand. I'm close, if he goes even a hair faster, I'll come, but I don't want to come, I want more. I want him to keep going, keep ramming into me, keep rubbing, keep kissing down my neck. I can't seem to get enough of him, and it's three, two, one…

"Liam, I'm coming, fuck, Liam…don't stop," I yell, holding on to the headboard as he hugs me flush against him and lets me ride out my orgasm. We're both covered with sweat, and even after he feels my body begin to go limp, he keeps patting and thumping on my clit with his hand like a drum because he's not done with me.

"Are you ready to go for a ride, love?" The question is rhetorical, because he doesn't have to ask; I'm always willing and ready to ride with him. I look back and nod, acknowledging that the gentle portion of our lovemaking has ended and the rough ride will now begin. He pushes my upper body down and with my ass propped in the air he starts fucking me like a jackhammer. Once he starts thrusting into me, he can't stop—he becomes possessed. I reach under to fondle his balls, which drives him mad until it's three, two, one… "Oh, fucking Lord! Oh fucking, baby…ah, yeah…ah…SARA!" And he flops.

He rests his whole weight on top of me and there's no doubt that I love this predictable fool more than life. I stay quiet, letting him crush me into the mattress because he's not fully coherent after climaxing. If I were to ask him for my own island right now, no doubt he'd say "*Ace.*"

Liam rolls off of me ten minutes later saying, "I can't believe I get you for four uninterrupted weeks. No meetings, no court, no one taking away my ballerina. Just us, love." He continues to talk as my cell phone starts to vibrate on the nightstand. He spoke too soon. "Don't answer! I didn't finish you off yet. I need to kiss kitty for being rough. I'm sure it has to do with the wedding anyway, and whatever it is it can wait."

"No, it's seven in the morning. Nobody would call this early unless it was important. Don't be a child, I need to get it." I'm already reaching for my phone as I see Jeff's name with JJ's picture flashing. I leap off the bed to answer the phone as my heart stops beating at the thought of something bad happening to our kids.

"Jeff, what's wrong?" I say, with fear gripping my voice. "What?!... When?...Oh. My. God," I chant over and over. I feel Liam at my side instantly, holding me, supporting me. "I'm sorry," I say before hanging up.

"Sara, love, talk to me. Was that Jeff? What did he say? What happened?" Liam frantically questions me.

I look up at him as the words fall out of my mouth. "Jacqueline passed away last night."

"What? Oh fuck no, that's awful." His shoulders slump as he lets go of me. His eyes turn to the floor at my feet and without looking at me with a deep breath, he defeatedly says, "You're going back aren't you?"

Look for Book III from the
Audio Fools
Series

Jeffery Rossi's Story

Coming in 2016.

Other Titlies by Tali Alexander

At 29, she has two beautiful kids, a live-in nanny, housekeeper, cook, and every imaginable luxury in the posh Upper East Side townhouse she shares with her drop-dead gorgeous husband, Louis Bruel. His company, Bruel Industries, owns a big chunk of New York City's most sought-after real estate, and together Emily and Louis embody the perfect hot fairy tale couple for ten happy years of marriage.

But when Louis mysteriously starts pushing Emily away, becoming distant and secretive, she is forced to search for the truth among the lies, scandal and heartbreak of his past that threaten to shatter her world. What she finds out will test the strength of her love and her vows to the man of her dreams.

Can Emily and Louis rewind far enough back to a time when life was simpler and love was all they needed? Follow their story with the help of some of their favorite songs from the 80's to discover just how deep and how far love will go.

Available Now

A Acknowledgments

W ell here we go again…

What a year I've had! In my wildest dreams I wouldn't see my life taking this path. I have been blessed to have the opportunity to let my heart and mind express themselves creatively with my writing and be able to share it with countless readers from around the world. My words get to travel the globe and have an effect on people I would never meet otherwise.

A person doesn't know how loved he/she really is until the people around them believe and support them when no one else does; and I'm very much loved. I wouldn't be able to follow my dreams without my ironclad support system starting from my saint of a mother and ending with my rock star husband. Writing stories is not always the toughest part it's having the ability to stand by your art and be strong enough to accept the praise together with the criticism that comes with it.

I don't write to change the world, I write to help you and me escape this world and live in someone else's world for a bit. Thank you for your support and for purchasing my books. I hope you feel compelled enough after reading my work to tell me your thoughts as it's the only way you can touch me back.

Thank you to my army of loyal readers. Thank you to all the people who stand by me cheering me on when sometimes all I want to do is give up and run away: Megan Cunningham Vohs (the sun), Jenny-Lee Ching (the moon), Robin Stranahan & Joanna Mongelluzzo (my stars), Jen Lynn, Amy Bustard, Heather Lane, Ursela Uriarte and many many more. A special thank you to Irene Myers, who goes to battle for me everyday, and makes sure we both get out alive.

To the amazing authors and bloggers who give me much love and priceless advice; Tarryn Fisher, it's no secret that I love you. If it wasn't for you I'd quit a long time ago. I look up to you and I thank God for your friendship and guidance every day. Thank you to: Natasha Tomic, Maryse Black and Vilma Gonzalez for all the hours of free therapy. To all the wonderful shoe designers, without your stunning shoes there would be no book. To my hard working beautiful muses, you know who you are, I thank you for allowing me to stalk you and in some cases pick your brains.

I'm nothing without my editors. Marie Piquette, you're amazing. Kristen Clark Switzer, you rock, you are my rock and I hope we can continue to rock together for many more books to come. Julie from JT Formatting, thank you for making this book look pretty and dealing with my OCD. Andrei Bat the cover to LIES IN REWIND exceeds all of my dreams and yet it's as if you visited my dreams and plucked it right out.

Please enjoy and stay tuned as I continue writing you another fantasy...

Tali Alexander

1. https://www.goodreads.com/work/quotes/171430
2. http://talialexander.com/the-eurythmics-here-comes-the-rain/
3. http://talialexander.com/journey-dont-stop-believing/
4. http://talialexander.com/depeche-mode-just-cant-get-enough/
5. http://talialexander.com/police-every-breath-take/ /
6. http://talialexander.com/tears-for-fears-everybody-wants-to-rule-the-world/
7. http://talialexander.com/belinda-carlisle/
8. http://talialexander.com/cindy-lauper-girls-just-wanna-have-fun/
9. http://talialexander.com/fleetwood-mac-little-lies/
10. http://talialexander.com/roxette-must-love/
11. http://talialexander.com/blondie-call-me/
12. http://talialexander.com/culture-club-karma-chameleon/
13. http://talialexander.com/the-weather-girls-its-raining-men/
14. http://talialexander.com/tina-turner-we-dont-need-another-hero/
15. http://talialexander.com/wham-wake-me-up-before-you-go-go/
16. http://talialexander.com/chicago-look-away/
17. http://talialexander.com/guns-n-roses-welcome-to-the-jungle/
18. http://talialexander.com/howard-jones-things-can-only-get-better/
19. http://talialexander.com/prince-and-the-revolution-when-doves-cry/
20. http://talialexander.com/rome-promise/
21. http://talialexander.com/peter-gabriel-in-your-eyes/
22. http://talialexander.com/bonnie-tyler-total-eclipse-of-the-heart/
23. http://talialexander.com/phil-collins-in-the-air-tonight-official-video/
24. http://talialexander.com/irene-cara-what-a-feeling/

25. http://talialexander.com/mr-big-to-be-with-you/
26. http://talialexander.com/howard-jones-no-one-is-to-blame/
27. http://talialexander.com/modern-english-melt/
28. http://talialexander.com/roxette-listen-heart/
29. http://talialexander.com/marvin-gaye-sexual-healing/ /
30. http://talialexander.com/bad-english-when-i-see-you-smile/
31. http://talialexander.com/sting-englishman-in-new-york/
32. http://talialexander.com/eric-carman-hungry-eyes/
33. http://talialexander.com/dead-or-alive-you-spin-me-round/
34. http://talialexander.com/omd-if-you-leave/
35. http://talialexander.com/the-human-league-dont-you-want-me/
36. http://talialexander.com/aha-take/
37. http://talialexander.com/stevie-nicks-edge-of-seventeen/
38. http://talialexander.com/def-leppard-love-bites/
39. http://talialexander.com/thompson-twins-doctor-doctor/
40. http://talialexander.com/soft-cell-tainted-love/
41. http://talialexander.com/lionel-richie-all-night-long/
42. http://talialexander.com/cutting-crew-just-died-in-your-arms/
43. http://talialexander.com/u2-i-still-havent-found-what-im-looking-for/
44. http://talialexander.com/kc-sunshine-band-please-dont-go/
45. http://talialexander.com/tina-turner-whats-love-got-to-do-with-it/
46. http://talialexander.com/sinead-oconnor-nothing-compares-2u/
47. http://talialexander.com/pat-benatar-love-is-a-battlefield/
48. http://talialexander.com/flock-seagulls-ran-far-away/
49. http://talialexander.com/cyndi-lauper-time-after-time/
50. http://talialexander.com/cher-turn-back-time/
51. http://talialexander.com/bette-midler-wind-beneath-my-wings/
52. http://talialexander.com/barbra-streisand-barry-gibb-what-kind-of-fool/
53. http://talialexander.com/madonna-live-to-tell/
54. http://talialexander.com/pat-benatar-belong/
55. http://talialexander.com/diana-ross-and-lionel-richie-endless-love/
56. http://talialexander.com/willie-nelson-always-on-my-mind/
57. http://talialexander.com/starship-sara/
58. http://talialexander.com/whitesnake-here-i-go-again/
59. http://talialexander.com/scorpions-still-loving-you/
60. http://talialexander.com/mr-mister-broken-wings/

61. http://talialexander.com/abba-the-winner-takes-it-all/
62. http://talialexander.com/tom-petty-free-fallin/
63. http://talialexander.com/soul-ii-soul-back-to-life/
64. http://talialexander.com/foreigner-waiting-for-a-girl-like-you/
65. http://talialexander.com/berlin-take-breath-away/
66. http://talialexander.com/celine-dion-the-power-of-love-official-video/
67. http://talialexander.com/heart-alone/
68. http://talialexander.com/bon-jovi-livin-on-a-prayer/
69. http://talialexander.com/bryan-adams-run-to-you/
70. http://talialexander.com/laura-branigan-how-am-i-supposed-to-live-without-you/
71. http://talialexander.com/thompson-twins-hold-me-now/
72. http://talialexander.com/the-eurythmics-sweet-dreams/
73. http://talialexander.com/echo-and-the-bunnymen-lips-like-sugar-official-music-video/
74. http://talialexander.com/the-cure-just-like-heaven/
75. http://talialexander.com/madonna-crazy-for-you/
76. http://talialexander.com/the-spinners-working-my-way-back-to-you-girl/
77. http://talialexander.com/simple-minds-dont-forget/
78. http://talialexander.com/phil-collins-against-all-odds-take-a-look-at-me-now/
79. http://talialexander.com/chaka-khan-through-the-fire/
80. http://talialexander.com/inxs-never-tear-us-apart/
81. http://talialexander.com/crystal-gayle-eddie-rabbitt-duet-you-and-i/
82. http://talialexander.com/pat-benatar-invincible/
83. http://talialexander.com/rick-astley-never-gonna-give-you-up/
84. http://talialexander.com/taylor-dayne-ill-always-love-you/
85. http://talialexander.com/diana-ross-when-you-tell-me-that-you-love-me/
86. http://talialexander.com/fine-young-cannibals-she-drives-me-crazy/

"Nothing really to tell, what you see is what you get."

I am every woman out there that has fantasies in her head. I am a daughter, a granddaughter, a sister, a wife, a lover, a mother, and a friend. I happen to also be a Doctor of Pharmacy and a business owner by day, and now a writer by night. Writing and reading help me escape the scary world we live in. I hope my stories help readers experience many different emotions and ultimately, I hope I make them smile…

Writing keeps me sane. I hope reading does the same for you.

Many Thanks,

Tali Alexander

Goodreads
https://www.goodreads.com/book/show/20804287-love-in-rewind

Twitter
https://twitter.com/Tali_Alexander

Pinterest
http://www.pinterest.com/talialexanderbo/

Facebook
https://www.facebook.com/TaliAlexanderAuthor

Instagram
http://instagram.com/talialexander

e-Mail
TaliAlexanderBooks@aol.com

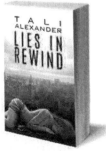

Made in the USA
Lexington, KY
15 June 2016